David Roy

HOBART BOOKS

THE BOMBER

COPYRIGHT © DAVID ROY 2021

ISBN 978-1-914322-02-0

The moral right of David Roy to be identified as the author of this work has been asserted by him in accordance with the Copyright, Designs and Patents Act 1988.

All Rights Reserved. No part of this book may be reproduced in any form, by photocopying or by any electronic or mechanical means, including information storage or retrieval systems, without the prior permission of the publisher.

First Published in 2021
by
Hobart Books, Oxfordshire, England
hobartbooks.com

Printed and bound in Great Britain by Clays Ltd, Elcograf S.p.A.

April

He had decided to become a suicide bomber, but when it came to it, when he set the bomb down, primed and ready, knowing that it was going to kill maybe a hundred people, something inside him changed and he knew he wanted to live instead. It was a snap decision, but it felt right. There might have been a way to 'un-prime' the bomb but that was not a contingency that had been looked at. Besides, he didn't actually object to killing hundreds of the infidel, he just wanted to live.

There were five minutes to go until the bomb went off and he wondered if there was somewhere he could take it, somewhere it could go off and not kill anyone. But the city was very busy; every square inch was packed with people. It was fine. If they had to die, then they had to die. It had been a purely hypothetical consideration.

In the end he opted to leave it where it was and beat a hasty retreat. Whatever happened was Allah's will. Everything was His will. He could shrug off personal blame.

When the bomb finally exploded he would be long gone, but he knew that he would be watching the results of his handiwork on the television that night. He walked away swiftly and kept walking when he finally heard and felt the blast. Screams and sirens did not deflect him from his controlled escape. He tried to look shocked as he entered the hotel's cramped lobby, but no one was there to witness his act.

His hotel room TV was elderly but worked spasmodically with a piece of folded card tucked under the Freeview box. He had no idea why this was effective, but it was. The room was grotty, supposedly themed like a Vietnamese house, but his bedding stank of sweat as if it had never been washed between guests. He laughed gently; he hadn't expected to return and had left a brief note for the police in which he claimed responsibility for the bomb on behalf of ISIS. He snatched it up as he slumped on his bed and then rolled it up like a joint as he replayed the bomb attack in his mind.

He felt a tickle of excitement at the base of his scrotum as he looked forward to watching the news.

There were no advertisements as the broadcaster rushed through the headline story. The bomb had achieved better results than he could have hoped for; one hundred and eighteen dead, many more wounded. He knew that some of those would die too. 'Dead' had greater impact than 'wounded', although the latter group remained behind, scarred mentally and physically as reminders of the terrible deed. But it was the dead who counted; their unintended sacrifice lived on as some sort of warped virtual memorial, whereas the merely wounded disappeared back into society with scars that could have come from a car crash or some other civilian accident.

One hundred and eighteen with more to come. Obscurely he hoped that it would become a round figure; dare he hope for one hundred and thirty? That number appealed. It was neat. He sat up in bed now as the cameras zoomed in on stretchers being carried out and hastily shoved into waiting yellow ambulances with their ill-matching red stripes.

Clouds of grey smoke surged through the station doors, testament to the inferno he had created inside. The reporter spoke breathlessly, lest any viewer be unaware of the drama of the situation; the idea was to draw them in, keep them tuned to that station. He – his name was Andre – owned the news, had made it his, as if he was 'in the know' to the detriment of every other reporter.

Subsidiary explosions occurred every few minutes making the reporter duck involuntarily, but bravely he stood his ground. The Bomber laughed at his antics; the man was in no danger. It gave him an idea for future attacks – a secondary bomb in the makeshift press area. He smiled at the thought and then silently punched the air as the reporter announced that The Bomber had been killed in the attack. It was a genuine thrill to hear his own death being announced! Andre spoke gravely and with authority of the difficulty involved in establishing the dead terrorist's identity. Andre, it seemed, had killed him off and yet here he was watching the whole thing from the comfort of his stinking hotel room. There was no limit to what he could do, now that he was dead!

It was the detail captured by the camera that Andre loved. They were telling his story to the world, showing every subtle nuance: the survivors led away draped in foil blankets, the queue of ambulances awaiting their turn at the end of the crowded street. When the reporter moved it was with a weather eye on the ground, strewn with glass and rubble. They – the news people – told his tale beautifully. What was good for the TV company's ratings was also good for The Bomber's cause.

There would be flowers to come (more great TV), eventually so many that they blocked up the station's entrance and stopped the emergency workers and building contractors from doing their work. But these soft infidels loved their flowers. They all wanted to help. They all wanted a share of the grief. They wanted to stand united until the novelty had worn off and they got back to the business of making money, ignoring the world's problems and getting fat at McDonalds. Their hypocrisy infuriated and entertained in equal measure.

As he watched, a section of the station's façade collapsed with a rending crack, sending a cloud of dust billowing into the confined street. There were screams. It was beautiful. He could almost taste the dust on his lips.

He smiled broadly as he rolled a joint.

Chapter One

The wind tore through the streets laced with chill rain that hit the pavement sideways and darkened it with a merging pattern of grey fingers that entwined to become a thin damp mass. Like Pavlov's dogs, the people of London unleashed their umbrellas, furled like sails then allowed to blossom as time-lapse flowers. Others ran. Still others crowded under canopies, collars pulled tight, and then stood dumbly, a human haemorrhage on the pavement. It was only rain, not a downpour of acid or a plague of locusts. From his office window, Tom watched the scene and gently shook his head. In minutes, the rain had gone and the clouds gave way to blue skies. He stepped back and turned his gaze to the television which occupied one top corner of the office. He watched the news for a moment before returning to his seat.

'It always strikes me as strange that we find things out by watching the TV like everyone else', said Tom. He pushed his chair back until it was resting on two legs and then braced his knees against the edge of his desk. He thought about nipping outside but he had told everyone that he was giving up the evil habit. Giving up wasn't working out for him at all. The truth was that, when no one was looking, he still smoked. His workmates were so bloody judgemental that he couldn't bring himself to admit his weakness.

'They don't always get it right', said Claire. She looked at him and then looked away again.

'*We* don't always get it right either', countered Tom. He had learned to keep his criticism of the department to a select circle of friends who could be trusted not to tell tales. Claire was one such. Matt and Wendy, sitting nearby, were not. He caught the latter looking at him over the grey rim of her computer monitor as she typed, attempting to look busy. She had reported him once for an acerbic comment he'd made and this had led to a verbal warning and a considerable cooling of relations between the two. Where once she had been alternately moody then flirty, moody and then flirty, now she was just moody. He loathed her and distrusted her. In fact, he distrusted anyone who said they liked her. For him, her mere presence was toxic. He wished she would leave and go off to have nasty children with whichever poor sod eventually married her. It still irked him that she had behaved so oddly and yet had offered no word of explanation for this, as if it was her right to mess with his head.

It was worse that she had on occasion tried to make amends, making him a coffee at a period of intense stress and even buying him an ice cream during last year's long hot summer. She did things so that he was unable to refuse her supposed kindness and then resumed her usual inexplicable moody stance as if he had once again offended her. When he was feeling charitable, he thought perhaps she was mad, maybe a psychopath or 'something of that nature', and although he didn't actually think she would report him again, he saw no reason for trust. He didn't plan to give her an excuse either. He would be very circumspect in future.

A mound of paperwork sat on his desk awaiting his attention. Reports from around the world, but mainly from Britain, landed there like huge butterflies and hung around until he had assembled the will, and the time, to action, file or disregard. At times he functioned mechanically, giving little thought to the hysterical content he was forced to look at. Most sightings of terrorists turned out to be nothing of the sort, or came to him far too late to do anything about them anyway. There was an unending, sticky morass of paranoid sludge entering the building and it all had to be dealt with in some way. Nothing could be ignored. Sometimes he wondered if it was all landing squarely on his desk and no other. There was certainly plenty of it.

The news still showed the aftermath of the Antwerp bomb. It followed an increasingly familiar pattern with the harassed reporter adding layers of conjecture to the existing speculation, which was itself laced with guesswork and handwringing, professional anguish.

He switched the TV off and then surveyed the office to see if there were any objections raised. There were none. They were all pretending to be busy and, although this sort of event was their bread and butter, it hadn't officially become their concern yet. Even when their section supervisor entered the office, it was only to tell them to be on standby; the bomb had exploded in a foreign country after all, not a great priority at the minute. Tom suppressed the urge to make a facetious comment, something to the effect that he was *always on standby*. But he desisted, purely because no one cared for his attempts at humour.

There was a routine to be followed and they would wait patiently for that routine to be initiated. When an operation went live it could be quite exciting but in between times the work was a grind. For now, the air of affected disinterest that typified their daily grind was perfectly maintained; no one got excited... about anything. Now and again, Tom wished that someone would show a spark of human emotion and stop pretending that they were superhuman, that they operated without flaw. It was the sheer fastidiousness and lack of humour that grated with him. No one dared crack a bloody joke any more.

The coffee machine made a noise as if reminding everyone of its presence, a sort of robotic clearing of the throat. It had the desired effect and Tom stood making his usual insincere offer.

'Anyone want a coffee – no? – okay then.'

No one spoke or even looked in his direction, reinforcing his view that they were a bunch of miserable bastards. He made his way to the coffee machine, thinking in purely esoteric terms of the bomb that had exploded across the water. If events followed their normal course, then it would eventually become something they would have to pay attention to. Antwerp was relatively close.

The machine coughed and wheezed but produced a drinkable concoction; not as good as the bigger machine in the rest room, but adequate.

He contemplated life as he waited. What was supposed to be exciting, challenging and prestigious work, seemed humdrum for much of the time. This was, *a good job*, and yet somehow his workmates sucked the life out of it with their seriousness and pomposity. They were so self-important, that they lapped up each new morsel of bullshit and repeated the same old buzzwords *ad nauseum* and without any sense of irony. In part they hoped that their bosses, layer upon layer of them, would see some spark of genius in their inanity.

No one else shared his view that there was an entirely ridiculous thread to much of their work culture and for a lot of the time he seriously wondered what good they were doing. They were supposed to be on the front line of the *War on Terror* but often he felt like any old civil servant, sitting in front of any old computer, doing any old job. Tom sometimes wondered if he might have enjoyed working for the Job Centre more. At least there was a human element to that, he supposed.

He could picture himself doing the same thing in thirty years, hunched over a computer, wearing a shabby grey cardigan and brown cords, gradually dying of baldness and despair.

At midday he stood and announced to his work colleagues that he was leaving the office to purchase his lunch.

'Would anyone like anything?', he asked, certain that no one would. 'A crocodile or a cream egg from the Polish shop? A handful of twigs? A barrage balloon?' His suggestions fell on deaf ears. No one was listening; they never did. He forced a sarcastic smile. Tom thought his workmates hated him. 'If I die while I'm out, I want you to have my pen, Claire', he said.

Claire didn't look up.

'Ta', she said.

Wendy didn't look up either, or speak, and so he pulled a face at her, which he knew was childish and the sort of behaviour that gave him a bad name. Tom knew and accepted that he was not highly regarded by this bunch. However, he was convinced that with a different set of colleagues, even ones in the same job, things might have been better for him.

Tom gave off an air of 'triviality' but he couldn't bring himself to be anything other than the person he was. In their eyes he was a lightweight, not to be taken seriously and someone who, by association, might be bad for their careers. Even Claire.

Clearly, it wasn't enough that he was good at his job, although slightly plodding in nature. To race ahead in his career, as any young man should want to, he needed to appear stern and single-minded. There was no place for the office comedian here. Tom needed ambition. He needed to drink at the pubs in Pimlico and to lust after a German car. He needed to be a graduate of Oxford or Cambridge.

But sadly, surrounded by the cream of Oxford and Cambridge, he felt like a bit of a nobody. He checked that he had cigarettes in his possession and left the building.

***

No one doubted that the bomb had been planted in the name of Islamic State, and so it proved. In a world increasingly desensitised to terrorist violence, the Antwerp bombing still came as a shock though, largely because of the number of victims; one hundred and thirty-one killed in the end, plus another fifty-seven severely injured. Antwerp was a cosmopolitan city and a port, one of the gateways to Europe and so, as intended, the casualties were a mix of nationalities, races, religions and backgrounds. Two Muslims died and some amateur commentators unfairly described this as collateral damage, almost as if they had deserved this fate. Two British backpackers also died. One American male, three French women, and twelve Dutch children on a school visit added their names to the roll of death. Twelve Belgian rail employees died and two Belgian cops. The rest, including the two Muslims, were Belgian commuters.

The Bomber also died but traces of his body couldn't be found. The station's CCTV was studied at length by a team of Belgian detectives, but although the damage wrought by the explosion was plain to see, the actual point of detonation was in a hitherto unnoticed blind spot between the ticket counter and the long internal boulevard leading to the platforms. The Bomber, whoever he was, had picked his spot well and that he had died was of no consolation to the police since he and every other suicide bomber was replaceable. There was no shortage of volunteers for the job.

It was twenty-four hours before his room was searched. The hotel owner had moved in to clean up after his departure, discovered his rolled-up note and, in a state of panic, had rung the police. The note was unsigned but claimed the crime in the name of the Islamic State. A forensic team took away every item in the room, including the remains of his final joint and from this a tiny sample of DNA was extracted. An Interpol search of DNA records led them to Britain – Scotland to be precise – and two detectives, who could barely be spared, were dispatched to the flat of a young woman named Shannen Cassidy who lived in Perth.

***

Jack Sullivan had left the army in 2014 with no real idea how he was going to fill the void in his life. The army had been his mother and his father but after six years with these uncompromising parents he had had enough. It took a while before he fully understood that civilian life had its very own set of limitations: you still had to get up in the morning, you still had to press your clothes, and going to work with a hangover was still terrible news for all concerned.

However, things never got *so* bad that he thought about rejoining – that particular metaphorical ship had sailed – but there were plenty of times when he wondered if he should have stuck it out in uniform for another few years. Quite how that would have changed anything he didn't care to think about, it just seemed like an alternative. For Jack the problem was that upon leaving the army, one merely left behind one well understood set of rules whilst having to learn and adhere to another. You exchanged one set of workmates for another. Everything was the same but different.

Those six years of military servitude had given him a short-lived sense of entitlement, which was not backed up or facilitated in any way by subsequent events. He wasn't a hero, nor was he exempt from participation in civilian norms such as working, paying taxes and going to the doctor with acute diarrhoea or other common ailments. All in all, civvy street was a bit of a disappointment and with the passage of time things got worse as people forgot about his contribution to world peace and about the perceived danger of the life he'd led. If anyone had ever seen a heroic aspect to Jack Sullivan, they had forgotten about it by now.

There was a paradox with which he lived; simultaneously admitting that he was no hero and yet wanting people to give some consideration to the possibility that he might have been. Had they done so, he could have spent time explaining to them why he wasn't heroic at all, whilst dropping tiny crumbs of the notion that he was being falsely modest. But since no one asked, there was never an opportunity to drop any crumbs of anything.

It was all, as he had said so often, bollocks.

There were days when it all – life, that is – seemed a bit negative, like the day when he got a letter saying that a previous employer had overpaid him and wanted its money back. The letter was unsigned, which both angered him and made him resolve to ignore it, neither of which paid off; they still wanted their money back. The episode filled him with dread, angst and a feeling of persecution. *Why couldn't they leave him alone?* After all he had done his bit...

He wanted to be left alone, respected but not bothered by small matters, so when he started receiving junk mail from SAGA, a holiday company for pensioners, he was angered rather than amused. He was only twenty-five at the time. He was a veteran of the army, not of life itself.

But life went on. By the age of twenty-six, he still had his own teeth, wasn't bald, or fat and had a job which just about covered his rent and beer money. It wasn't the life he had dreamed of, but it was the life he had. Things could have been worse.

Like many ex-soldiers, Jack had left the army with something of a thirst and when he drank to clear his mind – beer, rum or vodka were his favourites – Jack vowed to make a change in his life, although the exact details of that change eluded him. Anyway, the following morning, through a fug of toxic confusion, the whole notion of change had always evaporated, leaving him deflated and uncertain once again. Booze wasn't the answer. It merely gave him a false and temporary impetus to seek something better.

When his father died the previous year, Jack inherited a modest sum of money and with it he bought a car and a caravan. He packed in his job – there were no regrets from either side – moved out of his flat, diverted his mail to his mother's council bedsit and went travelling around the country. For some months, without really meaning to, he 'fell off the radar', the timing of which was odd, because for the first time in his life he actually became important. Jack Sullivan, suddenly and unwittingly, mattered again.

***

The MV Odessa was built in South Korea and launched in 1999. She was five hundred and fifty feet long and weighed fifteen thousand tonnes. Odessa was steaming from Sevastopol to Western Sahara when it went missing. No warning signals were sent. Russian and Turkish aircraft were sent to look for the missing vessel, a search they would give up after ten days. There was no oil, no bodies and no wreckage. It was simultaneously a puzzle and a source of delight for conspiracy theorists, who, with the advent of the internet, had become a virtual community of their own.

A lost ship threw up all sorts of possibilities. That a ship – a huge object, thousands of man hours taken in her construction, so much steel, so many miles of wiring and pipework – could sink in such circumstances made some of these possibilities seem... possible. The internet was filled with forums dedicated to theories created by ill-informed but desperately passionate lunatics who could explain away every curious event of the last hundred years. The apparent loss of the Odessa was just another log on the fire; they would be disappointed if it ever turned up.

When questions were asked by the various official bodies drawn into the investigation, the one that cropped up with the greatest frequency was this; what was the Odessa carrying? In the first instance, no one knew the answer.

***

Detective Constable Stevenson listened to his DI and thought carefully about the job he was being given.

'Can I take someone with me, Ma'am?', he asked. The police force in Scotland were terribly depleted in numbers. They had rid themselves of eighty percent of their civilian support staff to cut costs and put serving officers back into pen pushing duties. There were more cuts to come. Two officers going out in place of one was not to be taken for granted.

'I was going to suggest that you should. Tricky bugger, young Shannen is. Could say anything if you go there alone.'

'I thought she was a reformed character?', said Stevenson, half-jokingly. Shannen's barrister had made that particular claim the last time she'd been in court.

'Yes. They all are', said the DI, drily. 'Take Liz Truscott with you. Don't spend too long on this by the way. Probably a load of crap but we will be seen to be helping our European cousins. Looks good for us. Especially me.'

Stevenson knew his boss wasn't joking when she talked of good publicity helping her career, but he respected the woman's forthright evaluation of her own future, one in which she intended to 'get on' before retirement, thus boosting her pension pot. So far, she had worked her way up without trampling on her subordinates, which was not an easy feat. It was rare enough that anyone even attempted it.

Stevenson collected Truscott from her desk and explained the job they had to perform. She was only too glad to be able to leave behind a pile of burglaries and claims of domestic abuse to get out of the office. The pile would still be there when she got back of course. If anything, it would get bigger.

The drive to Shannen's flat was a short one.

'So, what's she done exactly?', asked Truscott. She was English and not entirely trusted or liked by some of her colleagues for that reason. She was learning patience and expected that someday their attitudes might change. She certainly hoped so. *Give it time*, she told herself. The police force was no longer the male-dominated employer it had once been, but English officers in Scotland were still a relative rarity. Now and again she intercepted a look which suggested that she was viewed as a spy or an infiltrator of sorts, sent by the English to keep an eye on things.

'Drugs, a bit of prostitution, selling dodgy videos – you name it. Not exactly a criminal kingpin. We are just trying to find out about her drug dealing.' He looked over at Truscott as he drove. 'We won't get anything from her', he added, dismissively.

They passed a row of cottages, a park and a retirement complex before turning off and heading past the retail park until they reached Shannen's estate. It was grimmer than grim.

Her flat was on the middle of three floors. The block must have looked great on the architect's drawings in the 1960s, with trees, mature gardens and maybe a plush Rover saloon parked outside, but the reality was rather different. Time had not been kind. The trees were there right enough, but what had once been a garden was overgrown with weeds and filled with enough garbage to prevent the council from being able to cut the grass safely. Rat-savaged bags of rubbish stood in line outside the block's main entrance and just around the corner, the fire-blackened remains of a Nissan Sunny Coupe could be seen. Once someone's pride and joy, it had been taken for a spin by the local youths, returned and torched. In their defence, there was nothing to do *except* steal cars since they had burnt down the youth club.

'Nice round here', commented Truscott.

'This is the impoverished end of crime. These people don't make a good living from their misdeeds.' Both police officers were familiar enough with the estate; burglaries, drug dealing, domestic abuse and twocking were prevalent offences. General drunkenness was a popular pastime but one which was dealt with by uniformed officers, few in number and with better things to do.

With a sigh, they made their way to the buzzer, pressed it and waited. Smartly dressed, they stood out, but being so was part of the job too and neither officer was required to lower their personal standards just to fit in with the greebos they encountered each day. A Vauxhall Corsa with faded red paintwork and inhabited by three dopey-looking youths drove slowly past in an unintentional pastiche of some American gangland scene. *They were pimps and hoodlums cruising in their Caddy, looking for bitches and carrying heat...* except they weren't anything of the sort. They were pimply young men with lank hair, two GCSEs to share between them, no jobs and a crappy car with no MOT and bald tyres. and which was running on three cylinders with the sound of a misfiring Centurion tank. It was pathetic for now but they would go on to cause the police plenty of headaches in the years to come, having served their crime apprenticeship on the estate.

'In some South American countries, they have special police squads who pick up kids like that and make them disappear', commented Stevenson. Truscott nodded but said nothing. They buzzed again.

'Maybe we should have booked an appointment to see her', said the female officer sardonically.

'Busy lives these people lead.' He rolled his eyes as he spoke. His sympathy for the plight of the estate's denizens was superficial at best but he would be as polite and respectful as he could manage.

They had buzzed for a third time when they finally got a response, a sleepy voice, saying, 'What? Who is it?'

'The police, Shannen. We need a chat.'

Stevenson heard a grunt and an indistinct swear word but she buzzed them through nevertheless and then greeted them at the top of the stairs wearing an off-white dressing gown and pink flip-flops. Shannen was twenty-two, looked thirty-five, was overweight, yellow of skin and carried the perpetual frown of the apathetic disenchanted. Her hair was scraped back in an untidy bun, exposing a forehead full of black heads. An enormous cold sore marked out the left corner of her mouth, and when she spoke, she did so with an overly large tongue that seemed to get caught on her yellow teeth.

She didn't say much but made it clear that they were to enter her flat, if only because entertaining the filth wasn't something you did in view of your neighbours. Not round here. The hall carpet crunched gently underfoot and Liz had the disconcerting sensation of walking across a thin crust of… crustiness. The two cops exchanged a look; this was the sort of home where you wiped your feet on the way out. It smelt of nappies, baby sick and piss.

'Have you had a baby, Shannen?', ventured Stevenson. He'd known her for some years, firstly when she was still at school and slim. Her weight gain and the overpowering baby smell made the question redundant; of course she'd had a baby.

'No', she said, plainly.

Or maybe the question wasn't redundant after all. Truscott's lip curled as they followed Shannen into her pokey living room.

'Do you have a dog then?', she asked. The smell was troubling her.

'Not allowed', said Shannen sourly. She slumped onto her scabby sofa but didn't offer a seat to the cops.

'Can we sit Shannen? We just need to ask you a few questions. You're not in trouble.'

'Aye. Sit if ye can find somewhere tay sit. The council doesn't give me much tay sit *on*', she complained. Truscott sat in the room's only chair – a ragged velour monster in brown – and Stevenson perched on the chair's arm. The room was dominated by a huge television with Freeview, X-Box and all the trimmings. A couple of sticky game controllers sat on the floor next to an ashtray and the plastic rings from a four pack of beer. A large veneer sideboard sat along the wall, filled with photographs and ornaments which gathered dust. Mark was drawn to matching Daniel O'Donnell pepper and salt pots. They were discoloured and dirty. A single, spectacular cobweb joined the sideboard to the ceiling. Truscott cocked her head to one side to better see the layer of fluff that surmounted twin picture frames of Shannen's family.

'So what do youse want?', she asked.

'We are trying to establish the identity of someone you supplied drugs to.'

Shannen sat back and folded her arms defensively. Her dressing gown gaped momentarily revealing a black thong. Stevenson looked away before he threw up.

'I don't do any of that now. Good girl, me.'

'Have you got a job?', asked Truscott, trying to gain the woman's trust.

'Nah. Nae fucker'll give ye a job round here. Once ye get a bad name that's it.' The female police officer tried to look sympathetic.

'But you have your own place at least', said Stevenson.

'It's a fuckin' dump', said Shannen, ungratefully.

'Anyway. Before – when you were selling drugs – you sold some to a person we are interested in.'

'Which person?'

'Well that's the thing. We don't know. It is someone who's been involved in a major crime. He smoked a joint and on that joint we found some of your DNA.'

Shannen raised her eyebrows at this and said, 'fuck me.'

'So, if you can help us with that…'

'Listen. I sold drugs to lots of people. I can say that now cos I've already bin tae jail fer it…'

'Have you sold drugs to anyone foreign?'

'English?', she asked with a hint of mischief.

Truscott sighed and answered. She wouldn't take the bait.

'Maybe English but possibly from somewhere else.'

'Nah.'

'You sure?', asked Stevenson.

'Well, it's not much tae go on, is it?'

The two police officers exchanged another look. They wanted to share as little as possible, but in fairness the woman needed more than that sparse description.

'We don't know his name, where he is from, or what he looks like.'

'Oh aye, I remember him now', she said sarcastically. Shannen looked at them with amazement. Their questioning seemed to get ever more ridiculous. Truscott spoke now, sensing that Shannen's cooperation was wavering.

'Okay. He may have been a Muslim.'

Shannen smiled.

'Does that narrow it down?', asked Stevenson, hopefully.

'I suppose so', replied the woman but the smile never left her face. 'I sold drugs to whoever, ye know? And some of them were Pakis. But I didnae exactly take names and addresses. I didnae run a loyalty scheme.' She laughed. 'What's in it for me? And don't say the chance to prevent a...'

'This person we're looking for was a suicide bomber but no one has any idea who they were.'

It was Stevenson who had spoken and Shannen regarded him seriously now.

'Christ', she said, clearly taken aback. 'But not bein' funny or nothin' but if they were a suicide bomber them what does it matter who they were? I mean they're deed, aren't they?'

'Presumably. But it would still be useful to know who they were, Shannen.'

'Look. I'm not a big fan of the polis, ye know, but I can't pick out one particular person... not from what youse have said. If I knew somethin' I'd tell ye.'

'So, no one stands out? No one who sounded foreign, who acted strangely. No one who was nervous... Anything?'

'They all act nervous', said Shannen with a giggle. She pulled her dressing gown tightly around her neck as if they had been trying to peer down her top. 'And they don't talk much, so as fer them bein' foreign…'

The two cops shared a sigh and then stood. Stevenson handed over a card with his details on.

'If anything comes to you, Shannen.'

'I'll let youse know….'

They thanked her and left.

Outside they paused.

'What do you think?', asked Truscott.

'Biffer.'

Liz shook her head and said, 'not about Shannen Cassidy. About what she knows?'

'She knows nothing. Did you expect her to?'

'I suppose not. Are you allowed to call her a biffer?'

***

Chapter Two

Tom returned to his desk with a ham sandwich, a bag of chicken crisps and two small energy drinks, one for lunch and one to counteract the mid-afternoon torpor. He thought he heard Wendy tut as he sat down. Claire looked over and smiled. In part, the energy drinks were intended to be a replacement for nicotine; he was determined to replace one habit with another. He logged back into his computer, aiming for a working lunch, but was called away immediately. With regret, he shoved his 'meal' to one side and followed his boss into the little cubby hole office he occupied in the corner of the bigger, communal floor space. The door shut softly behind him, enveloping both men in silence.

Normally he was only summoned when he was in the shit, and that hadn't happened for over a year. He tried to recall the event in question and then remembered that it had been a case of letting his flexi-time build up beyond the acceptable limits. He needed to put in long days just to get through the mountain of boring crap that was shoved onto his desk but he had accrued too many theoretical days off. It wasn't the first time it had happened either.

He blew out air from his cheeks as he sat. He hated the way they tried to make it all so civilised; an old-fashioned army-style bollocking would have been better. Get straight to the point and get it over with. Tom braced himself to make an insincere apology but still he couldn't think what his latest crime had been.

'Have a seat', said Andy. That was another thing he hated; first name terms with people who despised you and whom you despised in return. 'Andy' was actually Andrew Forsyth, Cambridge-educated Toff and general super hero for hire. Or was it Oxford? The rest was correct. Public school, first fifteen, floppy hair, Rolex and Jaguar. Forsyth wasn't ex-army, which he found odd; a few years in the 15th Foot and Mouth (Sheep Shaggers) would have looked great on his CV. That was the one advantage he had over his boss, the single cachet in his possession; prior to losing a foot in Afghanistan, he had served in the Intelligence Corps, who, as modern myth had it, 'made shit up'.

'Tom, we have a job for you. I think you'll like it', began Andy. He enjoyed building the tension when he spoke. It was like being interviewed by a Channel Five documentary maker, creating a half-hour programme from scant material.

Tom smiled. It was a genuine smile – not one of the fake ones he had perfected over the years – a smile born of relief, since he clearly wasn't in the doo-doo for once. When Andy judged that the correct amount of tension had been achieved he continued. 'A ship has gone missing somewhere in the Med. You might have heard about it on the news.'

Tom hadn't.

'Yes, I saw something about that. Dutch?'

'Russian.'

'Yes.'

'A number of agencies are looking into it but we want someone of our own keeping an eye on things.'

'Okay. So, what do we know?'

'The MV Odessa. Registered in Sevastopol but Russian owned. Sixteen years old. Completely seaworthy as far as we know. Insured. Legit. Disappeared on Tuesday. No distress signal. No wreckage – at least not yet. No bodies. There is nothing to say that the Odessa ever existed apart from her owner's paperwork. There were twelve crew on board and sixteen paying passengers. She hasn't docked anywhere else. She was heading for Western Sahara in Africa with a cargo of waste.'

'Piracy?', suggested Tom.

'Not a common occurrence in the Med but not impossible. However…' Andy held up a finger as if to prevent an interruption. 'In cases of piracy, the ship's master is generally able to get off a distress signal.'

'Industrial espionage?'

'Possible. Likely even. The owners apparently are being a little bit evasive about the exact nature of the cargo. If someone was going to steal a cargo, would they bother with a cargo of waste? But one man's waste is another man's gold mine.'

'So, if we knew what the cargo really was, we might be a bit closer to finding a…'

'Motive? I suppose so. A motive for taking the ship. It could be an inside job.'

'It could be', agreed Tom.

'It could be that the ship is still afloat but just not in the right area. The Mediterranean is a big place. Anyway, that's what we know. Over to you. See what you can find out.'

He dismissed his underling. Tom left the office with a mix of feelings but mainly confusion. If he had to pick his two main emotions at that moment, he would have selected confusion and flattery. It was clear that he had either been chosen for this job because of his ability, or because the job itself was a crock. As he stood, he was tempted to ask which it was, but had it been the former he was hardly portraying himself in a good light by questioning his boss's choice.

For once, someone spoke to him as he regained his seat.

'In the shit again?', asked Claire, but there was no tone of censure in her voice.

'No. Actually I have been selected for a job which requires my peculiar talents.' He paused briefly for his colleagues to scoff but when they didn't, he carried on. 'Don't you want to know what it is?'

Wendy said nothing, which he hoped was a sign of annoyance – annoyance that he had been picked in preference to her – but Claire and Matt obliged him by looking over.

'What is it then?', asked the former.

'I can't tell you', he said. Matt looked away with a tiny, dismissive shake of his posh little head. He found Tom tiresome and didn't even try to hide it. Claire muttered something as she returned to her work. It might have been the word 'arsehole'.

He pulled a face. Claire was his only ally and yet, as usual, he had managed to piss her off. It was a strange set of talents he had.

The early spring sunshine had gone, blocked out by a thickening cloud bank, and rain hung high in the air awaiting the impetus to harness gravity and soak the city. Tom pulled at his shirt collar and then undid his tie. This was about as rebellious as he ever got, certainly in terms of the dress code. His prosthetic foot seemed to irritate the stump of his leg on days like this. Humidity was the culprit, he told himself. He knew that simply because he'd heard someone else promulgate that as a possible explanation. It might be true, he supposed.

'We need a downpour', said Matt to no one in particular. Tom smiled indulgently. Everyone is a meteorologist on days like this, he thought. He blew air from his cheeks and tapped out a little tattoo on his tummy as he decided where to start.

Lloyd's Register. He would ring them and get clearance to examine their database. Tom hesitated. There was something wrong with this situation. He looked over at

Wendy. She glanced away quickly but she had definitely been looking in his direction. He thought back to the time when she had first joined the section. Frequently she had smiled at him (his mates would have said 'given him the eye', but it was a phrase he couldn't bring himself to use) and been, he supposed, overtly flirty. There had been a definite spark there but not for very long, and after a little while it had turned to enmity. When he tried to pinpoint the change, he was able to pick the exact moment her feelings had altered; when he had asked her out.

From that moment on, things had never been the same. He would never understand women. She had been handed what she seemed to want – handed it on a plate – and not only had she turned him down flat, she had actually begun to loathe him.

He sighed and tapped his finger on the edge of his desk before lifting the phone and ringing Lloyd's. He waited for three rings before the phone was answered, explained who he was, gave a password and waited again as he was passed on to the relevant section. A new voice, that of a female, came on the phone and for a second time Tom explained who he was although he was not required to repeat the password. He then made his request; that the Lloyd's Register database was made available to him. The request was granted and today's password was given. There were official channels and there was the old boy network and, depending upon who you were, either worked just as effectively, but Tom restricted himself to the former in any case. The latter was more of a public schoolboy thing, from which he was quite naturally excluded.

Armed with the password he logged on and then, after a short delay, entered the name of the ship, MV Odessa. The details appeared on screen at once and he sat back ready to work his way through them. He fired a glance towards Wendy and for a second time she hurriedly looked away. Whatever she was playing at, she was being none too subtle about it.

Tom sighed once more. Something still troubled him.

***

25

Jack had finally driven up to John O'Groats after weeks of prevarication. He didn't actually enjoy towing the caravan but it was a necessary evil for the life he had chosen. He'd spent two months in Northumberland and had become quite comfortable with the caravan parked in one corner of a farmyard. He'd worked as a labourer in return for electricity, a pitch and one hundred and fifty pounds per week. It meant early starts and anti-social hours but when he took into account the free meals – three a day – it was a good deal for someone with four GCSEs, two medals and an occasional bad back.

Already he was rueing his decision. His stomach rumbled. Even giving up on the three meals was a wrench; three good meals – farm-cooked food – was worth a few quid alone. Plus, he had to find another job. And he had liked it there. He had his car, his little caravan, a nice straightforward job, free food and the company of people who seemed to like and accept him. He knew he would be missed but living and working on a farm was not the life he had intended to lead and it was that knowledge that had forced him to pack up and move on.

The regret would wear off. He told himself that repeatedly. It was some reassurance that the move couldn't be avoided if he was to lead the life he had craved: the freedom of the road, no one to answer to, no pressures, no one reliant upon him, bar Jack Sullivan. If only he hadn't liked it so much at the farm, he thought wistfully.

He paid a deposit and set his van up before setting off to reception to ask about work.

The lad at reception scratched his head in confusion.

'Work? A job?'

'Yes. Just labouring. Anything really. Odd jobs', said Jack, hopefully. It was immediately clear that the young lad was the wrong person to ask. But it was equally clear that he didn't want to *appear to be* the wrong person. Jack guessed that he was about seventeen, probably a college student studying for 'A' levels in History, Drama and Media Studies. He had long, unkempt hair, one ear ring and probably wanted to be a Goth but lacked the courage and disregard for his Mum's opinion to go all the way and wear make-up and do whatever other miserable shit they did to themselves. His name badge proclaimed him to be Phillip, although it looked as if he had tried to score out the second 'L'.

However, Philip with one 'L' was not to be defeated by the problem he had been given.

'Well, there might be something...', he said scratching his head again. Jack was about to say that he would return later, when the lad had his most brilliant idea of the day.

'I'll go and get the boss', he said. Jack smiled – college was clearly paying off.

He had spent *his* 'college years' as a junior soldier and, although he wasn't always sure that it had paid off in terms of transferable skills, he was confident that it had equipped him with a modicum of common sense, a commodity which seemed to be in increasingly short supply. *Or was he just getting old?*

'The Boss', was a frowning man in late middle age, tall, grey, but with a full head of hair and a vestigial mullet.

'Hi', he said.

'I've moved onto one of your pitches, down near the cliff edge. Just wondered if there was any work.'

'Might be. What can you do?'

'Labouring, driving, odd jobs.'

'Bar work? Might have some shifts but nothing regular.'

'Never done it but I would have a go.'

'Only other thing is moving some static caravans but you would need an HGV licence...'

'Got one!', said Jack, happily. 'The Boss', shortly to become *his* boss, looked pleased and relieved.

'Well, that's bloody good news. Consider yourself hired.' They shook on the deal, which Jack thought was a little premature considering they had not talked about pay, conditions, taxes and so on, but he couldn't really argue. It was, he thought, further proof that there was work out there if you set your sights low enough. 'If you stop by in the morning with your licence and stuff, we'll get you started.' He looked his new employee up and down.

'You're English?'

'Yes.'

'What are you hiding from?'

'Nothing.'

The boss lifted one eyebrow, seemed about to speak and then closed his mouth like a sprung trap.

***

Her barrister had told the judge that she intended to go straight and it was true enough at the time. She wanted something better for herself. The judge had welcomed her decision, congratulated her but sent her down anyway, which was more than a little disappointing at the time. But her two-month sentence had given her the opportunity to think and to realise that prison life was not for her; she was much softer than she ever let on. She didn't like the communal showers, or having to clean the toilets. She didn't like the threatening, oppressive aura of the place. The single 'friend' she'd made inside had tried to hit on her and had then beaten her when her advances had been rebuffed. Shannen wasn't gay. From that moment on the place had seemed full of dykes... They came out of the woodwork when you least expected it.

So, prison had done her some good, insofar as she knew she didn't want to go back there. The whole idea of going straight had great appeal but the problem lay with actually doing it, especially when she came from a family of unsuccessful career criminals. For instance, her dad was in jail for grievous bodily harm. He had beaten up a nightclub bouncer in Aberdeen. No one, not even he, could explain why he was that far north in the first place. He was a well-known drifter and ne'er do well, but he certainly hadn't been looking for work on the rigs (or doing anything for that matter), which was the main reason why someone might end up in the city.

As for Shannen's mum, she had a suspended sentence for shoplifting. She'd avoided prison simply because it was the first time she'd been caught, no mean feat after a lifetime spent thieving. Shannen's little brother Kai was going to court in a couple of months charged with arson. Kai had burned down a barn killing three cows and causing nearly half a million pounds of damage. Two witnesses could describe him, both approaching and leaving, the scene. On the approach he was carrying a petrol can. CCTV had caught him lighting the fire.

His brief thought she could get him off.

In addition, Shannen had two cousins in and out of prison and an uncle who'd been shot dead in Glasgow. All were involved in drugs. She was bitter about her pedigree but leaving it behind was not easy. Becoming someone other than Shannen Cassidy wasn't straightforward.

The main thing she needed was a proper job. At school, she had done well in her food tech classes and, if she could even find it after all these years, she had a grade 'C' on her GCSE certificate for the subject. All her other grades were 'F's, 'G's and 'U's. There were other problems too. Time spent in jail didn't look good on her application forms, but she had been warned never to leave it off for fear of instant dismissal if she was found out. She had long since realised that she was in what she called a Catch *23* situation; she couldn't get a job with a conviction and she would get sacked from a job if she was caught lying. All the same she wanted to do something with her life.

With a heavy sigh, one laced with defeat, she raised herself from the sofa to find a pen and paper. Maybe if she recorded her thoughts, a solution would become clear to her, but even that nearly broke her will, for the pen and paper were hard to find. In the end she used the plain side of an ASDA receipt and the stub of an Argos pencil.

'Fuckin' great', she said but she sat down nevertheless and, leaning on a copy of Cosmopolitan she'd filched from the big recycling bin downstairs (the magazine was still being recycled, she told herself), she prepared her notes. After a brief, thoughtful pause she decided to list the pros and cons of her situation. This would enable her to formulate an action plan. The pros and cons thing she'd done at school in PSHE lessons. Everyone called them 'pish' lessons, because of the letters PSHE and because of the content, but here she was, nearly ten years later, putting something she had learned at school into action. The thought pleased her.

Shannen put the tiny pencil between her lips like a cheroot.

Pros and cons. For and against. Good and bad. She sighed again. One side was going to be much longer than the other that was for sure.

***

Chapter Three

The Bomber kept on the move but always blended in with his surroundings by being polite, respectful and ordinary. He couldn't change the colour of his skin, which he would have done had it been possible and if it had given him an advantage in the prosecution of the war against the infidel, but he could make himself look utterly conventional. From Belgium he had moved to Holland and from there to Germany, settling in to work at a friend's bookshop in Essen. The pay was crap, almost non-existent in fact, but he had a place to live, cover and a communication link to his masters, which, if sparingly used, was completely safe.

His 'friend' was a lady in her sixties, who supposedly knew nothing about his background but had once hinted at membership of the Baader-Meinhof gang. *Why had she brought that up if she didn't know about his links to IS?*

She was a silly old bitch and used to flounce around the flat in a semi see-through nightie as if he might be attracted to her lumpy form, but he certainly wasn't. The best he could manage was to ignore it. He indulged her, listened to her inane stories, smiled, bought groceries for them both and worked in her shop, covering the shifts she couldn't be bothered with. He spoke German well and she spoke English badly. She talked about Socialism and he listened politely, but her dogma meant nothing to him. Had she not served a purpose he would have ended their arrangement at once. But the truth was, she provided good cover – the best really. No one would seek him out here, even if they ever realised that he had survived. Belt and braces; a stupid expression but apt.

He was on his phone when the man came into the shop. He looked up and waved a hand as if to say, *I'm here and I will serve you if you need me to.* The man browsed, picking up paperbacks, mainly translations of US crime thrillers. He was tall, bearded, mid-thirties, dressed in a single-breasted suit which looked expensive but slightly old-fashioned. His brown shoes gleamed.

The Bomber saw him as a normal customer, just any old person. He looked up from his phone – he was texting a woman called Collette he'd met last week in a night club – and kept an eye on the man but without suspicion or, truth be told, interest. Working here bored him almost to death. He didn't read much and wouldn't have bothered with any of the trash in the shop if he had. The work of the infidel, it was like living in the midst of all hellish temptations but he was resistant to anything American, repulsed by every aspect of their culture. He failed to see the attraction on any level and found himself detesting their easy ways and their slackness. The mistake of the Europeans was to slavishly follow the American lead, whether it be in music, films, books, even their food. It would be their undoing. Where America led, Europe would follow and that included the carnage wrought by Islamic State. They had done it to themselves; how could they not see that Islam had no need for the West and its decadent ways?

He prided himself on his knowledge of the subject. There were so many who rallied to the cause without really understanding it. They had no knowledge of the Jews and their crimes, or of Israel's subjugation of the Palestinians. They didn't understand how America propped up oil-rich, Islam-poor nations like Saudi Arabia with weapons and shiny trinkets exchanged for oil. The Saudis played a game in which they stepped between the cracks and gave support to both sides. But that wasn't good enough. There should be no hiding place, although he was astute enough to know that they couldn't afford to offend the most powerful nation in Islam.

He had a dreamy look on his face – quite silly really – when the man approached the counter with two books. One was by Robert Ludlum, the other by Harlan Coben, both

Americans. The man handed the books over and reached for his wallet and withdrew a credit card. He noticed how blue his eyes were, typically German, he supposed.

They chatted for a few seconds and then the man said, 'you did well.'

The Bomber looked up from the till as it spewed out a receipt. Anyone watching would see only a minor commercial act being carried out and nothing more sinister. 'Many dead and many injured. This is the only way we can fight our war at present and you, my friend, are in the front line.'

He nodded. His previous encounters had been with a different man and he was wary of traps. This man didn't look like an IS commander but he had obvious authority and certainly wasn't a mere messenger either.

'There is another job coming up. Something bigger than anything we have attempted before. We want you to lead this next attack. You have all the skills we need and one particular advantage that money and training can't buy.'

'What is that?', he asked, although he felt he already knew the answer. His pulse raced and he felt that peculiar tickle at the base of his scrotum.

'You are already dead.'

***

Odessa was a standard 15,000 tonne freighter with a mixture of hold space, a deck area for containers and a few cabins. The South Koreans built good, serviceable ships cheaply, and to the detriment of other shipbuilding nations. No one bought ships from the British any more, not even the British themselves. The only country producing more ships than the Koreans was China. By shipbuilding standards, Odessa was cheap to buy and economical to run, which was all a shipping company really required from its vessels. It was expected to last for twenty-five years and then be sold on to another, lesser operator, or possibly scrapped. The yards in

South Korea had certainly thrived in recent years and there was nothing wrong with their products.

Tom was checking the histories of several other South Korean ships of identical design, of which there were eleven. Two sailed under Greek flags, one under a Polish flag, two under British flags, one Moroccan and the rest, including the missing ship, Russian.

No major insurance claims had been made against any of the vessels and all the operators seemed to be legitimate. In short, the MV Odessa was utterly unremarkable apart from the fact that it had disappeared.

So far, so bland, but he loved a mystery and looked forward to the moment when he was able to explain the ship's disappearance. If he could do that, the credit would be his and no one else's.

Internationally, a number of agencies were already engaged in a search for Odessa, including the authorities in Gibraltar who would be able to spot the missing vessel if it attempted passage of the Straits. All the major ports – those able to accommodate a ship of this size – were alerted, and SAR aircraft from several nations still patrolled. Tom was now patched into the appropriate maritime emergency database and would be alerted at once if the ship, or any signs of it, were spotted.

With that all done – and there wasn't much else he could do from an office in London – he began writing his initial report, filling in the scant details he had at his disposal. That task, quickly carried out, made him pause and think about the reason for their interest in the missing ship, namely that she had disappeared without any warning signals being sent out. He sat back in his chair and tried to imagine Odessa's last moments. He clicked on his monitor, bringing up an image of the ship, and then pictured it steaming through the Med, its master and crew completely unconcerned and certainly not contemplating the need to send a distress signal. They didn't do it – didn't send a signal – so they perceived no danger. He was fairly sure that the relevant signal was generated by the mere push of a button and yet no one had pushed that button. So, what *had* happened?

He screwed his eyes shut until the ship's outline was indistinct and imagined it sailing through the Mediterranean. In his mind, it was flat calm – which reminded him to check the actual weather conditions – so what happened next? What happened with such suddenness that the officer of the watch or one of the crew couldn't send a distress signal? Pirates? Few pirates operated in the region and their approach would be spotted long before they managed to board the ship, thus enabling an electronic message to be sent. Also, he was fairly sure that merchant vessels could defend themselves against pirates these days – didn't they carry a complement of armed guards, usually ex-soldiers? He would double check. It occurred to him then that nobody could possibly know at what time of the day it had sunk/disappeared, ergo; these events might have happened at night. Tom made a note to check if such a thing was possible.

He scratched his neck and screwed up his eyes again. *The Odessa was sailing though the Med. Flat calm, no pirates. What happened?* She didn't just sink and she didn't collide with another ship. Not in broad daylight, if that was the case, and not without at least one vessel sending a distress signal. So, what else? An explosion? He sighed and pursed his lips. It was possible. Probably depended on the cargo to some extent. *Could the ship die with such suddenness that no trace was left?* He remembered the story of HMS Hood, pride of the Royal Navy, sunk with just one lucky shell from her nemesis, the Bismarck. There had been just three survivors from a crew of nearly fifteen hundred. Could something like that have happened here?

He couldn't quite imagine a warship of any nation opening fire on a merchantman without having good reason and without the incident being reported. No doubt a modern destroyer could launch a missile which would easily and swiftly sink a freighter but who would do such a thing? And why?

He put a finger to his lips. Did Libya have a navy? He added that query to his list. Despite his doubts, he felt like he was at least coming up with one workable theory. The other Mediterranean nations had navies – well, most of them – but it could only be a warship from a country which had somehow put itself outside of the greater community of nations that would pull off such a stunt.

He made a quick enquiry about Libya's naval capability and discovered that the country's navy had been sunk more or less in its entirety by NATO in 2010. That seemed to get them off the hook.

The idea that a naval vessel had sunk the Odessa was only a theory but it was one which lent itself to the facts of the ship's disappearance. Only a strike by a missile could ever really bring about such complete and rapid destruction that it would be impossible for the master to get off an SOS. What other scenarios fitted? Granted he wasn't an expert in maritime loss, but even Tom knew that ships generally took time to sink.

He typed it up in his report. Words. His bosses loved words. Sometimes it seemed as if quantity counted for more than quality. He was considering which buzzwords he could lever into his writing when the urge to drink coffee overtook him. He stood, made sure his computer was locked and then left the office for the restroom upstairs. Tom preferred the coffee up there and the fact that he got away from his fellow office drones. He knew that it made him seem anti-social – after all, why would he choose to mix with the rest of the riff-raff from other sections when they had their own coffee machine? – but he liked the exercise and the chance to meet other people.

Occasionally, feeling a bit down about his situation, he wondered why his closest workmates didn't make a bigger effort to get to know him and understand him, but they seemed to dislike him unconditionally and be prepared to let that dislike fester. He didn't matter to them on any level. Tom didn't understand it.

But as he climbed the stairs, he was still mulling over the problem he'd been tasked with.

The most important Mediterranean nation was undoubtedly Italy, but they were a responsible country and, had one of their warships been involved, they would instantly have admitted their error. France likewise was a big player in the region but again, they would have admitted responsibility. To think that either nation would have done otherwise was lunacy. They could both be ruled out. Turkey? Like the other two nations it was a NATO member and keen to be an integral part of everything thathappened in Europe. Turkey could never carry out the sinking of a merchant vessel and not admit to having done so. Increasingly modern, they had the capability but not the will to commit a crime of this nature.

He walked into the restroom and made straight for the hot drinks machine, which, for fifty pence, produced a rather good facsimile of filter coffee. He selected a cappuccino and smiled at his remembrance of a Tony Hancock sketch in which he orders a similar drink in a café with the words, *'Cappuccino, no froth.'* Tom didn't think he'd even seen the sketch but the words stuck with him nevertheless.

He wasn't alone. A young black woman from another section sat there with her sandwiches and her own coffee enjoying a late lunch. She nodded to him and returned to her Kindle. She was of striking appearance, a bit like Graces Jones but more petite, prettier and generally less peculiar looking. When his drink finally arrived in all its frothy fury and after a series of pops, plops and wheezes from the great machine, he took it over to the small window which gave the room its only view of the city. The rain had stopped but London looked grey and washed out despite the sunshine. But he wasn't really looking at the view. Rather, he was looking *into* it, but seeing nothing except the outline of Odessa as she ploughed through the sea and then suddenly disappeared. A ship-to-ship missile was a definite possibility. What about a torpedo? A submarine could have delivered the necessary element of surprise. Even then the resulting explosion would have to be so destructive that the crew was killed instantly. How else could you explain the fact that no distress signal had been sent? *The push of a button, that was all it took. Getting a coffee from this machine was more involved than warning neighbouring ships of the danger you were in at sea.*

The restroom door opened and closed behind him but he didn't turn, assuming that it marked the departure of his colleague from the other section, rather than a new arrival. It wasn't a popular place, thanks to its grim décor. Often, he spent long minutes alone.

'Hello there. Escaping?'

He turned to see Claire standing before him.

'Just needed a break. Coffee?' He nodded towards the vending machine and rattled some change in his pocket.

'I'll get my own', she said. He felt rather deflated but when he looked at the coins in his pocket they only came to thirty-nine pence, eleven pence short in any case. As the machine produced her brew, she asked him how he was getting on.

'Fine', he said and pulled a face.

'Working on the ship thing?'

He wasn't really supposed to talk about it.

'Well, I...'

'It's okay. Why else would you be ringing Lloyd's? We're all colleagues. No one will blab.' She smiled and then winced as she took her first sip of coffee. 'Tastes like pee', she added.

'Yeah, it's the ship', he confirmed. 'Not sure why I was given it. Bet Wendy's pissed off.' Their mutual dislike was well known but the others had always seemed ambivalent about the woman. Increasingly, he saw her as a void, a patch of nothingness in the office, irrelevant, unpleasant and dull of mind.

'She'll get over it.'

'We don't get on', he said.

'She thinks you're an arsehole.'

'Do you think so too?', he asked knowing that she didn't.

'Yes.'

'Oh.'

'Only sometimes. Sometimes you just seem like a slacker. And, you know, when everyone else is working hard and you are cracking inane jokes it gets a bit…'

'Fucking annoying?'

'Tiresome, I was going to say, but, yes.'

'I can't help it', he said. 'I'm not good with tension and everybody being so bloody serious all the time. The world would still turn without us.'

'But would it turn safely?', she asked, gravely. He wasn't sure if she was being serious.

Tom stood back and looked at her as if for the first time.

'What? What's that supposed to mean?'

'You see? Now you're being an arsehole.'

'I'm sorry but all this is po-faced bullshit. We're just rearranging bits of paper.'

'We're tracking enemy agents.'

'We're writing things. Looking at things…', he countered almost desperately.

Claire shook her head. A strand of her hair clung to the corner of her mouth and she swept it away with the back of her hand.

'If you don't like this job you could always do something else like drive a truck or deliver letters for Royal Mail.'

'No, I couldn't. I've only got one foot, remember?'

Claire blushed slightly, a mix of anger and frustration tempered with embarrassment.

'You know what I mean', she stammered.

'Was I being an arsehole again?', he asked after a pause.

'No.' Her annoyance seemed to be wavering a little. 'No, maybe *I* was. I'm sorry.'

'Don't worry about it.'

He knew that Claire had recently split up with her soldier boyfriend. Tom looked at her, debated about asking her out and decided against it since he had done the same thing with Wendy. To have asked both of his female work colleagues out and to be rejected by both smacked of terrible desperation, and if she did turn him down, as he expected she would, he'd have to become gay and ask Matt out. He didn't even like Matt…

'What were you thinking about? Your mind was elsewhere.'

'Oh nothing. I was thinking about nothing', he lied.

Claire seemed to want to reply but held back.

'You look as if *you* have something you want to say', he said.

'I was wondering whether to ask you out for a drink or the cinema', she replied.

***

Shannen looked down at her flip-flopped feet and the nasty-looking leggings she wore. If anything symbolised the need for change it was these two items, along with the unwisely chosen crop top and the cheap-looking tattoos. She bulged in all the wrong places and none of the right ones, although it hadn't always been so. She still had a couple of pictures of her as a young girl, looking slim, relatively pretty and happy. Could she be that again?

She knew she was a super-slob by anyone's standards. No wonder she couldn't get a job. Mind you, when she considered this further, she could also point to the fact that she never even got an interview and if she ever did, then they would have taken one look at her and known she was a *wrong'un*.

She had to make some changes. Shannen looked at her list, which, predictably enough, was longer on the deficit side. Good things first – the pros; she wasn't in prison, she had an address, she had a CV and she had a GCSE certificate. Four things. That wasn't too bad on the surface of it. On the bad things side – the cons; she *had been* in prison, there wasn't much to show on her CV (a two-week spell in a café), there wasn't much to show on her GCSE certificate, she knew of no one who would give her a reference and she didn't really have many nice clothes to wear if she ever got an interview. But chief amongst her difficulties was her time in prison. *She wouldn't have given herself a job*, which all things considered was pretty damning. She sat back on the sofa, looked at the kettle and the bag of reduced-price doughnuts on the breakfast bar and decided that the new Shannen began with a diet.

She added that one word to her action plan – diet – and then considered what else she might need to do. Shannen scratched her eyebrow, her nail catching on the piercing she'd had done there a few months before. Well, that could go! She didn't bloody like it anyway. What else? Her wardrobe wasn't exactly inspiring but there was a new branch of Primark recently opened and they did good outfits for not much money. Maybe with a new outfit she'd get a job and with a job she could afford to go to the gym and buy better food. It might be the start of something. She felt quite excited. Excited enough to drink coffee, eat a doughnut and have a fag…

But she resisted. One of those could be her treat. With her new outfit she could go around the shops and ask for jobs – nothing like showing willing, she told herself. Start at the bottom, stacking shelves. Suddenly, she really felt good about herself. This was the moment when she put the past behind her. New outfit – new Shannen. Adrenaline coursed and she wanted to add to her list. What else could she do? She was determined to make this work. She hadn't always been a horror, although someone had once told her, to her face no less, that she was a 'minger'. The insult had pierced her heart but worse than that it had stuck and given her something to live down to. After all, what was the fucking point if you only ever amounted to that?

She cast those thoughts aside, but they came back with the immediacy of elastic. She wanted something to do right now that showed she had turned the corner and was fighting back against the crappy hand her parents and all her crappy uncles and her crappy brother had dealt her. And then, like *one of them bolts from the blue*, it came to her. She'd go to the cops and give the name of the man they were looking for.

She just had to figure who exactly that man was…

***

Jack liked the new place well enough, although the fierce winds which blew in from the sea rocked the little caravan at night. He felt like he was adrift on a stormy sea but it was a strangely comforting feeling, just so long as he didn't actually take off. He had found all the facilities, the sluice and the pan bash, and had spent a couple of quiet evenings in the site's little pub. It was nothing special but they were friendly and, importantly for a pub, they sold beer, something which he had hardly touched on the farm. The family hadn't been drinkers, a fact which had actually come as a relief to him for there had been times recently when he'd thought he was drinking too much. It was easier to abstain when in the company of abstainers. He didn't want to be a boozer but the occasional beer would do no harm, he told himself.

The work was okay but he couldn't see it lasting. More to the point he *knew* it wouldn't last. So far, he had loaded three old static caravans onto the back of a flat-bed truck and taken them to either the scrappies, or to an industrial unit which specialised in refitting and reselling caravans. There were another two vans to go but once they had been taken away then what remained? He needed work and hoped that something else could be found for him. He was optimistic. Jack thought they *would* find something for him – he was a useful man to have around, even if he said so himself. Jack of all trades.

In the meantime, he was beginning to enjoy his new home. It was intoxicating, as if he was living at the edge of the world and that he could step off into any adventure he chose. From this point you could get on a boat and finish up anywhere. The fact that he didn't intend to do so mattered not. It was just the thought that there was no limit, no boundaries that excited him.

But it wasn't really an adventure he sought. Not right now, at least. Jack wanted time. He wanted to be able to think. He wanted to know what direction to take his life and for now he wasn't bound by anything. He wasn't trapped. He hadn't become a drudge. He could get up one morning, drive away and start again. It wouldn't always be that way – he accepted that – but for now it was just right. In fact, it was perfect.

Who else had this sort of freedom? When you're born, you are dependent upon your parents, and when you are growing up and at school, you are bound by rules, rules and more rules. When you join the army it all gets ten times worse. Plus, you are trapped for however many years you signed up for.

When he thought about it, as he did often, he knew that in many ways he hadn't really minded being in the army, despite the bullshit, the hardship, the uncertainty, boredom and occasional danger. His time in uniform had been so unlike Call of Duty that he could never quite explain it to a young person in a believable way. Their minds were not open to the possibility that he hadn't spent years on the rampage with automatic weapons, spraying bullets, killing dozens of enemies with ease.

He wouldn't have swapped those years for anything and the two medals he had, whilst having little financial value, showed to whoever cared to listen that he had done his bit. It was more than most people could say even if it didn't always count for much in civvy street, as he had found.

Jack accepted that the world did not owe him a living just because various people of roughly Middle Eastern origin had tried to shoot his arse off. He further accepted that in most situations he could name, those experiences counted for absolutely nothing. It didn't even guarantee him free drinks in the pub these days. But that was the past and he felt that the deeds of his past had given him the right to decide upon the future he wanted, right down to the last detail. And now he could plan that. He could choose his moment… he just needed an idea, inspiration, and that, so far, eluded him.

His freedom never felt greater than when he sat in his caravan, staring out to sea and feeling privileged to have that view all to himself. When it rained, as it did almost every day, that only increased his sense of wellbeing, especially when he was inside, with a hot drink in his hands and experiencing that pleasant tiredness brought by exposure to salt air. He loved the sound of the rain pelting the metal roof and sides of the caravan. It brought a calmness to him, descending like a soft blanket around his shoulders. He had never slept so well in his life, nor wakened so refreshed.

Each day brought parties of hardy visitors, keen to say they had experienced Great Britain's most northerly point. He supposed they felt like explorers, whereas he, after just a few days, felt like an old-timer or a pioneer. *Maybe he should have built a log cabin…*

Sometimes, he would simply watch the waves rolling in and try to predict where they might break. The beauty of the game was that it didn't matter if he got it right or wrong.

***

Chapter Four

He hated the café but it had been chosen as their rendezvous and he had no option but to turn up there and wait for his contact. Sometimes he thought that this was the most dangerous time, when he was most likely to get caught. This was when they might be filming him and waiting to move in, not when he was delivering the bomb – from their perspective that was much too late. No, this was the dangerous time and even though he was, to all intents and purposes, dead, his contact was not and it was the contact who brought the danger with him like a shadow.

He had to admit the security services were good. They had the resources to keep tabs on people and they were in for the long haul if needs be. *Just look at Osama Bin Laden. They had waited and waited, then bam!*

He allowed himself the small conceit of admiration for the capability of his foes, which wasn't the same as admiration for their worthless cause. They were worthy adversaries in this great game and he was thrilled to think that he was becoming an ever bigger player. They didn't know it yet, they didn't know about him, but his time would come and his name would be spoken with awe.

His enemies, on paper, held all the trump cards, but in many ways the relative simplicity of the IS operation was its strength. There were no pitched battles to be fought and no radio leaks, few digital intercepts. The Americans – and they were of course the main players in this big game – had been beaten in war by a bunch of sandal-wearing peasants in the jungles of south east Asia in 1973. It had hurt them, injured the national pride and it could happen again. He could play a big part in that.

Patience was required.

He thought this particular café to be a ridiculous choice. It was a meeting place for every nationality, for every type of dealer, for would-be hoodlums, gangsters, fraudsters. They insisted that to meet here was like hiding in plain sight. He wasn't sure about that, but what options did he have? He didn't have the power or influence to change anything or to make the big decisions. He was still the little man in their eyes, although in time that might not be the case. Maybe he'd work his way to the top.

He sipped a coffee. They called it an Americano and he could have spat on the floor for its name alone rather than just its insipid taste. The Bomber preferred Turkish coffee, although he recognised it as something of an affectation; he had attended university in Ankara – just a year – and enjoyed the subtle punch it delivered. No chance of getting Turkish coffee here. Inexplicably the Germans loved everything that came from America, the country that had twice defeated them in the war. The humiliation! *What was wrong with them?*

He sighed and drummed his fingers nervously on the table as he waited. This contact would be one of two men and he never knew which was coming or why they bothered to alternate. Security? They never said. He thought that the whole procedure looked suspicious and had to remind himself – *hiding in plain sight*. Yeah, right.

In the booth opposite, two young women gabbled away excitedly. Half a dozen large shopping bags sat at their feet as if *they* worshipped the customer and not the other way around. He was repelled by the shortness of their skirts, by their make-up and jewellery. They were the sort he really didn't mind blowing up. An image of scattered shopping amongst the human debris – dresses and shoes, legs and heads – flitted through his mind. He saw Andre, the reporter, talking about the tragedy of it all as the cameras homed in on the stupid things that people, now dead, had bought. It was a metaphor for the pointlessness of life in the West.

Just minutes before they had been shopping for clothes and now they lie dead...'

He smiled. That would be his work. He would produce that result time and again.

***

Mark Stevenson got to his desk and resisted the temptation to slump for just long enough to retrieve two co-codamol from his top drawer. He downed these with a painful wince and followed up with a long drink of Lucozade.

'Is that better?', asked Liz.

'Not yet. It takes a while.'

'On the pop?'

'Nah. Just my monthly headache. I've been getting them for years.'

'You should go to the doctors.'

'I've been. He says I am just a washed-up old git. No good to anyone.' He slumped finally as if the effort of talking had nearly killed him.

'Well, I suppose that's true enough. Anyway, on a brighter note, Shannen Cassidy would like to speak to us.'

He looked up.

'Really? The lovely Shannen? I thought that was a dead end.'

'Apparently not.'

'She has a name for us?'

'The Filth', said Liz.

'Ha. I meant she has the name of one of her ex-customers for us?'

'I presume so. We'll find out when we get there.'

'Right. Will you drive please?'

The car was a high mileage Vauxhall. It was looking a bit the worse for wear and smelled of cigarette smoke, which was odd given that smoking was forbidden in police cars.

'Stinks', commented Stevenson as he fastened his seat belt.

'How's the head?', asked Truscott. She had her hair tied back today. It suited her.

'Fine, I suppose. I'll have this headache all day.'

They pulled out of the station and onto the main road, past ASDA and the FIAT dealership. The sky was unending blue.

'Go to the doctor. I'm telling you. Men just don't go.'

'Beautiful day', he said.

'Changing the subject.'

'No, I was just commenting on the weather. It happens to be a beautiful day.'

An ambulance was parked outside one of the little terraced houses that lined their route. As they passed an old man was led out and plonked in the back next to his wife.

'That'll be us someday', she said.

'We're not married.'

They drove in silence for almost a minute.

'Are the headaches worse after you have been drinking?'

'I don't know. They are just headaches. I can't separate one from the other really.'

'You might have a brain tumour', she said as she accelerated round an ice cream van.

'Thanks. When I see an ice cream van these days, I always think they are dealing drugs.'

'Changing the subject again. You've been doing this job too long. It's almost a form of racism that. If it was a black ice cream seller, what would you think?'

'Drugs.'

'Institutional racism', commented Truscott.

'You tricked me into making that response. If I think that ice cream vans are places where drugs are sold then why should I think that one run by a black person is any different?'

She pulled up at a set of lights and waited as a trail of broken humanity crossed the road on their way to Poundstretcher Lane, an area of cheapo shops and charity emporia.

'Depressing', said Truscott.

'This is our underclass on the move, Liz. Their daily migration to the shops to get their six packs of Rola-Cola, their catering packs of cereal, discounted cider and drugs.'

'You can get drugs in Poundstretcher?'

'I wouldn't claim so in court', he replied guardedly. Truscott laughed.

'Nearly there.'

They pulled up outside Shannen's block and looked at each other.

'Let's go', said Stevenson without enthusiasm. 'This'll be some old bollocks she could have told us on the phone. She just wants to punish us for being cops. Having to endure all those baby shit smells all over again.'

They were pleasantly surprised when Shannen came down to meet them in what passed for a lobby, looking slightly more kempt than normal. They were even more surprised when the flat was odour free and rather tidy. This time, when they sat, she offered them a hot drink which they both declined for health reasons. Nevertheless, she spent some time fussing around in the kitchen and the two detectives briefly discussed the apparent change in her circumstances as she did so.

'Is this the same woman?', asked Truscott smiling evilly. She waggled one eyebrow.

'She's dressed, has proper shoes on, looks a bit cleaner and the flat doesn't stink of non-existent babies. Very strange. Plus, she actually asked us to come over.' He looked at his Citizen watch, a present from an ex-girlfriend. 'Mind you she'd better hurry up.'

As if on cue, Shannen rejoined them and sat heavily.

'Right. I think I know the person you are after.'

The detectives raised their eyebrows.

'Go on', said Truscott.

'It's risky if I tell you', said Shannen.

'I don't think it is. This person is probably long gone and I doubt if any of this will come back to you.'

Truscott interjected at this point, saying, 'there is a very remote chance of you being called as a witness but we can make sure you are protected if that happens. I seriously doubt if that will happen.'

Shannen still looked dubious but she nodded her assent.

'I'll tell you what I know. He was an Asian. A Paki, you know?'

They didn't correct her description but nodded instead. Racism was the least of her problems.

'Go on.'

Shannen sighed. Stevenson was unsure if this was an act or genuine apprehension on her part. He was well used to prevarication and witnesses holding out when they needed to just to get on with it. Lonely people were the worst, or those for whom being the witness to a crime was the single biggest event in their recent life. Shannen might be either, or both, and the fact that she had cleaned the flat, dressed properly and actually invited them round suggested that there was a degree of truth in his suspicions. She was keen to make an impression for some reason.

'He was from the university. His name was Khan or something. I would say he was about twenty. He had a beard.'

'Was he Scottish?', asked Truscott.

'I already said he was a Paki.'

'Was he a Scottish Pakistani? Did he have a Scottish accent?', asked the female detective. Stevenson sat back now and let her get on with it. She had some sort of rapport with Shannen, whilst he did not and never would.

'Nah. He just spoke like a Paki. He didnae say much.'

'Did he come here?'

'Aye.'

'So, he might be on CCTV?' She glanced over at her male colleague who nodded.

Shannen just shrugged. She didn't know if the flats even had CCTV.

'Is there a caretaker or someone we could talk to?'

Shannen shrugged again as if she had suddenly become bored. Liz knew she had to inject some fire into the woman's belly.

'This is really helpful Shannen. We're not talking about some little crime here. It's not shoplifting or stealing cars. This is an international manhunt.' Shannen sat up, suddenly important, at the centre of something.

'Yeah. Okay. Well, there's a man who lives in flat one which is right next tae the doors in the lobby. I think he puts the bins oot and mops the puke out of the lifts, stuff like that. He might know aboot CCTV'n'that.'

'Would you be able to describe the man?' The words seemed to partially deflate their witness once again but she answered nevertheless.

'He's aboot sixty, straggly hair, always wears a maroon cardigan with a sort of blue stripe around the neck....'

'No, I mean the Asian man.'

'They all look the same, don't they? Pakis, I mean.'

'Was he trendily dressed? He didn't wear traditional clothes I presume?'

'I can't remember.' She then gave a pretty detailed description of their suspect's clothes, belying her supposed ignorance on the matter. 'He had brown boots. Lace up ones. Came up his leg, you know?' She pointed to a spot on her shin. 'They were a bit scuffed but looked expensive. He had tight blue jeans and a brown belt. His jeans were nae hangin' roond his arse, you know like they American rappers'n'that.'

Stevenson smothered a smile. Despite her relative youth, Shannen was not an ardent follower of current fashion trends even allowing for the copy of *Cosmo* she had rescued from the recycling bin on their last visit.

'What else?', prompted Truscott. She fired a quick glance at Mark Stevenson to make sure that he was taking down the details in his notebook.

'He had a blue Superdry T-shirt. Just a little logo up here.' She pointed to an area just above her left breast. Truscott noticed that Shannen's bra was much too small for her ample chest. She felt a pang of pity for this directionless soul who was clearly trying to do the right thing for the first time in her life.

'And he had a leather jacket, like a biker jacket with a zipper. It was black and all scuffed but deliberately scuffed, you know? Like it came oot of the factory that way. It had beige stripes doon the sleeve. He had an earring, just a little diamond stud thing like a girl wid wear. A bit poncy. And his hair was short, sort of oily and pointy in the middle.' She made a sort of triangular shape with her hands. 'Like that footballer.'

'David Beckham?'

'Aye.'

'That's a good description. What height was he?'

Shannen shrugged.

'Tall, short, average?'

'Average.'

'Would you be able to identify him from a photograph?'

'Youse have a photy of him?', she asked in surprise.

'Well, we don't know yet. We will have to look for him – or someone will. But could we call you back to identify him if we find some photos?'

Shannen shrugged. She seemed to sense that her moment was coming to an end and that her new pals were going to leave. She wanted them to stay but that *was just silly and pathetic on her part.*

'How long ago was this, Shannen?'

Shannen shrugged again. Shrugs were part of her language.

'A week ago?', suggested Stevenson. 'A month?'

'Probably two years ago', said Shannen.

***

Tom made an unusual detour that lunchtime, making his way to Waterstones to buy an atlas and smoking both there and back. He would claim the money back on expenses. The search for Odessa had given him new impetus in his career and he had decided upon a working lunch, the atlas open before him filling up with breadcrumbs as he devoured his sandwiches. He brushed them away with annoyance.

The image of Odessa suddenly disappearing was ingrained in his head. He was waiting on phone calls from several friendly agencies, hoping that they would share their information with him. Sometimes they did and sometimes they didn't – that's how it was and one just accepted it. With the atlas open on a double spread of the Med, he began to trace the known journey of the Odessa and added to that the unknown segment, the latter going off in several different directions. She had sailed from Sevastopol in Ukraine, which immediately gave rise to suspicions that the Russians, with their evident ambitions in that region, were somehow involved. That they were contributing heavily to the search meant nothing. They could spare some of their huge Tupolev bombers for a few days to keep up the pretence of not knowing where the ship was or what had happened to it.

He sat back and put the pencil between his lips.

Were the Russians in the frame? Of course, they were. Maybe they were at the top of the list. Wendy was looking over at him. He gave her an insincere smile and she looked away again. Had he not known better he would have picked her out as a spy – for the other side, whoever the hell that was?

Who was the other side these days? Once it had been easy to pick out the Russians and point a finger and say, 'there is the enemy.' Now things were a lot less clear. Tom sighed and clicked his tongue. He wasn't enjoying his sandwich much, the bread was stale. He dropped it into a bin and felt instantly better about his health. He was going to the gym tonight. It was a good place to think.

Back to the map.

So, Odessa had sailed through the Black Sea, dominated, he supposed, by Russia, and then into the Med, past Turkey. He peered closely at the map for the next few details. The ship had travelled through the Bosporus Straits to the Sea of Marmara. From there it had made its way into the Aegean. On either side of the Sea of Marmara was Turkey. But Turkey was a friendly nation, not given to acts of international terrorism despite its largely Muslim population. In general, Turkey and the Turks felt that their allegiances lay with the West.

The Aegean was dotted with Greek holiday islands, popular holiday spots and the ship had been sighted sailing south, some distance off the Turkish coast before turning roughly south west to steam into the Mediterranean. At some point it had disappeared. He supposed that it was still sailing south west but there were no guarantees that that was the case.

He paused, scratched at the stump of his leg where once he had a foot and wondered how much further on he actually was. Several things occurred to him. The Russian bombers that were currently being used to find the ship or wreckage could just as easily have sunk it. That was one thing. If the ship had just suffered a catastrophic explosion that was another. If someone had managed to disable all of the vessel's communications then that was yet another…

The TV news still described the disappearance as an act of piracy but that was the least likely explanation. Obviously, the various intelligence organisations looking into the matter were not sharing their professional opinions as yet. The Odessa had not put into port or at least not officially.

What were the implications of that?

Simply that there was no form of mutiny or takeover involving the crew.

He cast his glance back over the double page on the atlas. Having this book, although old-fashioned in concept, enabled him to trace the ship's last journey and still be able to use his computer for report writing or research. The Lloyd's Register was open to him but it had already released most of its secrets as far as he could tell.

Who else might be taking an interest in the ship? The Greeks for one. The Albanians? The Italians? The Syrians, the Egyptians, the Libyans? Not the Israelis, surely? And the Odessa had not passed through the Suez Canal so he wasn't suspecting any Saudi involvement. Had it passed through that region then the Yemenis might have been likely suspects. But the Odessa had categorically not passed through the Suez Canal. On second thoughts he would check.

***

Outside Shannen's flat they paused. A few cars passed them, hissing through puddles. Across the road from them a mother berated a large, dirty-looking child who should have been at school. He looked gormless and unhappy. His mother wore an anorak with a fake fur collar, leggings and pretend Ugg boots, which was pretty much the uniform for the estate. Her hair was dragged back severely from her sallow-skin face and a cigarette hung from her bottom lip.

'So, what do you think?'

'I don't know, Liz. She *is* a link to this guy… but two years? It's a long time. Whoever he is, he could be anywhere now. His appearance could be different – probably is, let's face it – and the link between her DNA and his joint gets very much extended – sort of drawn out – in two years. Who knows where that cannabis has been in that time? If he was ever caught, he could say that he'd got the drugs from anywhere. A friend of a friend of a friend…'

'And she thinks he was called Khan and he was a Pakistani?'

'I doubt if he gave her a name and to people like Shannen anyone who doesn't have white skin is probably a 'Paki'. I'm not saying for one minute that she didn't sell him drugs but it's a tenuous link, certainly if it gets to court.'

'Maybe court isn't where this is heading. They just want to find him. Some of these people don't survive the arrest operation', she said without a hint of sympathy. 'Osama Bin Laden didn't go up before the magistrates did he? Or whatever they have in America.'

'Special forces, that type of thing?'

'Could be. He's a terrorist after all. I reckon he's the Antwerp bomber. This is something big.'

DC Stevenson pursed his lips and then said, 'We didn't ask the caretaker about the CCTV.

'Long shot.'

'Let's ask while we are here.'

They retraced their steps and buzzed Flat One. There was an almost instantaneous answer and it was clear that the caretaker had been paying close attention to goings on in 'his' flats.

They identified themselves and heard the main door click open; he was waiting for them, exactly as described by Shannen, standing between his door and the door jamb, protective of his home. Only when they showed their ID cards did the door open fully. He stood back and ushered them in.

The flat was neat but in need of some fresh air and a lick of paint. There was a faint aroma of stale booze.

'Thanks for speaking to us Mr....'

He didn't offer his name.

'I didn't catch your name', said Mark.

'I didnae tell it ye.'

Funny fucker, thought the male DC rubbing his forehead and sighing. It was a waste of time. But they were here now.

'Okay, we wondered about CCTV. We might need to have a look at any old recordi…'

'Who said I had CCTV?'

'Do you?', asked Truscott. She sat on the arm of a chair in his cramped living room as if she was intending to stay. She hoped to make him feel uncomfortable so that he might comply with greater haste just to be rid of them. It was a tactic which worked well; few people with anything to hide wanted to spend time in the company of the police and she was sure that he had something to hide. Men like him – late middle-age bachelors – had skeletons in their cupboards, always something and often collections of porn.

The TV was blaring in the corner, some perma-tanned, bouffant-haired loon was talking excitedly about antiques.

'Aye', said the caretaker.

'We might need to see it then', said Stevenson.

'Oh, might ye?'

Something inside Truscott snapped at that moment, some little elasticated restraining strap that kept her mouth shut in the face of provocation.

'Right. Enough of the funny answers mate. Start cooperating with us or I will drag you down to the station. Then I'll get a warrant to search your flat and confiscate anything we think we need for our enquiry. That means we might find your stack of kiddy porn because we'll have to look through the hard drive on your computer. How does that sound?'

The caretaker looked momentarily startled. Her words, so unexpected, had hit home with force.

'I dinnae have a computer', he said but he was abashed nonetheless.

'Your CCTV?', said DC Stevenson reasonably.

'Okay. How long ago?'

The two detectives exchanged a look. The man on the TV stopped speaking for a moment as if he was listening in.

'Two years'.

'We had a new system put in six months ago', said the man running a hand through his unruly hair.

'Oh', said Mark in defeat.

'But I kept the tapes from before so you might be okay. It might be recorded over but it might not. If it is still there, there are dates and times on the tape.'

Mark blinked in surprise.

'Can we have the tapes?', he asked cautiously.

'Aye. No good to me. Mind, it'll take days to go through it all.'

'That's fine. We'll manage. If it's there, we'll find it', said Truscott sounding relieved. She almost regretted her previous hard tone now that he was being so bloody helpful… but not quite. He was still an arse.

The caretaker looked dubious but he stood and led them into the hall and then out of his flat into the lobby. His carpet slippers made no sound on the tiles. From his pocket he produced a bunch of keys and easily selected the correct one to open an understair cupboard.

'In here', he said. The room held the usual items of caretakery – mops, sprays, buckets, a sink and cloths. It stank of furniture polish. DC Stevenson closed his eyes but when he reopened them there were still about twenty boxes of video tapes stacked against the back wall. He nearly swore.

'They're not all full', said the caretaker.

'That's a relief', joked Stevenson.

'But most of 'em are', said the caretaker.

***

Chapter Five

'You want to go to Paradise?' The man smiled cruelly revealing perfect white teeth through his tidy but greying beard. The Bomber supposed he must be nearly sixty but he wasn't fat, didn't wear glasses and still had the air of a fighter about him. Not someone to mess with certainly, and yet he sat there so calmly and with endless patience as if every task could be finished in the afterlife if it couldn't be completed on earth. He was... at peace, and yet his business was that of violence and death. *How did he reconcile that?*

'Of course', answered The Bomber. It seemed like the only answer he could possibly give. What else could he say?

'You could be there now and yet you walked away. You walked away from Paradise...' He paused as if there was more he could say, but he was evidently pleased with his turn of phrase and wanted it to hang in the air for full effect. All of a sudden, it seemed like an act.

The Bomber felt uneasy.

He took a sip of his coffee – proper coffee, a double espresso – and as he did so he let his brain work out the details of his next statement. Care was needed. This was a test. He didn't understand the need for a test or quite what was expected from him so he took his time.

'If I had died then I couldn't have done any more. I decided to forego my passage to Paradise so that I could kill more of the infidel.' He was relieved to see the man smile and nod his head in agreement but his next words were at odds with his body language.

'I don't believe you', he said sharply. He narrowed his eyes as he spoke and kept his gaze fixed on The Bomber as he sipped his coffee.

'My sacrifice was to go on living in this world of greed and corruption but to give myself more chances to bring about its destruction.' He uttered the words with a sort of hushed passion but they certainly hit the mark. The man was beaming at him, his eyes glassy with emotion.

'You are exactly the man we need', he said.

'Need for what?'

'You are going to kill more of the infidel than you could ever imagine. We are putting together the most devastating bomb ever produced and you will be the man who delivers it.' He could barely keep the excitement out of his voice but his words were lost in the general chatter of the club. They were safe here, with other Muslims and all the others, especially since they conversed in English, a foreign language.

The Bomber nodded uncertainly. *The most devastating bomb ever produced? That couldn't be right, surely? More devastating than a nuclear bomb?*

'Is it a Russian bomb?'

'No. Well, not exactly. You might say that they have had a hand in it.'

'Okay. Well I am honoured to have been chosen.'

'I am happy for you. You will make history. Nothing that has gone before will come close to this.' The stranger was still nodding and beaming like a man suddenly revelling in his daughter's choice of husband. The Bomber felt a surge of pride despite his doubts. It couldn't possibly be a bigger, more destructive weapon than something possessed by the Russians or the Americans, but even so...

'You won't survive this one though', said the man. His tone was mock serious; he was holding his smile in check, a comedian about to deliver the punchline.

'Pardon?', asked The Bomber.

'This time you won't survive', explained the man. His smile had slipped. 'This bomb? Much too big for you to survive. You'll be in Paradise soon enough when it goes off.'

***

Tom felt nervous. More than that, he felt ridiculous that he felt nervous; he was after all an international man of mystery dealing death and... destruction to the Queen's enemies... from his desk... between bites of his curling sandwich from the deli across the street... the one where the woman who served knew all about the occupation of her customers. But none of that had anything to do with his nerves. He was meeting Claire tonight for a trip to the cinema and maybe a drink afterwards. *And what was wrong with that?*

Plenty. He could write a book – a short one admittedly – on the things wrong with the situation he was in.

Where to start? For one thing he wasn't sure how much he actually liked Claire. She was pretty and quite petite. She was intelligent. She wasn't exactly witty but on occasions she forced a smile at something he said, although he couldn't rely on it. Often, she ignored him. She dressed nicely – much more nicely than Wendy who looked okay but gave little thought to her appearance. Claire didn't wear too much make-up, which was another definite plus point. She was quite reserved and he liked that. She had a nice voice, no strong accent. In short there was a lot to like and when he thought about it carefully, as he was doing now, waiting outside her flat in a taxi that was costing him a fortune, there wasn't much he could fault her on. And yet there was something missing.

He simply wasn't attracted to her. He wondered if that would come in time. Maybe it was enough for now that she was attracted to him. But his sense of foreboding would not leave him. Perhaps the biggest problem was with going out on a date with a woman who sat six feet from you at a bank of desks in a rather confined office. If it went wrong – and that was beginning to feel like a self-fulfilling prophecy – then there was no escape from the subsequent ill-feeling. They might glower at each other for hours on end and make everyone hate them as their enmity sucked the life out of the place.

But that was another thing. Claire wouldn't sit back and let everyone hate *them*. She would make sure that they hated *him* and tell them why they should hate him. He hadn't even done anything wrong yet!

Tom was reassured a little when he saw her coming down the short flight of steps from her block looking quite stunning and quite pleased to see him. He silently reprimanded himself for his silly, unfounded worries. She had asked *him* out! How badly could it really go? This date was what she wanted!

'Christ almighty, give yourself a break', he mumbled as he got out of the cab.

'What's that guv?', asked the driver but Tom didn't hear. Claire seemed to appreciate the kiss on the cheek and the fact that he held the door open for her. Things were going well but, like a punch, all his previous doubts surfaced.

'Are you well?', she asked brightly as they pulled out into the evening traffic.

'Fine. Booked the tickets.'

'What are we going to see?'

'That one about Stephen Hawking. You haven't seen it have you?'

'No. It gets good reviews. Eddie Izzard.'

'Redmayne', he corrected.

'That's it, Redmayne Izzard.'

She was quick, he'd give her that. It was a short journey through the city. He marvelled at the numbers of people out enjoying the early summer heat. The bars had put tables outside, everyone wore shorts and the drink seemed to flow. He wondered how it would seem when they came out of the cinema but he didn't blame anyone for taking advantage of the sun. No one knew when summer started or ended these days. One day in April might be the sum total of British summer.

They enjoyed the film but didn't speak and Tom had maintained his sophisticate qualifications as a sophisticate by resisting the pick'n'mix.

They streamed from the cinema with the chattering hordes. She took his arm, a level of affection he hadn't entirely expected, and they made their way into the cool night air, joining the revelling crowds of mid-week drinkers. The pubs were still busy. The city had an ephemeral continental air; the surroundings suited well enough but the weather was marginal for much of the year.

They found an empty booth in the first pub they came to and claimed it as their own.s Tom pushed his way to the bar to get a pint of beer and a glass of white wine. He returned grinning sheepishly.

'What?', she asked, looking up at him.

'This', he said nodding at the drinks. 'It's a bit of a cliché.'

Claire was going to make a joke about her drinking the pint and letting him have the wine but she lost the will to say anything even as the words arranged themselves in her brain. Suddenly, after a day at work and a trip to the cinema everything became tiring.

'Nice pub', she commented. Tom replied with unintended grimness.

'Filled with the mid-week crowd, worried about going to work with a hangover, thinking, *can I have that last drink – the one for the road – or is that the one which tips me over the edge and gives me a hangover.'*

'Quite the philosopher. Is that what you are thinking about when you are sitting at your desk at work?'

'I suppose so. Sometimes at least.'

'You never really know anyone do you? Not when you just work with them. I didn't know your mind worked like that.'

'I suppose I am a bit of a people watcher, an amateur student of the human condition.'

She laughed at his self-analysis.

'Those two over there', he said nodding to the next booth. Claire glanced over at a middle-aged couple enjoying a drink but barely speaking or smiling.

'What about them?'

'They are the empty-nesters. Children left home, off at university, only come home when their washing needs to be done or when the money has run out. Mum and dad have lost their reason for staying married and only go out to the pub together to break the monotony of watching repeats of *Morse* on the TV. They are totally bored with each other. They have everything they could ever want but it's not enough.

'She dreams of running off with a toyboy called Pedro…'

Claire snorted with laughter at this point.

'But contents herself with buying jewellery from the internet which gives her thirty seconds of pleasure as she unwraps it and then a week of depression and guilt because she has wasted her money on something she didn't need. In the meantime, her wrists get heavier and heavier as she adds more and more accoutrements to them: bangles and beads and bracelets. She paints her nails and reads Cosmopolitan, pining after her lost youth and wishing that she could do it all over again and do it differently.

'They watch those advertisements for bloody awful river cruises that come on the TV after Coronation Street and each wonders if they could spend a solid week in the company of the other as they drift slowly up the Danube watching sheep graze on the banks in the drizzle. Could they tolerate their fellow codgers in the bar at night with their Cotton Traders pensioner shirts and their glasses of brandy and fake Rolexes, their sunburn and coiffured grey hair? They wonder if they have become as dull as these people on the cruise they haven't even signed up for yet.

'He wants a 3 series BMW but has to make do with a Nissan Primera. *Great car the Primera; roomy, well-equipped and reliable*, he tells everyone but he doesn't really like it at all. And he wants to play golf but can't hit a ball straight, besides which he doesn't want to turn up at the club in a Primera. When he gets the BMW then he can join the golf club. With a BMW it won't matter about being able to play well. But already he is worried that he might not be able to afford all the extras or the metallic paint for the BMW when he goes to the show room. He might have to order a plain white one which doesn't even have leather seats…'

'You know all this for a fact?'

'Just look at them. Tell me it's not possible.'

She smiled; it was more than possible.

'They're not love's young dream, I suppose', she said before adding, 'what do you think of your workmates? I hardly dare ask'.

'They're okay.' He said cautiously, suspecting a trap. He took a sip of his beer. He counted himself as one of those who didn't want to go to work with a hangover.

'So, you can manage a complete run-down of the characters and lifestyles of people you don't know at all but when I ask about people you do know, you come up with 'okay' and nothing more.'

'You really want to know?'

'I asked', she said. She watched him from over the rim of her glass as she drank.

'I don't think much of them. They are pious and arrogant and up their own arses. They have God complexes and think that they are the only ones with anything to say or who make any contribution to life. They are boring fantasists, who read spy stories and then criticize them for being inaccurate. They love having secrets but let slip enough to keep people intrigued even though they can't give anything away. Everyone knows what they do but daren't ask. They dream of going to dinner parties and of delivering some subtle, yet stunning icebreaker comment about their work. The men lust after a fast car that they can't actually afford and the women lust after a man with a fast car he *can* afford. They like skiing holidays because it's a bit James Bond. They drink cocktails for the same reason.'

'Blimey', she said.

'You asked', he replied with a shrug.

'I did. Don't you think our work has any value?'

'I do but we don't have to make it sound so bloody ridiculous. We're civil servants with offices, computers and little pads of post-it notes. Wendy for instance is an arrogant, opinionated moron. Intelligent but with no common sense.'

'Are you better than her?'

He sensed that the conversation was heading into conflict. He reasoned, however, that this date had been her idea and she had also been the one who instigated this line of conversation therefore she would have to put up with how it turned out.

'Am I better than her? Probably not in terms of doing the job but I am a better human being than her, certainly.'

She was temporarily floored by his argument.

'Oh', she said at last. 'I am used to thinking about us in terms of work.'

'And I think about people in terms of the people they are. Work is only one aspect of who we are. There are other ways to judge people. Other criteria that are just as important. And all this shit we are bombarded with about how dangerous Britain would be if it wasn't for us and that we are unsung heroes... It just sounds like horseshit. I mean they really labour the point, don't they?'

'But it is true', she protested, laughing.

'I know it is but I don't need to be told every day. Just let me get on with it. I'll be fine.' His situation angered him sometimes but he had kept his temper. He was relieved to see Claire still smiling; Tom wasn't confident about being a dream date for any attractive, intelligent young woman.

'No one else thinks like that', she said.

'Well, maybe they should.' He lifted his pint to his lips. 'It's like you said. Sometimes you just don't really know people. You didn't know I felt like that.'

'I suppose not.'

'Now, *you* are a good employee because you get on and do your work without complaint.' He watched the late middle-aged couple as they left their booth. He felt sorry for them and their respective plights; a lack of love and fulfilment for her, the lack of a BMW and golf club membership for him.

Claire scowled and he quickly qualified his statement.

'That's not a criticism by the way. What I mean is that you play the game. You do what needs to be done and say what needs to be said. All of the things that torment me, you don't even notice and it is much better for you. I'm out of step, you're in step. Me hating the people I work with is pointless and worse than that it makes it look as if I am the one in the wrong. I'm the arsehole, not them.'

She smiled sympathetically as he tried to find a way to bring the conversation back to something slightly more uplifting than his battle with the world. The more he thought the emptier his mind became.

'How did you lose your foot?', she asked, deftly changing the subject. He was glad she had.

'Mortar attack in Iraq. Everyone assumes I stood on a mine because it is a missing foot. The base I worked on got attacked. I got caught in a building which collapsed. The rubble came down on my foot and they had to amputate it. I got flown back to UK, fitted out with a prosthetic, and that was that. I maybe could have stayed on in the army but I'd had enough so I left. No regrets.'

'No regrets? You must regret losing your foot surely?'

He blew air out from his cheeks and answered.

'I suppose so, but I was lucky. I could have been killed and I wasn't. I still lead a normal life but with a bit of a limp. Others were much worse off than me. So, I don't play on it.'

'You have never talked about it', said Claire.

'People don't ask because they think I'll be too upset to talk about it but actually I'm not bothered either way.'

'And how did you end up in intelligence?'

'That's what I did in the army. Got offered a job when I came out. The old boy network. Great when it works in your favour. Terrible when it doesn't.'

She nodded her understanding of the concept.

'The old boy network is fine if it selects the correct people and not a load of duffers. They recruit from Oxford and Cambridge because they supposedly have the best graduates', she said

'Which were you?'

'Ha. Durham. Occasionally someone else slips through.'

'You're not exactly a slacker though. I think you're marked for great things.'

'And you're not?'

'I'm not a graduate. I was just a sergeant in the Intelligence Corps. I'm lucky to be working in such elevated circumstances.'

'You put yourself down.'

'I don't really. It just happens to be the truth.'

A group of men – they looked like rugby players – standing in a crowd around a pedestal table, laughed uproariously at some profane joke. They created an explosion of mirth. Their sound filled the pub for a moment, drowning out any other sounds and making speech impossible.

'Rugby players', said Tom with a hint of disapproval.

'Not your type?'

'No one is my type.'

'You aren't a rugby player?'

'Not with one foot?'

She rolled her eyes.

'When you had two feet', she said with slight exasperation.

'No. I boxed for a while but I gave it up when I was nineteen.'

'Why?'

'I didn't like getting hit.'

Claire laughed.

'You see, me not being a graduate means that there is only so far up the greasy pole I could ever go. So, I could do as much crawling as Wendy or Matt but I would probably stay exactly where I was. So, although I don't mind getting on with my job, there is no long-term plan for my career and if they needed to make redundancies, I'd be one of the first out of the door.'

'You act like there is more to life and I'm not saying that I disagree but what else is there? For you I mean? You don't have kids, or anything, or your own house.'

'Yes, when you put it like that my life is pretty useless. I might as well end it. Thank you for making it so clear to me.'

'I didn't mean that. But your attitude is more like you would find in someone married, who had a great hobby or great holidays.'

'Or two feet? Besides I could say the same about you. You're knocking on a bit now – twenty-five or so – no kids, no husband…'

Claire rolled her eyes again.

'Maybe I'm on the lookout for a husband', she said mischievously. She gave Tom a look.

'Choose wisely, is all I can say. There are a lot of poor ones out there. What sort of thing are you after? Rugby player, own teeth, Audi, Ray Bans, Union Jack flip-flops, likes beach holidays and has a subscription to Men's Health?'

Claire laughed.

'You put a lot of effort into your disparaging comments', she said, wiping away a tear.

'It's a gift of sorts', he said modestly. 'I am a prospective husband, you know.'

'Yes.' Claire said that one word with no inflexion at all.

'You're not giving much away.'

'I did ask you out for this date…'

'How do you think it's going?'

'Not bad', she said coyly. 'I've been on worse.'

Buoyed by apparent success, Tom delved a little deeper. It was a mistake.

'You were engaged once.'

Claire's face clouded over at once whether with anger, sadness or despair he couldn't tell. She looked away, breaking some sort of spell. He knew that he had erred for this was plainly a sensitive subject for her. The trouble now was how to patch up the conversation and carry on as if the words had never been said. As ever on these occasions his mind went blank. He had some sort of social affliction, the reasons for and the effects of which he barely understood. It was an insidious blight on his life, attacking him when he was weak. As a sergeant he had become a member of the Warrant Officers' and Sergeants' Mess, which had involved him taking part in endless social gatherings with layers of rules and customs to be learnt and adhered to. He dreaded mess evenings and when his supply of small talk had dried up, he felt the strongest desire to slink off back to his room and go to bed with a paperback novel.

'I'm sorry. That was obviously the wrong thing to…'

'Can we just change the subject?', she said. Claire oozed tension. Her jaw was clenched tight and Tom wanted to leave at once. He hadn't even asked for the bloody date…

'Can I get you another drink?', he said, but in his mind, he was saying, *I'll ring for a cab.*

***

A police van came to pick up the boxes. The caretaker didn't offer to help take them away but stood there with his arms folded looking rather pleased with himself.

'He was probably supposed to dump these himself and now we are doing his work for him', commented Stevenson. 'We're going to end up putting these in a skip. There is no way we can look through this lot. This is months of footage and we don't even know if this bugger is on it or not.'

'Maybe the DI will give us a team of helpers', said Truscott.

'Us two? Are you joking?'

'If this is important enough…'

'Don't hold your breath.'

'I don't know Mark, she sounded pleased when I spoke to her on the blower.'

They returned to the station to be greeted by the DI on the station steps, looking agitated.

'Mark and Liz, we've hired the Guild Hall round the corner. They're installing video players and monitors as we speak. You're going to have five constables assigned to you and we are getting a team from Belgium over and an inspector from Holland too. Send the van round there and start unloading the tapes and getting them into some sort of order. I'm going to be overseeing this but you two know what is going on at this end of things so you will have to brief our new team. This is a big deal all of a sudden. Are you up for it?'

Both constables felt crushed by the sudden weight of responsibility.

'Absolutely, ma'am', said Truscott.

***

Chapter Six

The plane tickets had been shoved through the letter box in a white envelope with a single name written on it – Khan. He lifted it from the mat, hefted it in his hand as if it was a weighty item and then took it to his room. It was then that he began to suspect that the parcel had been tampered with. He sat heavily on his bed, rather dismayed; this might be yet another complication that he could do without. *Could someone have seen enough to read the destination on the ticket and who would that person have been?*

He'd been slowly coming to terms with the impending end to his life. Although he had set out to be a suicide bomber, the success of his single mission had filled him with such pride and happiness that continuing with life seemed rather attractive now. He wasn't being flippant when he thought that perhaps Paradise could wait. There were things to do on earth.

The fact that he could carry out more missions was secondary to the thrill of living. After all, who wouldn't want to be him? He was central to the greatest battle in mankind's history. He was in place to be a successor to one of the great fighters like Osama Bin Laden. He had been chosen to deliver the greatest blow, something which would easily eclipse the attacks on the Pentagon and the World Trade Center. His name would become synonymous with Jihad…

But he wanted to be around to see it. It wasn't just self-aggrandisement or pride, he told himself, it was more than that. He just wanted to know that he had succeeded. And if he was dead then how could he know? Nothing had matched the thrill of seeing the effects of the Antwerp bomb, and it had been a world first – a suicide bomber being able to witness the effects of his attack.

He thought about Osama Bin Laden again and an image of the great man flashed through his mind: beard, kindly smile, dazzling white robes and AK47. He hadn't died in the attacks he had orchestrated. He hadn't planned to die at all, at least not in connection with the war against America, and no one thought any less of him. The great had to live to orchestrate the war. You didn't use your generals in bayonet charges... He worried now that his death would be a waste of his talents.

He wasn't having second thoughts, he reminded himself. Not exactly. He would still carry out his mission. He looked at the envelope again. He didn't want to make the existing tear any bigger but he held it open carefully with a finger and thumb until he could see inside. He could tell that it was an airline ticket – AirWest – but not the destination. However, as he twisted the envelope in his attempts to see inside, he made a worrying discovery. The gap between the main body of the envelope and the flap was big enough to, with a bit of a shake, dislodge the ticket. He did so. One edge of the ticket protruded. He used finger and thumb to gently slide the entire thing out and into the palm of his hand. And there was the destination – Tripoli.

For a moment he felt as if the noose was tightening, that someone – someone deadly – was on to him. If someone had the gumption to open the envelope and to check out its contents, then they would only have done so knowing that he was a *person of interest* or however they phrased it. Not everyone had their mail tampered with.

Or was he flattering himself? He sucked on his teeth as he sat there and turned the ticket over and over again in his hand. *Was anyone onto him?*

How could they be, especially after his recent demise in the Antwerp bombing? His nerves began to settle. True, they might be looking for him because they were on to his contact, whoever had put the tickets through the door, but if that was the case, they would have come for him by now. They certainly couldn't wait until he had disappeared in Libya.

He rubbed his hand down his beard, a repeated but unconscious movement, redolent of a cat preening itself. He felt that the immediate threat had passed, or more accurately that the threat had existed in his mind only. But still he turned the package over and over and still he asked himself the same question, *had someone opened the parcel?*

He pursed his lips and glanced at his watch, a gold Rolex he had bought in Saudi Arabia. He remembered explaining to his fellow students that it wasn't a fake but they just didn't believe that an impoverished student could afford to spend ten thousand pounds on a watch. Of course, he *wasn't* an impoverished student! They didn't quite grasp that either. He had lived in student digs but his rent was prepaid and he always had plenty of cash in his bank account.

So, if the outside world wasn't after him but the package had been opened and somebody now knew his destination, then who – and more importantly, what – was he going to do about it? Just then he heard a noise.

Someone was on the landing, and since he lived here alone…

Slowly he sat up. His landlady was at work. She didn't come back until close to tea time. His mind was racing, each sense on alert. He could smell nothing and the sounds that had first alerted him to danger had receded. The Bomber tilted his head towards the door and listened. He held his breath. No sound now, but they were there alright.

He licked his lips as he looked around the room for a weapon but close quarter fighting wasn't really his thing. He told himself that he was a strategic weapon, not a tactical one, and at ten stone he didn't have a lot of weight to throw into a scrap. He'd only had one fight in his life with some obnoxious fat kid from a housing estate who didn't like 'Pakis'. He could have run and the fat kid would never have caught him but he stayed, fought and got pummelled. It wasn't all bad news for it had given him anger and hatred, and when the time came to channel those emotions, he was ready. More than ready as it happened. The Jihad had given him a focus and now it would make him famous.

But only if he survived to launch the big attack, whatever it was, and that would not happen if the person on the other side of the door was an assassin. It was all becoming very real now, very immediate. He wasn't watching these events on the television, they were happening on the other side of a cheap plywood-framed door. A few millimetres of wood separated him from a killer's bullet or knife blade, and he was unarmed.

He'd fired a gun in the training camp in Iraq, just a few rounds from a Russian sniper's rifle – a Dragonov, an unwieldy beast – but he didn't have anything now, not even a handgun. His killer would be armed. What would be the bloody point otherwise? His mouth was dry.

A bedside light? It was a ceramic orb with a cheap wire and cloth shade and about as deadly as a watermelon. His shoes lay next to the bed. A pair of red Converse. Terrifying. He heard another noise and became fixated on the door handle, expecting it to rattle at any moment. Nothing. No repeat of the noise either. Maybe if he rushed them. They wouldn't be expecting that.

He resolved to go on the offensive. He would attack the attacker. Allah would protect him, sparing him for greater battles to come and he would prevail. Courage came to him in a tremendous wave. All the same he winced as he sat up and one of the elderly bed springs made a noise like a catapult. It might have been funny. Take away the fear and the real possibility of throwing away his newly discovered destiny, then yes, the noise was very comical indeed. He froze and remained frozen until his muscles began to ache from the effort of keeping him immobile.

Whoever was outside was taking their time. They were a cool customer. Much cooler than him. He began to feel like an amateur again…

***

It had been three days since the ill-fated date but things had been okay at work. They had the second drink and then, by mutual consent, taken a taxi back to their respective Pimlico flats. There had been no peck on the cheek this time and certainly no hint of an invitation inside for a 'coffee'. Tom smothered a smile as he recalled that awkward evening. Claire made out like she was the girl for him but so what? He genuinely didn't care. He was mildly worried that she might be a complete miserable bitch towards him at work as a result of the flop date but that hadn't happened and, after an initial hesitancy, things had got back to normal very quickly, that is to say they practically ignored each other.

There was no suggestion that another date was in the offing, which was fine with him. Okay, she was pretty, intelligent, witty and they had actually enjoyed their time together until near the end of the night, but there was still something missing. He supposed that he didn't quite trust her and when he gave the matter further consideration, he became more certain that his instincts were right. He *didn't* trust her and he was pleased that his reservations had firmed up. It wasn't a lack of trust in her ability or her loyalty to the Queen, it was more prosaic than that. She wouldn't be – and he hated the phrase – but she wouldn't be *there for him*. How quaintly American.

But it was true. There was something missing from her personality, something shallow about her as if her emotions were blunted. He could imagine buying her flowers and her forgetting to put them into a vase with water and then going round to her flat and finding them dead, next to a pile of washing up or down the side of the fridge. Or he might buy her a watch for her birthday and when the battery died she would put the watch in her bedside cabinet and simply do without a watch not even thinking about the effect it might have on his feelings.

In short, she was a bit of a bitch. Maybe not as bad as Wendy, who was completely untrustworthy and not even terribly bright in his opinion.

Both women were good-looking, and when he thought about them he was reminded of the old joke;

Three women go for a job as a secretary. They are interviewed by the three senior managers – all men – and give their reasons as to why they should be given the job. The first candidate could type two hundred words a minute. The second used to be a PA in a rival company and knew lots of company secrets. The third had a first-class honours degree from Oxford.

When the most senior of the managers is asked which one he thinks should get the job, he silently considers the three candidates and then says,

'I'll have the one with the big tits.'

Was that ever a true reflection of the selection process through which job candidates went? Obviously, it shouldn't have been but just supposing his two female colleagues had got their jobs based on their looks. What would have happened to them if they'd had faces like slapped arses and arses like the blunt end of an oil tanker? Or facial warts? Or hairy moles in the centres of their foreheads? How much use was an Oxbridge degree when you weighed in at twenty-stone despite drinking three two litre bottles of Diet Coke everyday?

'You were off in another world there', she said from across the bank of desks. He was stirred from his reverie by the words, brought back to the present, the here and now.

'I was thinking about this, er… ' He pointed dumbly to his desk and the paperwork it held. 'This, er thing I am doing.'

'Fancy a coffee?', she asked brightly.

'A coffee? Yeah, whatever. Tonight?'

'No!', She wrinkled her nose and shook her head as if his words were absurd. 'Now.'

'Yeah. That's right. Now. Okay. Let's go. Get your coat'n'that', he said distractedly.

'Get my coat?'

'You know. *Get your coat, you've pulled.* That's a joke.'

Claire shook her head in dismay. Tom was being an arse which was quite characteristic. She had hoped that maybe she would understand him a bit better having socialised with him but that was not the case. If anything, she understood him less but she wasn't ready to give up yet.

The restroom was empty as usual, just Tom, Claire and an overflowing waste bin. Tom deposited a few coins in the coffee machine and waited for it to produce two melting cups filled with artificial tasting, but to him, delicious coffee.

'So how are you keeping?', he asked to fill the dead time between coin insertion and drink receipt.

'Fine. I wanted to say sorry about the other night', she said to his back. He turned moments later with two hot drinks and a surprised look on his face. He wasn't used to anyone apologising, especially not someone like her who could afford to be off with him, and frequently was.

'It's fine. My fault for being nosy. I think I ruined the evening.'

'No. You didn't ruin it. I ruined it. I should stop being over-sensitive and just get on with it.'

Tom sat down opposite her and smiled, but felt no intimacy at all. There was nothing between them. He wasn't even sure if she would ever even be a mate, not even one of those mates who you knew were essentially no good but who were a laugh on a night out. She might not even be the sort of mate who you wanted to see once every ten years for about five minutes. He had plenty of those already, mainly old army buddies with whom he now had nothing in common. Tom had moved on. Sometimes he felt as if he had moved on from everything.

However, for ease of working with her, it was better that they be on good terms. It saved any unpleasantness. So British that: *unpleasantness*. It was a word which, in the mouth of Brit, could describe anything from a disagreement over a hedge boundary to a nuclear war.

'How has your day been?', he asked, injecting a cheery note into his torpor.

'Just the usual, Tom. Nothing special.'

The use of his first name jarred slightly; they weren't normally used in the office except when picking out one possible conversant from another.

She put the same question to him and he answered in much the same vague manner. The conversation was forced, unnatural, joyless, pointless.

'Are you getting anywhere with it?', she asked. She made the words sound purely conversational, as though she was entirely incurious, but was she trying a bit too hard? *Was this studied indifference a bit too much of a put on?* There was something about the way she asked and then instantly looked away, studying what was a totally blank wall as though it held great fascination for her. He wasn't supposed to say anything about the missing ship, not even to her. He didn't want to come out with any of that 'need to know' bullshit they loved and yet she really did *not* need to know.

'Erm bits and pieces. It's nothing much. Just keeping me out of mischief.' In fact, that day he'd had a call from an Israeli intelligence officer telling him that they suspected that the Odessa had nuclear waste onboard, hidden amongst the other crap it carried. The Israelis, efficient and reliable as they were, often kept their cards close to their chests but on this occasion had decided to share. The officer's words had chilled him.

'This is a bomb my friend and if you ask me, they are going to plant it under your arse, there in London.'

They weren't always right but often enough for him to take the warning seriously. The two men agreed to keep in touch and set up a discrete channel of communication which cut through some of the formal bullshit they would otherwise have to endure just to make a simple call. He gave his name as Herv Ankoplar, which he had to spell for his British colleague and which looked like an anagram when jotted down on paper. So far, he'd made VERA POLAR but he had some letters left over; H, N and K. RE HANK V POLAR... that didn't make much sense.

'What are you thinking about? Have you got epilepsy or something?'

'I was just thinking about work.' He ignored the nasty slight.

'Are you a bit stuck?', she asked solicitously. She might have been talking about a crossword he was attempting. No one got *a bit stuck* round here.

Tom beamed at her.

'No, no. Nothing like that. It just takes time. Quite complicated.'

He thought that he might have intercepted a look of disappointment, anger or frustration or possibly some subtle blend of all three. To keep the peace, he considered telling her more than she was supposed to know but he reminded himself that he wasn't actually too bothered if she was disappointed, angry or frustrated. She wasn't supposed to be asking about these things anyway. Claire should have understood the reasons for his reticence and allowed him to avoid the subject. Had the boot been on the other foot she might well have been aggrieved at his unasked-for probing about a case she was looking at.

A short awkward silence ensued but then she smiled with affected stoicism and said, 'despite the other night, do you fancy coming out for a drink?'

Tom didn't. No matter how he tried, he couldn't see past the many reservations he had about this otherwise alluring woman. They were not a match. She would be high maintenance, demanding and awkward. She was too ready to take offence, too shallow, too keen on her work. There was just something missing. Many things missing.

'Okay. Just say when.'

'I'll text', she said.

He noted that whilst he had agreed to this date it had immediately been put on her terms, to her timetable. They would go when it best suited her. That was how it would always be and she would sulk if that was not the case. With sudden clarity he realised that she had been a spoilt child, indulged by everyone around her and that the traits she had developed had been carried over into adulthood. She was used to getting her own way and her personality was most unattractive when that didn't happen. It wasn't hard for him to imagine her being a bit of a bunny-boiler.

'Okay.' He drank from his coffee, hitting what he thought of as a thermocline, an invisible but quite defined border between the cooler top half of the drink and the hotter bottom half.

Claire was looking at him expectantly as if he had told her a joke but then forgotten to deliver the punchline.

'I don't have your number', she said finally. She was on the cusp of exasperation; that was another thing that would never change about her.

He gave her the number and she put it into her phone with the deftness of a teenager. She could barely remember a time when mobile phones had been the preserve of the wealthy or the foolish lover of gadgets.

They chatted about inconsequential things. She was lively, interesting and happy. She had a beautiful smile which she used a lot and she liked to laugh. Claire was everything a woman should be. Tom desperately hoped she wouldn't text him.

***

Mark scratched his head and sighed. His sigh turned into a groan.

'What's up with you?', asked Liz. 'Your piles playing up again?'

'I'm looking at all this lot. I feel like my entire life has been taken over by video tape. This is a slim chance you know. Has anyone considered the possibility that he might not be on any of the tapes or that it might be really indistinct if we do get an image?'

'They have. They must have, but someone is keen for this to happen so we just go along with it. Just play the game, Mark, play the game.'

It was 08:30. The uniform constables, now out of uniform, sat at their monitors, trawling through hours of grainy, low quality video footage of a mostly empty lobby area in the flats on the estate in Perth. At the start they had cracked a few jokes or laughed at some weird behaviour they had witnessed but it wasn't funny any longer; none of it was funny. Watching drunks trip over the welcome mat or piss up against the door of the understair cupboard was no longer amusing. Watching the same drunks on another night puking on the stairs, or watching the caretaker in his maroon cardigan with the blue trim round the neck, cleaning up the puke a few hours later was not entertaining. On yet another night one of the drunks – and there were several habitual pissheads, video tape regulars – had curled up and gone to sleep next to the bottom step, lying there for six hours as another might sleep next to his partner.

All life was there, captured in glorious black and white. One tenant was obviously a prostitute judging by the haphazard trail of male visitors she attracted to her door. The flats seemed to have their own gay couple, two butch-looking men, builders or similar, finding solace in each other's company in this most unfriendly place. The police officers were soon able to separate the tenants from the visitors and got a feeling for the flats' natural rhythms, the comings and goings, the goings and comings. It became predictable. It became boring, so boring in fact that it became stressful. They started each new day brightly enough but within an hour their task was extremely tiresome.

This was the crime fighting equivalent of factory work with monotony piled on monotony. Their collective sense of purpose dissipated with each false alarm, with each rewind and fast forward. Images of unrelenting sameness burned themselves into their minds, be they of the same patch of corridor, the lobby and doors or the lifts. Each tape was slotted in with a feeling of foreboding and with no expectation of a result.

The visitors were the usual mix but predominantly white, male and young. There were few Asians, few Blacks and a disproportionately small number of women. They hoped that their target would at least stand out if he ever appeared. The quest had begun with tapes from thirty months previously but the tapes ran up to a period ending six months ago. Due to the sheer mass of material they still had no idea if they were looking at a complete record of that twenty-four-month period.

But they knew it must have been important work, for coppers were in such short supply that they were rarely spared for anything other than patrols, paperwork and court appearances. At no point were they told about the reason for the work they were doing, although it was something to do with the Antwerp bombing. They guessed that they were looking for an associate of the dead terrorist.

There were still occasional moments of levity. One of the constables had managed to spot himself on a tape, knocking on a flat door. There was no answer. He recalled that it had been in connection with a stolen motorbike from nearly two years ago. *'Is that what I look like?'*, he had asked in dismay, fearing that he was less handsome than he supposed. Another such moment was when they caught the caretaker peeping through the prostitute's letter box. He was there for over a minute, bent over like a crone before he moved on. Caught on his own security system. *What else had he got up to?*

Peppered throughout the coverage was the figure of the caretaker, emptying bins, mopping, brushing, polishing. He was more industrious than anyone had thought…

The Dutch and Belgian team were staying at a local hotel, being brought into work each morning in a minibus for a nine o'clock start. They all spoke remarkably good English, chosen for that reason, supposed Mark and Liz.

The Dutch inspector was called Pieter. Balding and a bit overweight he was nevertheless charming and professional. He often alluded to the fact that his retirement beckoned. His look was dreamy when she spoke of handing in his gun and growing tulips, although his Scottish colleagues had begun to think that mention of tulip growing was allegorical. Perhaps 'growing tulips' meant doing nothing. Pieter had spent much of his career policing Amsterdam, a fact which had made him detest both drug users and drug dealers. He was never going to be a fan of Shannen Cassidy should the two ever meet.

This morning he looked stern.

'Might I take the briefing this morning?', he asked Liz.

'I'm sure the DI won't mind', she said.

The team assembled at the guildhall stage where Pieter sat with a sheaf of notes in his hand. He liked informality so long as it didn't interfere with the job getting done – the outcome was more important than the process.

'As you know, lots of people are working on this case. It is an international affair simply because these radicalised Muslims can be anywhere or travel anywhere to carry out their deeds. So far, we have been concentrating on establishing the identity of the Antwerp Bomber. Our Belgian colleagues are involved because the bomb was in their country. I am involved because it is feared that IS will target the Netherlands next. You are involved because there is a link to Scotland, namely the drugs sold to The Bomber by Shannen Cassidy.'

His tiny audience were rapt although he had said nothing new.

'But things have changed. We had hoped to learn about the cell this man worked for by finding out as much as we could about this particular bomber – the one who died in Antwerp – only we now know, or we think we know, that he didn't die at all.' Pieter paused to let the meaning and implications of his words sink in.

'The Belgian forensics team have found no unaccounted-for traces of DNA at the scene. In other words, all the remains found have belonged to one of the victims. So, unlessThe Bomber was vaporised by the explosion, he wasn't actually there at the time of detonation. We can always find traces ofThe Bomber in these cases. There was no unaccounted-for DNA at all. This wasn't a suicide bomber.

'Whether this marks a change in tactics for IS I couldn't say. I'm not sure if that is even our concern. But what *is* our concern is that we must try to get this bastard before he does the same thing again. We must assume that is the idea. Why else would he choose to survive unless he was being used for another attack? So that means it is a manhunt and all we have to go on is his link to Shannen. I suppose we might be working against the clock but there is no way of knowing if that is the case at the minute, so for now we get cracking and see what we can turn up.'

With Pieter's message ringing in their ears the team returned to their monitors in the hunt for the Antwerp bomber. It seemed like they were in for a long haul with this one. There was very little to go on but it was down to them to methodically assemble a trail to follow, working against the clock as they did so.

***

Jack had done a few shifts clearing glasses and washing pots in the restaurant. He didn't enjoy it exactly but he got paid, had a free meal, and a free pint of beer at the end of his shift when the place had emptied out. That free drink in particular brought with it a great sense of wellbeing, of a job well done. He had sweated and, in his books, if you worked hard enough to perspire then you had earned the right to replace your missing body fluids with beer. He had quickly become friends with Penny, the slightly, but only slightly, overweight bar maid with the pretty face and dirty laugh. She was just the right side of forty and bucolically attractive. The others were pleasant company too, except for the cook who was a miserable bastard who had apparently modelled himself on Gordon Ramsey or some other surly TV egg boiler, and who thought it was okay to swear and shout at his underlings. He and Jack had exchanged severe looks and he guessed that the cook had got the message that Jack wasn't going to be messed with.

'So, what are your plans?', asked Penny as she sipped on a half pint of cider.

'That's the thing. I haven't made any. That's why I am here, to give myself time to make plans, to figure out what I want to do. I don't want to get trapped in a job I hate and not be able to get out for fear of losing my pension or something like that. I want to know exactly what I want to do and if I end up trapped, I won't mind because hopefully I won't *feel* trapped.'

She nodded and said, 'not many of us get the chance to do that.'

'I know, but I'm not married, no one is depending on me, I have no mortgage. I can afford to be selfish about it and not hurt anyone else.' He smiled. 'So, what brought you up here? You are plainly not Scottish.'

'To get away from it all', she said simply. He sensed that there was more to say but that it might have to wait for another night. For the first time he sensed tragedy or something like it. Already he knew he would miss her when he moved on as he would do someday but he had become used to saying goodbye and consoled himself with the thought that it was better to have met the people he had met than to have passed them by on life's journey.

'Who would have guessed we'd end up here?', he asked, gazing out over a stormy sea. Crooked lines of creamy surf moved shoreward like advancing infantry and he found himself mesmerised by them. 'This is the end of the world.'

'I suppose', she said. 'So, what do you think you want your life to be like?'

'That's it. No idea. I was in the army but after a few years I knew that I didn't want to do that any longer. But as I am making my mind up no one else is suffering as a result of my indecision. And no one can complain that I don't earn much. All I need is enough to look after myself.'

'So someday you plan to have the detached house and the 2.4 children and the Ford Focus?'

'It sounds awful when you put it like that, like living death, but we all fall into that trap eventually. Maybe you fell into it and then escaped again?'

'Something like that.' She spoke nicely, sounding intelligent and educated.

Penny had finished her drink and stood, yawning.

'Tomorrow is another day. It might be the day that our dreams come true', she said. 'But before that I am going to bed.'

Jack watched her go and wondered if the life he wanted even existed. After all, she was yet to find *her* perfect life. Maybe no one ever truly succeeded in finding happiness.

***

Chapter Seven

Herv Ankoplar had spent two days looking at the names of the crew onboard the MV Odessa. The skipper was a German, the first mate was Danish, the rest a mix of Filipinos, Chinese and Greeks. The Captain was Schumann, first mate was Hansen. The remainder had the sorts of names he thought befitted their nationality, except for one. Ossama Bilal didn't sound like he quite belonged on that crew and Herv tried to convince himself that he didn't think that just because of the man's first name which reminded him of another famous Osama, albeit one with slightly different spelling. But it was hard to think of someone called Ossama Bilal and not conjure up an image of Osama Bin Laden.

The shipping company representative had been awkward at first, not fully cooperating and not releasing the details he required, but Herv made a breakthrough via the simple expedient of threatening to send a team of commandos around to kill them all in their beds. This seemed to concentrate his mind greatly and all of sudden the information he required was at the man's finger tips. He could hear them at work on the keyboard. They were all the same these dodgy shipping companies, easy to intimidate. What he had not said was that he might send some commandos around anyway.

They had references for the officers and men and all their paperwork was in line with international regulations. Herv knew nothing about these regulations – he could always double check later – but he knew that the man on the phone was past the stage where he might try to mislead him; in fact he would be looking over his shoulder for months to come.

The sticking point came, as he expected, with Ossama Bilal, who didn't possess the correct papers, had no experience of seamanship and who should never have been aboard.

'So, he didn't possess an Ordinary Seaman Certificate or its equivalent?'

'No.'

'Do you think that might be why your ship has gone missing?', he asked sarcastically. The frightened Russian had no answer. 'I'm surprised that the skipper agreed to sail with him but then this is a dodgy little racket going on.'

He had his man on the ropes.

'So, this cargo was quite legitimate?'

He had to explain the meaning of the word 'legitimate' which was funny in the circumstances. There was a pause on the line. The man was thinking about how he could distance himself from the ton of shit thatwas likely to fall on the company he worked for. Herv merely wanted confirmation of their suspicions. With that in place he could order that things be moved on rapidly.

'Sometimes I think we get waste products from nuclear power factories. It is cheaper to take it to Africa than to reprocess it. That is what I think. No one tells me these things but I am suspicious of it nevertheless.' He sounded cautious, scared even.

The Israelis kept a close eye on nuclear materials, constantly in fear of a catastrophic attack on their tiny country. One decent nuclear weapon could kill them all. Just one. Jerusalem, Tel Aviv, everywhere, wiped out. God knows they had enough enemies. The security services had long suspected that Russia was not keeping a close enough eye on the by-products of its nuclear industry and this was the proof he needed to recommend further action. Without it he would not be listened to by those who could make the appropriate decisions about further action.

'Is there anything else you might like to tell me? Something that you have remembered perhaps?'

'I will get in trouble with the company.'

'Which will be much worse than getting into trouble with Mossad, I am sure.' He sighed heavily down the receiver. 'Where do you think the ship has ended up?', he asked finally, not really expecting an answer.

'My er… theory is that it is at the bottom of the Mediterranean. I think that Bilal disabled the communications, killed the crew and waited for another vessel to come alongside. I think the waste was cross-loaded and the Odessa sunk. I think that the other vessel made its way to Tripoli.'

'How do you know this?', asked Herv in astonishment.

'I don't know anything. It is a guess. You mustn't say how you found out this. It is just a guess anyway', said the man. He tried to sound dismissive, when in fact he was rightly frightened.

'Thank you, my friend. I can try to help you. What is your name?'

The line went dead. Herv shook his head. So much fear in the world…

He tapped a few numbers into the phone.

'Tom, it's Herv. How are things going for you?'

'I'm fine.' Tom stood as he talked and moved to another room, aware that his colleagues were looking at him suspiciously and with resentment. *Or was he just paranoid?* It was more than possible.

He gave the Israeli a run-down of his work. He imagined his counterpart in a white shirt, perspiring despite the languid blades of a desk fan pushing out a current of humid air.

That morning, his immediate boss, Andrew, had told him about a police investigation into the Antwerp suicide bomber. He had smiled when he found out that the man wasn't dead at all.

'Did you hear about the Irish Kamikaze? He flew twenty successful missions. Ho, ho etc.'

Andrew looked at him as if he was mad. Andrew's point was that someone, somewhere had decided that there was a possible connection between the disappearing ship and the non-disappearing suicide bomber. He instructed Tom to keep this to himself for the moment. Agencies jealously guarded their findings if they could, to ensure that the credit for whatever breakthroughs were made were ascribed to the correct people and no one else. It could become rather childish.

'Okay, about MV Odessa. We think that the waste was offloaded onto another ship and the Odessa sunk. We think the other ship ended up in Tripoli. When I have finished this call, I will be making my way over to the office of General Tal. I will be hoping to authorise a commando raid on Tripoli. I will keep you up to date on this Tom but be aware that things like this can escalate and you may find yourself answering to people further up the food chain than you are used to. This is a big deal my friend. Your career could be founded on how well you acquit yourself.' Herv fell silent.

Tom's heart sank as he heard those words. This sounded like more hard work than he was prepared for.

'Thanks. Thanks for letting me know, Herv. I will await your next call with interest.'

'Ha. Just another day at the office, saving the world from itself.' The line went dead. He liked Herv. Herv Ankoplar, he had decided, was just on the right side of cynical. A man after his own heart.

He left the side office and returned to his desk. He scowled at his work colleagues. Wendy was looking expectantly in his direction. Matt was typing away like a fucking drone and Claire was scribbling something in a pad.

He hated Matt. He hated his prematurely grey, semi-bouffant hair and the way that he walked with a slight stoop like a pretentious monkey. Worst of all he hated his little moobs. Matt didn't look like the brilliant graduate he was supposed to be.

'Some men are born mediocre. Some men become mediocre. But others have mediocrity thrust upon them', said Tom, as if to himself.

In the stunned silence that followed he began to update his report.

***

'Woah boy!', shouted the copper. He had the room's attention at once. It was 11:30.

'Here he is', he said triumphantly. 'Or someone anyway.' An instant crowd had formed around his monitor as he rewound the old VCR to the point where a young Asian man had first come into view. The machine rattled and squeaked as if it might suddenly die in a pathetic puff of smoke, but it kept going. 'Right. This is the spot', he said. 'You need to be looking in the bottom left corner. You don't get long and he is with another man. I've gone through this again and again to make sure', he said as the tape went forward frame by frame. The quality was terrible.

Frame by Frame. Liz noted the date –12th March 2014 – hardly daring to look away from the screen.

The copper jabbed a finger down with gusto.

'There', he said. He is only in a couple of frames. He is definitely of Asian origin but his face is obscured. He pressed again, advancing one frame. The man wore a hat and his head was turned part way towards the camera which was mounted in the corner of the lobby and towards his back. 'And that's about it', he said as he pushed the button a third time. The man was gone.

'It's the best we've got', said the DI, with evident disappointment.

The copper wasn't finished however.

'Don't forget, ma'am, this is just the footage of him coming in. We should get something of him coming back out and if you look at the man who is with him, his face is clear in a couple of the shots. This Shannen character might know him and if we can track *him* down, we're there, aren't we? He's bound to have a name for us.'

'You're right. Well done PC Bass. Let's all keep looking just in case there is a better shot.'

Liz took Mark to one side.

'What do you think?'

'I think we are going to have this taken off us and handed over to someone *really* important.' He made the really important person sound like they might not be any better at the required job than he and Liz.

'Maybe so. We'll see.'

***

Sayaret Mat'Kal is the most secretive part of the Israeli Defence Forces and it was this unit which would be charged with getting into Tripoli, finding the bomb-making material, and destroying it. If some of the terrorists involved in stealing the stuff got killed along the way then no tears would be shed. In part the IDF was fighting a war of attrition but it did so subtly, knowing that its activities were under constant scrutiny by the hostile Arab World and the ill-informed West. There was a long established, but hard to fathom, tendency for the sections of the West to berate Israel for any military action it took whilst overlooking the atrocities carried out against it. For the state of Israel, set up shortly after the conclusion of the Second World War in which six million Jews lost their lives, it seemed that memories were short indeed. That the Jews should be allowed a dusty sliver of land to call their own

– a land that in biblical times and long before the establishment of Islam had actually been theirs – had taken on the proportions of the greatest injustice ever known. The evil roots of anti-Semitism were long and too deeply burrowed to be easily disposed of. It seemed that one didn't have to be a Holocaust denier to harbour distrust of the Jews.

The plan was simple. The high standard of training of Israel's top troops meant that simple plans worked best; these men were adaptable, tough and resourceful. To alter a range of practised scenarios to suit the mission in hand was simplicity itself, almost a case of trying out Plan A, then Plan B and so on.

A C130 Hercules would drop a team of twelve soldiers onto the outskirts of Tripoli by parachute. They would make their way to the docks, where the ship holding the waste, which had been spotted by a US satellite, was waiting to be unloaded. The team consisted of a captain, two staff sergeants, three corporals and six privates. It could operate as three sub-teams each with an officer or senior NCO in charge.

A submarine was already making its way to the Libyan coast for the extraction of the team.

Herv Ankoplar sat in the control room listening as the raid unfolded, the details being relayed from Libya by the communications staff sergeant who was also a sub team leader. Herv tapped a finger against the seam of his trousers and avoided eye contact with General Tal who was even more apprehensive than him.

Ankoplar had served in the IDF, just as virtually every Israeli had done. As a junior officer in the Golani Brigade he saw his share of combat and understood the tension and fear that this team of young lions were facing as they made their way deeper and deeper into foreign territory. There was nowhere in the Middle East or North Africa where an Israeli soldier could expect a rapturous welcome if compromised. They *were* lions but they repeatedly found themselves in the Lion's Den with no friends to help them out.

Today, their mission was so secret that it had no code name, would never be acknowledged and, if caught, the troops could expect no support. All of this was understood before they set off.

They landed without opposition. Herv sensed Tal's relief. There were a dozen things that could go wrong but now that was not one of them. The twelve men located each other and moved in towards the docks which they estimated was a two-mile march. Herv looked at his watch – it was 22:30 – and then added forty minutes. They would be at the docks by 23:10 at the very latest. His coffee had gone cold. Next to him, Tal was chain smoking. It made him pine for nicotine but the battle to stop smoking had been amongst the hardest in his fifty-three years and he didn't want to suffer a late defeat.

'More coffee, General?'

'Yes please, Herv. We should have one of those coffee incubators.'

'Percolators', said Herv smiling.

'Just a joke, Herv. This is the worst part, don't you think? I'm not saying that their job is easy but at least they have things to concentrate their minds on. For us old, chair-bound warriors there is nothing to do but sit and fret.'

A message came through on the satellite radio link. The words were so clear that they could have been spoken from the next room.

'We can see the lights of the container port. There are derricks and a few ships. We can't see our ship yet, over.' The voice was hushed but clear.

Tal acknowledged the message and then sat back down in his chair to light another cigarette. He thanked Herv when the latter set a steaming hot coffee next to him. Another ten minutes passed before the next broadcast. The team were in the docks area. There was almost no security apparent and they had sent a single soldier ahead to identify the ship in question. Five minutes later its presence was confirmed and the team moved in. They expected to hear nothing more until the nuclear waste had been found. Tal and Herv Ankoplar exchanged a look but neither spoke. Things were going well but they were superstitious men and neither wanted to tempt fate.

***

The ship was small and streaked with rust. It was the type of vessel that plied its trade along the Mediterranean's coastal routes and was totally unremarkable in appearance. The team closed in, keeping close to the line of derricks on the quayside. The overhead lights were poorly maintained and, as fate would have it, the gantry illumination adjacent to the coaster was almost black. One of the soldiers was placed to cover the coastal side of the quay with his FN machine gun. He quietly laid his belt of 7.62 flat on the ground and snuggled his cheek in next to the butt. He was ready. No one would be interfering from that direction. The remainder formed a loose security ring as the captain and one of the staff sergeants stealthily climbed aboard. They knew what they were looking for, or thought they did: a small, red container, big enough to hold a small car and nothing bigger.

Inside the container they expected to find a series of drums filled with nuclear waste encased in concrete; very amateurish. They had been pleased to learn that the waste had been prepared in this way – the plan was to roll it off the ship and into the sea for all eternity – and anything other than a drum would have been impossible to roll. Once that was done, an anonymous call would be made to the UN explaining that the waste was lying in the harbour. IS could not possibly recover it or lay claim to it. The delay would totally botch their plan and bring a heap of unwanted scrutiny to those who had assisted them.

The captain and his staff sergeant ducked into cover the moment they had climbed on board. The shadows swallowed them whole. Both men sat perfectly still and listened. Nothing else, just listened, growing accustomed to the sounds of the ship: the creaks, the groans, the hums and shudders, so that anything else would alert them to possible danger. The little ship smelled of oil and salt water. They heard rats darting about on the metal deck.

When they were satisfied that their boarding had gone undetected, the captain inclined his head and both men stood slowly, pulling on night vision goggles and then walking slowly towards the freight deck. They seemed to rise from the shadows like phantoms. The container was in plain view. The sergeant pressed his pressel switch twice in a pre-arranged signal that the container had been identified. In Tel Aviv, Tal and Ankoplar exchanged a hopeful look but fell well short of feeling complacent. More coffee and cigarettes would have to be consumed before the night was finished.

The two soldiers moved in. The captain signalled that the staff sergeant should stand guard as he examined the container. He was dismayed to find that the lock was secured but that the wire and lead customs seals had been broken. In a legitimate shipping operation this might signify that the container had been opened and the cargo removed. He didn't give up hope; this wasn't a legitimate shipping operation – the exact reverse was true.

On his webbing belt the officer carried a set of wire cutters – more like bolt croppers, in fact – and he used these to snap the padlock, which fell silently into his gloved hand.

He took a deep breath before starting to unfasten the long, steel spars that held the container doors shut. He paused and looked backward to the ship's bridge where there probably should have been a look out. The bridge was in darkness. Thankfully they were dealing with total amateurs. The senior NCO gave him the thumbs up and he turned back to the doors. He made a mental note to bring penetrating oil on the next mission of this type if there ever was one. He winced as he twisted the handle and the lock began to screech as he expected.

'Fuck', he muttered. He twisted the handle by small increments and each harpy squeal of metal on metal became less pronounced until finally the door flopped open.

A gap of twelve inches was more than enough for him to squeeze inside. He saw the inside of the container through the green haze of his night vision goggles but there wasn't much to look at. In fact, there was nothing to look at. The container was empty, unsullied by not so much as a cigarette packet or a butterfly's cocoon. He cast his glance around one final time, sighed and withdrew.

***

Tal and Ankoplar sat bolt upright when the radio crackled.

'The container is empty. I say again, the container is empty, over.'

Tal scratched his head and pulled a face.

'Roger. Withdraw your men, out.'

He turned to Ankoplar.

'This is going to keep you busy Herv. If there is anything I can do, you know where I am. My men are at your disposal.'

'Thank you general. My next move is to inform the PM.'

***

The Bomber unlocked the shop and made as if everything in his world was fine. But it was far from fine. He thought he might have blundered terribly; this charade was just part of the cover-up. His mind was filled with images of failure. He pictured himself being led away in handcuffs, no longer a hero but an object of derision. *What sort of suicide bomber gets arrested?*

The bookshop was as he had left it the night before. He hated it more with each passing day, but it was part of his cover. He shuddered when he thought of what he had done but he would put on a brave face and welcome his customers with the same cheery demeanour he affected every day.

Such a nice young man. Always charming and helpful. Kept himself to himself. But by the time these words were uttered after news of his crime, he would be nothing more than tiny lumps of flesh stuck to smoking ruins of central London. His soul would be in Paradise. *Was that enough for him? Didn't he want a bit more time on earth?*

He was thinking of the inevitable TV programmes, the German equivalent of Belgium's Andre, interviewing neighbours and customers. *Such a nice young man.* He felt as if he could puke.

The Bomber switched the till on and took the float from the little safe in the back room. He intended to keep himself busy but as he put the coins in their respective segments of the drawer, images of his crime kept rolling in. He'd found his landlady – Ingrid – poking about on the landing and looking very guilty when he had opened the door to confront her. At that moment he knew without any doubt that she had opened the letter and consequently signed her own death warrant.

Ingrid knew that he knew. It was funny how the whole story was written across her face; the silly, nosy bitch. Why had she put him in that position? She opened her mouth to speak but his hands were around her throat and he was pressing down with all the power he could muster. She was bigger than him and she had struggled fiercely of course, but such was his anger and the rush of adrenaline that she stood no chance. Her arms flailed at his, trying to push him away, to break his grip, but her strength quickly waned. Her eyes bulged and her face reddened as if she might explode. Ingrid's knees buckled eventually and only the power of his grip kept her from falling to the ground. He kept pressing and pressing. He guessed that two minutes had elapsed before he let her down. She was dead. The Bomber kicked her limp body in annoyance and disgust.

He was out of breath and dizzy. He had never killed like this before. It was too close, too immediate, but worse than that it left him with a problem. He wasn't due to fly out yet, but if the shop didn't open suspicion would be raised. The only option was for him to open the bloody shop until he could get on the plane and that meant living with a corpse. When he had regained some of his composure, he went into the hall again. With great difficulty he took the body by the arms and heaved until he had dragged her dead weight to her bedroom. She lay there, dishevelled and, well... looking very dead, and he cursed her again.

Why had she been so nosy? She knew the score about these things. Discretion was everything. He loathed her even more in death than he had done in life, a feat he had not thought possible. *How long before she began to stink?* The thought of sharing a flat with her bloated corpse made him nauseous. He wondered about the process of decay and the smell and the juices that would leak from her body. He wished that he didn't think about these things but his mind was invaded, overrun with unpleasant images.

And now the books sat there dumbly in their orderly shelves. The Bomber wanted to pull them down and burn them, or throw them into the street. He wanted to scream about the unfairness of life and about the Jihad. He wanted everyone to know what he thought about, what drove him on and what awaited him in Paradise. He could easily have cried.

The shop was open, ready to trade for the day. He sat heavily behind the counter and began biting his nails, a habit he had given up many years beforehand. The plane journey couldn't come soon enough. As the street became busy, he tried to pin down the root of his worries. The answer came to him immediately and he was surprised by it.

He didn't want to die. That was all.

He thought by now he'd have come to terms with death, he was a suicide bomber by profession after all!

But he didn't want to die.

***

The DI looked over at Mark and Liz. They knew what she was going to say.

'Get over there at once, see what she knows.' They nodded but were already on their way towards the door.

They were there in minutes despite a build-up of traffic following a crash between a lorry and a van. Mark had grown up in Perth and knew his way around and so he took them down a maze of grubby side streets to emerge at the retail park, next to McDonalds. His stomach rumbled involuntarily.

They buzzed Shannen but there was no answer and they stood outside thinking for a moment or two.

'This doesn't happen on the TV', said Mark, philosophically. 'When the cops go around to someone's house they're always in, or escaping from the back door or something like that. They slide down a drainpipe, vault a hedge, steal a car… they don't just *not answer*. There is no plot development in simply having the two detectives turn up and for nothing to happen.' He sounded disgusted.

'Get you', said Liz jabbing him in the chest. 'Plot development! Are you angling for a job on TV then?'

'Yes. I want to be a fictional detective instead of a real one. You only work one hour a week and you solve every case.'

'The downside is that you have to be a divorcee with a drink problem and a terrible secret plus there is a lot of shouting involved in being a fictional detective. Everyone is so angry about everything. I don't think I could cope. The DI is always banging on about getting results and how the Super is on his back.'

'That's true. It might only be an hour but it is an exhausting hour. Too much tension for me. I'll just stick with working 168 hours per week like everyone else.'

They looked up at Shannen's window as if she might appear but her curtains did not twitch, unlike those of her neighbours.

'I could be a fictional something else maybe. What about a fictional nurse? They spend most of their time dealing with other people's marital problems or the fact that the consultant's son has only got three A grades in his 'A' Levels. That is a lot easier.'

' Firefighter?'

'Nah. Fictional firefighters do more work than real firefighters. I have a mate who is in the fire service. He only works two days a week and sleeps through those.'

Liz laughed as she pressed the buzzer for a second time. Still there was no answer and they were about to leave when Shannen rolled around the corner laden with shopping bags from a discount retailer.

'Here she comes now', said Mark. 'And she's been stretching those pounds again.'

'She's thrifty.'

'Dole doesn't go far.'

'She's trying', said Liz with a degree of sympathy. Mark gave her a look.

'Hi Shannen', he said. 'We need another word. Can I help you with those bags?'

Shannen grunted and passed him a full to bursting carrier bag filled with cordial, jam rings, tins of beans, white bread, pizzas, oven chips and wine.

He was tempted to ask how the diet was going, but Shannen had never claimed that a diet formed part of her plans for the future. So much for his empathy training.

They followed her up the stairs and she motioned with her head that they should enter. Liz noticed a thin patina of sweat on her top lip, a sort of pale, glossy moustache.

'What dae youse want?', she demanded. She was flustered, red in the face and less friendly than last time. The police were once again falling out of favour.

'We found CCTV pictures of that man we were looking for' explained Liz. 'You really helped us a lot but the pictures of him aren't very clear.'

'That's a pity', she said laughing. She seemed to wobble as she sat on her couch. Mark noticed that her feet were dirty when she kicked off her shoes. Perhaps she had taken the bin out in her bare feet the night before.

'But there was a man with him and we wondered if you could identify him?'

'Oh aye?', she said, uncertainly. Returning to form, it sounded as if she might only cooperate if some sort of incentive was on offer, but they had nothing *to* offer her. Liz carried on quickly as Mark retrieved a couple of camera stills from his jacket pocket and passed them over. He perched on the arm of her chair but Liz continued to stand. There was no offer of coffee this time and the flat had begun to smell again. Over the aroma of *Shake and Vac* something else came to him: vomit or shit mixed with the sweet odour of marijuana.

Dutifully she studied the picture and sighed deeply. Mark knew she was milking the moment rather.

'Aye. I know him. Tha's Malcolm Singleton.'

Mark noted the name. It was unfamiliar to him.

'But he'll no be able to help youse.'

'Why's that Shannen.'

'He's deed.'

'Dead?'

'Deed as a pancake. Car crash. He crashed his wee Vauxhall intae a milk lorry.'

'Oh', said Liz. She pursed her lips and shot a glance at Mark who merely shrugged. That seemed to be that.

Mark spoke next, 'is there anyone else who might know who this fell – this Asian – fella is?' It was a slim hope but he couldn't leave without asking.

Shannen's mind however, was elsewhere.

'Let's see that photy again', she said. Liz handed it over. Shannen frowned and tilted her head to one side for a second. 'Youse are in luck. I made a mistake. That's nae Malcolm. That's his wee brother. That's Gavin Singleton.'

Liz felt unaccountably relieved but she needed more.

'Do you know where he lives?'

'He lives wi' his ma in Dodge City. A dinnae ken the address mind.'

'Dodge City – Donald Park Estate?'

'Aye.'

'Thank you, Shannen. As ever you've been a great help.'

'How's the job hunting going?', asked Mark.

'Just the same', she said. He took that to mean she'd either given up or not started but he smiled encouragingly.

***

'Tom, the stuff we talked about has gone. We were too slow or they were too quick, however you want to look at it. Our men got there and found an empty container. The problem of course is that we don't know where it is now although what is going to happen to it is rather clearer.'

Tom was getting used to Herv's way of working. He was direct and quick off the mark. In a world of obfuscation and verbiage, Herv cut straight to the heart of the matter like a surgeon. In his world every second counted and he wasted no time on anything superficial. Herv Ankoplar was cutting through the bullshit to get his message across. There were no niceties he really wanted to observe; they only held things up.

'So, what could happen to the stuff next?'

'Good question. It could get broken up into smaller pieces and sent off in different directions. It could be flown out, shipped out or it could stay where it is either to let the dust settle or for it to be made into bombs and so on. Libya is the ideal spot for things to disappear from view. Naturally, we are asking our American friends to keep an eye out for it with their satellites but they don't know where it has gone either. My bet is that it will be moved to somewhere else in Libya. Who controls Libya? Anyone's guess. If you want to hide, then go to the desert. People have been doing it for years.'

'What should I be doing?'

'You're asking me?'

'I mean, if you wanted me to help, what would you want me to do?'

'Find the Antwerp Bomber.'

'Okay.'

'He's their new pin-up so to speak and this is their biggest project. Bear in mind that this is just my theory but when you add two and two and then think about how these people operate, it all makes sense.'

'And what sort of bomb could they make with this waste?'

'A dirty bomb. You've heard of them, haven't you? Conventional explosive leavened with radioactive material. You can blow that stuff to smithereens and put a whole town out of action for years to come. Not as good as an atomic bomb of course but the most potent terrorist weapon you can imagine.'

'This can't be made into an atomic bomb?'

Herv looked at the receiver of his phone with dismay before he answered.

'No, my friend but don't underestimate the potential of this type of bomb. Let me tell you something. You think back to the Twin Towers in 2001. That was the terrorist attack to top them all and it has never been surpassed. Hundreds of people have been killed by these barmy bastards but all of the attacks since the Twin Towers have been damp squibs in comparison. IS are losing ground – can you believe that? – they actually aren't winning and their greatest hero was killed by the Americans. They said he died like a coward – I don't know if that is true. I don't even know if they really got him at all. But whatever, IS need a new hero, someone whose image will serve to taunt the West. They want someone who galvanises their followers into action. But first he has to blow something up and it's got to be something big. Our little friend is hoping for one of those days when people ask, *where were you when such and such a thing happened?* Nothing less will do.'

'And you think the target is London?'

'You suffer from the curse of the so-called 'special relationship' with Washington. Your special relationship is bullshit. You realise that? It helps the Americans out and does nothing for you except make the Arabs hate you. Britain once had a good relationship with the Arab world and now you are sitting ducks.'

There was a short silence before Herv spoke again.

'No ducks have ever been more sitting than you', he added with a chuckle. 'So, Tom you gotta catch that bastard who blew up the station in Antwerp.'

Tom blew air out of his cheeks and rubbed his temples. He was beginning to feel out of his depth. The stump of his leg was aching. He associated that particular pain with stress.

'Okay Herv. You have put us in the picture. If we aren't doing so already, we will get moving on this thing. I am sure I will be in touch again soon.'

'I think you will, my friend. I think you will.'

***

Chapter Eight

Andrew listened to his subordinate as the story was delivered.

'I don't know this man, Ankoplar', he said at last.

'He sounded plausible.'

'I'm sure he did. They are normally on the ball, the Israelis. They must be bloody worried if they have us in the loop.'

Tom wondered what 'loop' he was talking about. Andrew's world was one of buzzwords and bullshit. Nothing happened in the future any more, it was always 'moving forward.' People didn't find out things these days, they had 'learning curves.' No one had ideas, they had a 'raft of ideas.' *A fucking raft?*

'So, you believe him?', asked Tom.

'It's a good theory. Quite believable. He certainly believes it or he wouldn't bother to tell us. I'm not sure about the link between Antwerp and some new 'dirty bomb' attack. He could well be right but I don't think there is enough to go on. But the point is I suppose that we are looking into both things anyway, so if a link does become apparent then so much the better and if not, then nothing is lost. We might need to cooperate more fully with the police in Scotland. At the minute they are doing their thing and we are doing ours.'

Tom nodded. He was only vaguely aware of the police operation north of the border. He couldn't quite see how they could cooperate more closely when they were separated by hundreds of miles but he didn't argue.

Andrew pursed his lips.

'I was thinking of expanding your team.'

Tom nodded. At present his team consisted of him and no one else.

'Maybe Wendy or Claire? What do you think? Have you a preference?'

'No.'

'It'll mean bringing them up to speed quickly. This thing is likely to spiral.'

'Either of them. Not bothered.

'Well, Claire has already expressed an interest in working on it, so can I tell her she's in?'

Tom really didn't want to work with her. He thought she might be stalking him.

'Yeah, that's fine', he lied.

'Great. I've got a side office lined up for you both so if you get set up in there, you'll have peace to get on. I'll get you contact details for the police up in Perth. Just keep me informed.'

With that he was gone. Tom noticed for the first time that he had a brisk, busy walk. He was a bit... camp. Could you be a *bit* camp, as in like a row of tents?

***

Claire listened attentively and then with the aid of a porter they set to work putting their office together. The office was clearly being set up with the thought that more staff might be added because every piece of equipment barring the photocopiers was duplicated. Four desks instead of two. Four computers instead of two. Four chairs…

'Bit of a dump but it'll do', said Claire. 'I think Matt and Wendy are a bit peeved at being left out.'

Tom shrugged. He didn't give a shit. In fact, when he thought about it he was glad that they were. He did not like them at all. Claire seemed excited by her perceived elevation, excitement that she kept in check with difficulty. Tom thought she was very childish. When the office was finished, she sat at her desk with a proprietorial air.

'Let's get cracking' she said. 'Where do we start?'

'We ring the police up north and see how they are getting on', he said.

'Let's do it.'

***

Pieter sat in the back of the car as they drove to Dodge City. The five constables drafted in to work on the tapes had been thanked and returned to their normal duties when no further evidence of The Bomber's presence in the flats had been found. Now they could concentrate on their normal work: drunks beating their wives, mothers beating their children and children stealing their father's cars. Domestic violence, neighbourhood disputes and robberies; it was actually more exciting than their recent duties.

The Bomber had obviously been more cautious on the way out than on the way in since there was no useful sign of his departure. It seemed like a sure sign of guilt, and not just the guilt that came with buying drugs.'This is a nice place', said Pieter.

Mark was dumbstruck but gave a tiny smile. Liz said nothing. She was English and had learned not to criticise anything Scottish. She presumed that Pieter was joking, either that or Holland was a bigger dump than Britain.

The car sizzled through the rain-soaked tarmac. Low, grey clouds collided and churned, spilling vast quantities of water onto the dark streets. People scurried from one shop to the next like rats. After a while the traffic was sluggish as though the rain had become treacle. A mood of slow despair fell on the town.

'I suppose some of it is okay', said Mark, qualifying Pieter's admiration. 'The bit we are going to isn't much to write home about.'

'Write home about?', queried the Dutchman.

'It's not something you would tell people about. It's a bit run down. I don't know if you have places like it in Holland.'

'Oh yes. We have people who take too much drugs and who don't work and want everything done for them. It is the same everywhere, I think.'

Mark nodded. He didn't know whether to be relieved or disappointed. Part of him wanted to believe that there existed societies in which everyone had a shared sense of purpose and worked towards some common goal of harmony. If that place did exist, then it clearly wasn't Holland. He wanted to think that there was a better world even if he was never permitted to live in it.

Pieter had more to say on the subject.

'I was in the marines for six years and when I left and joined the police, I got a shock. I was so used to people working hard and having a sense of purpose that when I came across the drug users in Amsterdam, and the pimps and the thieves, their lives just made no sense to me. I wondered why they even bothered to live. But over the years it just became normal and I came to accept that some people just didn't give a damn about themselves. Why is it like that and why do we allow it? I don't know. But you will find things like this place you are talking about everywhere, even in countries like Germany. We think of Germany as very orderly but it has its problems too.'

'Drugs are the worst.'

'You are right. They legalised soft drugs in Holland and now we are inundated with drug tourists. I hate to walk around Amsterdam with all the stoners. Off their faces, I think you say. It is not nice for the locals or for children to see it. But once you create the problem then you can't make it go away.'

The rain was still falling as they pulled up outside the flats. A newly burned out car was already rusting, half on, half off the pavement. The air still smelled of ash. All the windows had come out and the boot lid pistons had gone off like rockets, landing a hundred feet away.

The block consisted of sixteen floors of piss and misery. It was a cliché in itself. The smells, the sounds, everything was in place. It was a tenement for the modern age, a new slum to replace the old slum. No one had to throw buckets of piss into the street when they could piss in the lifts. That was progress of sorts, at least. If your bin was full you could throw the occasional filled nappy over the balcony onto the playground below. It was the natural order of things. Degradation led to degradation. Once the metaphorical and actual rot had set in no one gave a damn, but it was the same with any shared resource and with anything that wasn't in private ownership. Here the community had collectively shrugged its shoulders and handed responsibility over to the council. What they destroyed, the council would fix. The adults blamed the kids – the ones they had brought into the world – and the kids blamed their parents. Blame couldn't really be pinned on anyone.

Every crime under the sun had been committed here and possibly a few unique to Dodge City. The four tower blocks had a motley assortment of swings and roundabouts at their base which served as a handy meeting place for drug dealers and glue sniffers. Discarded beer cans, glue bags, condoms and empty wine bottles were littered like flowers. The playground apparatus was burned and defaced with foul language and idiotic gang slogans. Mark shook his head. No one ever did anything about Dodge City; it was genuinely lawless like its Wild West namesake.

Five dirty children dressed in Lonsdale and Nike lounged about on the climbing frame, spitting, smoking and swearing. One of them was a girl, slightly more kempt than the rest, dressed in jeggings and Converse. Her hair was dyed nearly white and a variety of facial piercings marred what might have been fine features. She was jailbait colloquially. They were all trouble, they should all have been at school and they had all been arrested at one time or another. Kids like these got so far through the judicial system before that same system gave up and spat them out just to start all over again.

The five children glared, their young-old faces filled with hatred and contempt. They were scarred by life, by drugs and by poor diet. Their chip shop pallor – a mild gangrene yellow – told its own tale of malnutrition. These were children who drank *Monster* for breakfast and cadged fags off passers-by. They were shop-lifters, stoners, vandals. They hated everything including themselves.

'This is a real shit hole', commented Mark. Pieter nodded his head.

'Yes. It is better to keep these people in one place though? Instead of spreading them around?'

'I suppose so. I'm not sure that it is a deliberate policy but that's how it works out. In amongst this lot there are decent people who probably live in fear. They can't just move out because the council has nowhere for them to go. Can you imagine being a young mum and dad trying to start out in life and having to bring your kids up round here? Bloody awful. Anyway, let's find the delightful Gavin Singleton.'

With silent assent they entered the piss-stinking lobby and selected the tenth floor in the lift. They were greeted with a clanking noise and a dull rumble.

'It's our lucky day – the lift is working', said Liz.

As they waited, yet another young truant came down the stairs on an expensive mountain bike. He shouted, 'fucking pigs' at them as he cycled off but they were encouraged when he got to the double doors at the far end of the lobby and fell off 'his' bike. Justice was served.

'Little twat', muttered Liz.

When the lift finally opened in front of them, they braced themselves and stepped inside like bold adventurers. It smelt of urine but they had become inured to that particular aroma by now. The floor was sticky and marked out with an archipelago of dirt-blackened chewing gum. The metal walls were scratched and defaced in marker pen; red and black proliferated. One notable slogan said, 'Neil Barrie still eats pies.' Another said 'Rangers fuck pigs.' Several said 'Fuck off.'

'At least they can spell', said Mark. 'Our education system isn't totally defunct.'

Liz pointed to the Neil Barrie slogan.

'What does that even mean?'

'Social comment', said Mark, feigning a superior attitude. The door drew shut with an awful squeal of unlubricated metal.

'Welcome to the socialist paradise of Dodge City', said Mark. The journey to the tenth floor was thankfully brief and the doors opened with less difficulty than before. Liz stepped out first and the two men followed.

'We weren't being gentlemanly there, Liz. We were just scared', said Mark. Pieter smiled

'I did wonder. Right, flat 106', she said glancing at a sign which pointed to flats 104-106 on the right. 'Let's go.' The floor was concrete and had been painted at some point in the flats' history. Only on the periphery was the blood red paint intact. The walls were daubed in the usual slogans, some poor attempts at street art, and two of the windows were smashed. One had been boarded up but the boards had been duly smashed. Pieter paused and stared at the ground before kicking at the corpse of a dead mouse. From around the corner – flats 101-103 – a baby cried. They heard its mother shouting before they went out of earshot.

Flat 106 had a blue-painted door with a spyhole. The doors were solid, more or less impossible to damage or to break down, although many had doubtlessly tried. Their main function, other than to secure the flat behind, was to act as a fire-resistant barrier. In the likely event of a fire the residents were supposed to stay in the flats and keep their doors shut, the doors holding back the flames until the fire brigade could extinguish them. Despite the violence and degradation of the block, this system had never been put to the test. Perhaps there was too much urine flowing for a fire to catch.

Mark knocked on the door and the three police officers listened for sounds of movement.

'I once worked in a sort of tower block and in the event of a fire, any disabled people were supposed to be put into a fireproof cupboard until the fire brigade came to rescue them', said Mark.

He yawned as he glanced around him.

'That's not true', scoffed Liz.

'That's what I heard.'

Liz shook her head in disbelief.

'A fireproof cupboard!', she scoffed.

Mark knocked again. No one ever answered their door first time. In these parts visitors were either trying to save your soul, sell you cheap electricity, repossess your 120 inch flat-screen TV or arrest you for drug dealing. No one came with good news. No one came by to socialise.

'If I had my gun, I could shoot the lock', said Pieter. Mark and Liz looked aghast but only mildly so.

'Joke', explained the Dutchman.

The need to shoot the lock or otherwise was obviated when, after a second knock, the door opened a crack. The thin form of Gavin Singleton appeared in the crack. He was dressed in the usual Lonsdale and Nike ensemble considered *de rigeur* for Dodge City, and when he spoke, having assessed the three smartly dressed people at his door, just one word was uttered.

'Filth?'

'I prefer the term police officer but yes, Gavin, we are from the police', said Mark with all the courtesy he could muster.

'It wasnae me', said the man.

With no knowledge of the crime Singleton was claiming not to have committed, Mark spoke.

'I beg to differ', he said. 'I think it was you, but fortunately we are here in connection with another matter. May we come in?' He was already pushing the door open, gently knocking the thin man off balance as he entered the flat with his two colleagues following closely behind.

Mark was familiar with the layout of the flats and made straight for the living room. He was joined by Singleton and the two detectives a moment later, by which time he was surveying the range of exotic plants growing in the room.

'Nice. Is this an Amazon Jungle theme going on here?'

Singleton frowned but said nothing. His bony shoulders protruded from his wife-beater vest. His skin was pitted with acne but otherwise grey. His eyes seemed dead like portals to a corrupted soul.

'I had no idea you were so green-fingered. This little crop must be worth a fair bit. Have you tried hydroponics? Ideal if you want to maximise the number of plants you can grow with limited space. You don't need soil you see. All the rage.' Pieter and Liz looked on but said nothing. 'Another thing is insulation. You need to keep this place nice and warm. The government used to do grants for it. Might be worth looking into. That would be funny – state sponsored cannabis farm. You might even get Lottery funding. They're really into all that bollocks. Just remember to call it a *community project*. They like that sort of shit', said Mark.

'What do you want?', asked Singleton, confused. *Was he in the shit or not?*

DC Truscott produced the photograph from her jacket pocket and passed it across.

'Recognise this person?', she asked.

Singleton smiled. 'Aye. It's me.'

The smile faltered rather when he saw that the other detective was now taking photographs of the living room with the camera on his phone.

'Don't mind me', said Mark, facetiously.

'What about the other man, Gavin?', continued Truscott. 'Do you know him?'

'Nah.' His eyes shifted in turn from Truscott to the Dutchman, to Stevenson and back again.

'Never mind. The only thing is that we are accountable for our time and our boss doesn't like us going out and coming back empty-handed. So, we're going to arrest you for growing illegal substances in your wee flat…'

'Mohammed Khan.'

'Good', said Truscott.

'Tell us as much as you can about Mohammed Khan.'

Singleton looked nervous now.

'You're afraid, Gavin. Why is that?' It was Pieter who spoke.

'He's a nutter. Seems okay at first but when you talk to him…'

'Tell us anything you can remember about him.'

'I think he was a student.'

'Was he Scottish?'

'No. He was a Paki.'

'Did he speak with a Scottish accent?', continued Truscott.

'No. English, but don't ask me where from.'

'How did you know him?'

'He was hangin' aboot. Said he wanted to buy some gear.'

'So, you took him to a place where he could get weed?'

'Aye.'

'How do you know his name?'

'We went to the park after and got stoned. Got chattin', y'know?'

'Okay. Anything else.'

Singleton rolled his eyes and rubbed his forehead, his few brain cells rattling around an otherwise empty cranium like boiled sweets in a jar.

'I think his middle name began with an 'I''

'How do you know that?', asked the female detective.

'His wallet had sorta gold writin' inside wi' three letters, M, I, K.'

'Mohammed, something beginning with 'I', Khan?'

'Spose.'

'Anything else?'

'He had a Rolex and it was a real one. So, he was fuckin' rich.'

'How do you know it was real?'

'Someone told me that the second hand on a real one goes round smooth. On a fake it sort of jerks with each second.'

'Have you seen him since that time?'

'I saw him about a week later but after that… nah. Don't want to either.'

'Why?'

'Just the stuff he was sayin' when he was stoned, y'know? Makin' oot that he was some big time terrorist'n'that. Why the fuck he was tellin' me like?'

'That's good Gavin', said Liz. 'If there is anything else let us know at once.' She handed over her card. 'I don't think you'll be seeing him again but if you do, get in touch with us straightaway. Really important that you do.'

She cast a final glance around the flat.

'This is just for your own use isn't it?', she asked. Singleton's mouth dropped open but he nodded his head.

'Good lad.'

***

The door hadn't been opened since he'd left her body on the bed. He looked at it for a last time without regret and hoped that she would remain unfound for weeks to come. There was no smell. He pulled a face, lifted his bag and swung it onto his shoulder.

'No going back', he said. He pulled the flat door closed behind him, scuttled down the stairs out onto the street, and headed towards the train station without a backward look. He had to be *Mr Inconspicuous* until he got to the aerodrome where a private jet was waiting for him. In a sense he was being treated like an honoured guest – he wasn't complaining – but it was all for security and not for his comfort. Would they look at him like he was a dead man? He wondered if these people knew who he was or what he was doing. He took a taxi out of town where he was picked up in a metallic blue Ford people carrier by two mysterious men who didn't bother to speak. They were dressed in black and wore sunglasses like movie villains; all very intimidating but more than faintly ridiculous too. He spent his life blending in and being forgettable and here he was in the care of two extras from some idiotic Hollywood action film.

He pondered his future as they swept through the town. The thrill of being the world's deadliest terrorist had gone and at times he might have accepted the offer to return to normal life had it been made. It never would be. It wasn't that he had lost his enthusiasm for Jihad but he had doubts about dying. He reasoned it through. There was nothing stopping him planting his bomb and then quietly withdrawing from the scene to watch the effects as he had done previously. He didn't have to die there and then. And if he lived to be seventy or eighty and died of old age, then the deeds of his youth would be quite enough to get him into Paradise. He had already killed over a hundred of the infidel. What was that worth?

The streets teemed with normal life; fat Germans making money, getting rich selling their ugly cars to the Americans. The only thing they had ever done right was to kill the Jews, and even then, they didn't get them all. The West gave him so many reasons to complete his work as a Jihadist; it was, he supposed, reverse inspiration. The Bomber smiled at the phrase. He liked that. *Reverse Inspiration*. He saw one of the men staring at him in the rear-view mirror and removed the smile from his face, feeling suddenly foolish.

The Bomber tried to regain that lust for the Jihad that he had felt, but its effects had dissipated somewhat and he supposed that having to kill the woman hadn't really helped. He prided himself on being a strategic weapon not a blunt instrument. To have to strangle an elderly lady, a fat old woman, wasn't really his type of thing. She had brought it on herself. He could not take the risk of her nosiness giving him away to the authorities but even still it shouldn't have fallen to him to commit that act. He could still see her bulging eyes, filled with terror, disbelief and disappointment. She wasn't ready to die.

They left the town behind and forged through the countryside, gaining speed as they made for the aerodrome. He tried to feel something, some emotion but inside he was empty, just a blank. Maybe a joint would have done the trick. Or maybe not. But something had changed.

Cows feasted on grass and he envied them for a second or two, but their fate was not better than his. Did cows go to Paradise? Another smile had crept onto his face and he wiped it away with near disgust. The man in the passenger seat lit a cigarette and The Bomber felt offended; his status was not sufficient for the man to ask if he minded the resultant smoke or not. It was then that he realised that these men were just hired. They were westerners, not Jihadists. They had a job to do. No questions asked, payment in hand... This sudden realisation made him feel naïve; there was so much about the world that he didn't understand. Suddenly, through eyes unclouded by marijuana he wondered if he was merely being used. Who really remembered the names of suicide bombers? Osama Bin Laden hadn't flown a plane into the World Trade Center and yet he was revered as the man who had masterminded the plot. Who could actually name one of the men who'd died? Even he couldn't and yet he was set to follow in their footsteps.

He was frowning now, burdened by the knowledge that he was trapped and that he was expected to die. Something had left his body, the thing that had made him want to die prematurely and go to Paradise. But how exactly did he put his concerns into words? *Surely he had done enough? Couldn't he be given some other job?*

They were here. Electric gates opened without fuss and they drove through. This was a well-practised routine, an escape route for well-connected criminals and gangsters... or anyone with enough money to pay. An aeroplane sat at the end of the airfield and the people carrier drew up alongside as the gates glided shut. He stepped out. The engines were winding up and a smiling hostess with a uniform waited to welcome him aboard. It was surreal. *No questions asked.* This was the top end of the criminal world he was stepping into. This was corruption, not holy war. This was a display of illegal money, thumbing its nose at authority. This was an escape route from Europe, an escape from justice. He didn't approve but now he knew that no one was seeking his approval. No one gave a damn about him.

He stepped aboard as one of the men in black loaded his bag into the hold. They had done this before, many times. These were well-practised, economical movements, almost military in their precision. The men had retreated now and as he entered the cabin, he heard the big car pull away.

'Welcome aboard', she said with a broad smile. She was, he had to admit, very beautiful, but undoubtedly mercenary in her outlook. Her blue uniform was tailored and everything about her from her polished flats to her hair worn up and tucked into a neat pillbox hat was immaculate. She was a lovely creature but also, he supposed, a slut. He felt a stab of jealous anger, both disgusted and intrigued by her.

He blushed and thanked her, feeling like a little boy thrust into the adult world with no explanation as to how he had got there or what was expected of him. He felt inadequate. Where had his dreams of glory gone? He wanted to get off the plane but the door was already closing and they were taxiing. Things were going too quickly. But even if he had got off the plane what was he going to do? His whole future, truncated as it was likely to be, was tied into these people for whom he worked. There was nothing left for him. He felt sick and depressed.

***

'So, we have a name', said Tom as he put down the phone. Andy looked over at him, eyebrows raised.

'The Antwerp Bomber', said Tom.

'Great. Give us the gen. You might as well bring us both completely up to date', said Andy. Tom nodded. He thought he had already done so.

'Well, the Israelis think that the missing ship is sunk but that another ship took off its load of nuclear waste. They have tried to capture this stuff in port in Tripoli but it had already gone. Their view is that the stuff will stay there for the meantime.'

'Why do they believe that?', asked Claire.

'No point moving it yet. They can let the dust settle and plan whatever operation they have in mind in Libya without much risk of being disturbed. Herv's view – that's our Israeli contact – is that anything can happen in the desert, anything can remain hidden.'

'Even with satellites flying over?', asked Claire.

'Unless the operators are looking for a specific thing, then I suppose so. So that's that. The police in Perth have come up with a name. They have been getting information from a former drug dealer called Shannen Cassidy and one of her ex-customers called Gavin Singleton.' Tom paused. Claire was making a note of the names. 'I don't think they are important Claire. Just a bit of colour', he said. Claire nodded and put her pad down. 'Anyway, between them they have a name – Mohammed Khan. I am sure that there are hundreds or thousands of men with that name but we have a possible middle initial – I.'

'Mohammed Khan', said Andy nodding. All of a sudden it feels like we have got somewhere. 'what could the 'I' stand for?'

'I am checking that at the minute but the only thing that springs to mind is Iqbal. Perhaps there are thousands of Mohammed Iqbal Khans or perhaps that is not what it stands for.'

'Or perhaps it isn't him?', suggested Claire. A look of perplexity crossed Andy's face.

'We have the DNA connection. It is by far the best lead we have.' He turned to Tom again. 'Good work. Anything else?'

'That's all for now. I'll put the name – both versions – into the database and see what it brings up.'

'Good. Keep me in the loop. We might be onto something at last.'

Andy left the room and Tom looked over at Claire.

'Are you glad you're on the team?', he asked.

'Yes. Yes, I suppose I am', she said. But she didn't sound it. He looked at her curiously. *This, surely, is what she wanted?* He doubted if he would ever understand her. He wasn't even going to try.

***

That the little bookshop on Brückner Strasse didn't open caused only the most minor inconvenience. Most people didn't even notice. The shop had done very badly from its inception, Ingrid barely covering her overheads and living off a dwindling savings account. She also got a small sum from various shady people for providing a room for… well, she always thought of them as fugitives.

One or two people tried the old wooden door, so badly in need of paint, but most took the fact that the little shop was bathed in near darkness as proof that it was closed. There were other bookshops, better ones too.

What did set a few alarm bells ringing was the build-up of mail behind her letter box in her flat. The previous resident had, before his arrest for internet fraud, been a dog lover. His dog had repaid that love by shitting on the hall carpet every day and ripping up letters as they fell through the letter box until eventually his weary owner had bought a cage... not for the dog, but for the letters. Ingrid, when she had taken over the tenancy, had not bothered to remove the cage; she simply took the letters out every day to prevent a build-up. But now that she lay dead on her bed the cage was filled up and the post man had begun taking her mail downstairs to the caretaker asking him to deliver it later. After just a few days the caretaker got fed up and then concerned. Ingrid was reliable and quiet. She caused no problems. The succession of dubious looking young men who passed through caused no problems either. In other words, she was a model tenant as far as he was concerned and something, therefore, was definitely up.

The flats had gone up in 1955 on the site of an engineering works bombed by the Americans in 1943, and he had been their guardian since 1987. He was proud of the fact that the lifts still worked and that his tenants were a good bunch. The owners had suggested the fitting of CCTV but he had told them that there was no need for such an expense. He didn't admit that he simply didn't want the extra responsibility. CCTV meant sitting in one place staring at a screen. It meant visits from the police when something happened.

He had pass keys for each flat. Ingrid's key was in his hand right now. With a sigh, he traipsed out of his personal flat and, despite the functioning lift, took the stairs to the second floor. What had started like a game had become a fitness routine and then in his later years a way of proving to anyone who cared to know that he was still alive. The only time he used the lift was when he was testing it or when moving heavy objects that he could not take up the stairs.

He was sixty-eight now. The stairs made him a bit breathless but didn't kill him, and when he could no longer do it – get to the top in one piece – he would retire. His wife had left him because he drank too much, never said anything nice and because he was boring. His children didn't visit for the same reasons; mere life was all he had left.

Before he did anything else, he knocked on a neighbour's door to check if they knew anything. The neighbour was Hans Mader, a lonely man in his early forties who worked for the railways. He left early and came back late. Like the rest of them he was a bit weird perhaps but caused no trouble. But it didn't matter because Mader wasn't in anyway. He wasn't surprised. He seemed to sleep there and nothing else.

The caretaker pulled a face and then moved down to the next door – Ingrid's. He knocked and listened for sounds of movement. He held his breath and put his ear to the door. Nothing. The caretaker drummed his fingers on the seam of his trouser leg. It was with difficulty that he managed to bend down to shout through the letterbox. His sixty-eight-year-old back wasn't very supple these days. Strange to think he'd been a paratrooper during his national service and now he could hardly bend over. He was glad that he could still get up the stairs however.

'Ingrid', he shouted. He rattled the flap of the letter box and shouted her name again. There was no answer. He groaned as his back began to protest, seeming to stiffen up as though it had been set in concrete. He tried to peer into the flat but his view was blocked by letters caught in the stupid cage which she didn't need and which had caused him this trouble.

'Ingrid! Are you in there!' He listened again but his back was about to break and with another groan he slowly straightened. He blew air from his cheeks and looked down at the brass key he clutched in his hand. Twice before in his tenure he'd had to enter flats only to find the resident dead. The first time it had been a young girl, once beautiful but now ravaged by heroin, and he had found her in the bath naked, bloated, horribly dead. An empty Vodka bottle lay next to the bath. He had spent a moment looking at her body and the scars it wore. He felt nothing but immense sadness.

The second time it had been an old man. He must have been eighty-five at least. The man was more or less a recluse and the rumour was that he'd been a prison camp guard during the war. No one knew the truth. Like the rest, he'd been no trouble, at least not until he had died. The man was at peace in bed. The room stank of 'oldness' rather than death. Before ringing for the ambulance he'd spent some time checking through the man's possessions. He didn't intend to rip him off... He really didn't *intend* to... But he was keen to find some clues to the man's past life. Maybe some medals or a pay book. Maybe a cap badge. In fact, he found nothing. The man's prior life was gone, totally gone. He had a few tatty old clothes, two ancient paper backs, no TV or radio and a kitchen cupboard full of biscuits still in unopened packets. That was what life added up to and it always ended badly.

Christ only knew what he was going to find this time.

The key stuck slightly. The spares never worked as well as the owner's personal keys but it clicked the lock open and he gave the door a slight push before calling out her name again. He had one foot in the hall but he paused, listened and then sniffed. The smell was the thing that would give it away. He'd been in the flat once before, when Ingrid's washing machine had sprung a leak and water had dripped into the flat below without her knowing. An emergency plumber had done the repair. All of the flats on the south side of the block were laid out the same way – the same way as his in fact – and he knew that the master bedroom was at the far end of the corridor. The remainder of the doors were closed: bathroom, toilet, second bedroom and living room/kitchen.

'Ingrid?', he called, more softly now. 'Is everything okay? It's Karl from downstairs. No one has seen you for a couple of days.' If anything, the silence seemed to deepen. He walked towards the closed bedroom door, only fifteen steps, and then knocked again. Now he could smell something and he knew what he would find on the other side of the door. She was dead... or someone was and you just couldn't mistake that odour for anything else.

'Ingrid?', he said as he pushed the door open. He had to be sure before he called the *Polizei*. 'Ingrid?'

Her body was grey and she was beginning to bloat. Karl gagged but, holding his breath, he took a step forward. He wasn't going to touch her but he wanted a closer look, just to make sure, he supposed. In death the lines in her face had vanished as if she'd had Botox but the bruises around her neck were lurid, browns, greens and blues mixed. Had she been strangled?

'Fuck', he said at last and withdrew from the room not bothering to close the door. With shaking hands, he rang for the *Polizei*.

***

The database onto which he logged was being updated and eventually replaced with something that would be harder to use and less complete; it had been that way for as long as he could remember, he seemed to recall it being called progress. The trouble with progress was that it wasn't the same thing as improvement. It should have been – the two words ought to have been synonyms but they weren't. Progress was brought about by people who would be out of a job if they didn't keep changing things, whereas improvement was often brought about by people who found ways of doing things more easily than that which was on offer from the people in charge of progress. There was no escape from it and, if anything, it was getting worse. The availability of greater technology brought with it a demand for greater, faster, more efficient progress and the results were always disastrous until the improvers had spent time getting it to work.

The current database only worked for him because he had figured it out over a period of years. It contained names of terrorists going back to the Mau Mau Rebellion in Kenya. The original records had been put in manually in the first instance, painstakingly typed in from the paper documents written at the time. It had been refined over the years until nearly everything was in rough chronological order but with an emphasis being put on the most recent terrorist campaigns. Tom wondered what would happen when the records were modernised for the hundredth time but for now he could type in a name and scroll through the results quite simply. The records also gave information about associates and links to other terror organisations as well as listing the agencies at home and abroad who were taking an interest in these people. Where available, photographs were included.

He felt hopeful, although he had discovered dozens of Muslim boy's names beginning with the letter 'I'. His fingers danced across the keys until he had brought up the name Mohammed Khan. As expected, he was faced with a great many entries. His next step was to add middle names beginning with the letter 'I'; Ibad, Ibn, Ibadullah, the list went on. He sighed. The office was empty and someone had switched off the coffee machine. Tom was quite alone apart from the Russian cleaner who paced back and forth with the world's noisiest vacuum cleaner. If suction could be matched to noise then this beast should have sucked up the entire office carpet, dirt and all.

He typed in the name, *Mohammed Ibad Khan*. Nothing came up apart from a message which said, 'no results found'. He tried again with *Mohammed Ibn Khan*. Nothing. He wasn't too discouraged. Each 'no results found' was narrowing his search. He tried another name and another and then another. After fifteen minutes he went to his original guess and typed in Mohammed Iqbal Khan, and here he found a reference to a man of that name. Tom told himself that it meant nothing, but in the light of previous efforts it gave him hope and he felt his pulse race at the thought of closing in on The Bomber. It had been a total punt, a stab in the dark, and yet here he was looking at the man's name on his computer monitor. He saved the name for later and continued his search, and by seven o'clock he had a short list of suspects. Eight names. Eight Mohammed Khans with a middle name beginning with the letter 'I'.

Now he had to eliminate them from his enquiry until he had narrowed it right down to one man if possible, but he was tired and decided it was time to go home. He and Claire could work at it tomorrow.

Chapter Nine

He had a list of just two names and two addresses. He memorised both sets of details and burned the paper they were written on. He'd been given two thousand pounds by an anonymous donor and a simple set of instructions. Very little equipment was required for these simple jobs. The equipment he did need was in his pockets.

His car was a stolen BMW 320i, black, satnav, leather. Its owner would never see it again.

It was a short drive and it was easy to find a broken street light to park under, not that this was the sort of place where people asked questions anyway. The block was a squat ugly thing, much like the one he lived in but less secure. He buzzed Shannen and pretended he was from the police. The door clicked and he entered. He was surprised at the advice he'd been given; pretend you are from the police. That wouldn't normally have worked, in fact it would have had the opposite effect, the target locking themselves in the flat. But fair's fair, it worked a treat.

Shannen looked wrecked when she opened the door, and the fact that he wasn't dressed like a cop didn't even register. This would be incredibly easy. He stepped inside, his nose wrinkling at the smell of shit, and softly closed the door behind him. Shannen stumbled ahead of him, her dressing gown swinging open. She giggled as she tripped and almost fell into her bedroom. Why was she taking a cop to her bedroom? No matter.

She sat on the bed and looked up at him as she shrugged off the dressing gown to reveal a grimy looking nightshirt that was nothing more than a long T-shirt really, which carried a faded *My Little Pony* illustration or something similar; he was no expert. He was puzzled by her behaviour but decided that it made his life easier.

'You're really off your tits aren't you? Get your kit off then.'

She pulled up the shirt and as she did so he thrust the knife blade into her heart. There was no sound and she fell back on the bed at once. He looked at the gap between her legs without interest and wiped the blade on the hem of her shirt.

With a little nod, he retreated and moved on to his next target. Easy money, he told himself.

***

Claire sat at her desk looking pensive.

'You okay?', asked Tom.

'Fine', she said, tersely. He decided to enquire no further than that; she was not in the mood for conversation or friendly concern… plus he wasn't *that* concerned anyway. Instead of following up his original enquiry he told her what he'd found out and what they should be looking at today. She nodded her understanding and logged on to her computer.

'I've written down the names of the first four for you and I'll do the second four. These are our best suspects. They are implicated in terrorist activity somehow, all connected to IS or Da'esh or whatever they're calling it this week.'

'I know. I understood the first time', she snapped. Claire stopped short of saying, *I'm not stupid*. Tom gave a tiny shrug and began entering details.

Mohammed Imran Khan was born in Pakistan in Peshawar, where his father and brother were GPs. He studied medicine in Birmingham, UK, but at some point he was radicalised, as they called it, and gave up his studies. Mohammed began collecting benefits and attending meetings in which young Muslims were encouraged to fight against the infidel. The security services kept an eye on him and a number of other young men. He rose to a sort of prominence when he bought a plane ticket to Pakistan, but he used it to return home and nothing else, and that was that for this particular Mohammed Khan. They had a complete record of his stay in Pakistan and there was nothing untoward; there was nothing in his recent history to suggest that he was involved in anything dubious.

Perhaps he had decided that Jihad wasn't for him. He was clearly an intelligent young man. It may also have been the case that he was so severely reprimanded by his father that the idea of holy war became untenable. Tom could imagine Khan senior as being a pillar of society and a strict head of the family. His younger son might simply not have dared to go against his wishes. Whatever the case, Tom now put him to the bottom of his pile of four potential suspects.

The next in line was also an Imran. This one was also a Muslim of Pakistani extraction but had been born in London. Once again, he was highly educated, having studied fine arts at university. Mohammed Imran Khan graduated with a first-class honours degree and immediately (and probably against the odds) got a job working for a London auction house. Not one of the best known but prestigious enough. He was a great success. His family was proud of him and he earned good money. Mohammed was engaged and looking at buying a flat with a bit of help from his father who owned a textile factory.

However, one day in 2011, Mohammed surprised everyone by getting on a plane to Pakistan. Nothing was heard from him for over a year and he did not seek out any of his relatives in that country. Father reported this to the police, hence this entry in the database. When he returned early in 2013, he was thin, clearly ill, but refused to talk to anyone about what he had been up to during his time abroad. He was interviewed by the police but he gave away nothing. Tom ran a hand over his mouth as he thought.

Was this the Antwerp Bomber?

He read on. After a few months he had recuperated sufficiently to get a job working for his father. He didn't even attempt to get his old job back. He had repeated bouts of illness and had never left the country again. Or not officially. Tom pulled at his bottom lip and then put an asterisk next to the man's name. Maybe.

He had the sudden urge to have breakfast. A little mobile deli usually turned up around this time and parked across the road. It all looked very French, complete with a vintage Citroen van. The pastries and croissants were always fresh and warm – they sold out in no time. The coffee was even better than the stuff out of the machine.

'Fancy a coffee?'

Claire looked up at him. Her face was creased with tension, which he put down to some sort of woman's problem. She sighed heavily as if in pain, and for a second he thought she might cry… but still he didn't dare enquire after her wellbeing.

'No thanks', she said.

'They do good croissants and stuff', he added but she shook her head in reply. He was still tempted to go himself but something stopped him.

Exercise was difficult and painful for him these days and he worried sometimes that he would begin to put on weight as he got older. Maybe it was good for him to resist the lure of French pastry which he presumed couldn't possibly be good for him. If it was nice then it was full of fat or carbs… or both in this case. His body could easily store both in rings of handy fat around his waist in preparation for the next ice age. With regret he opted to remain seated.

The next Khan was a British-born Pakistani from Preston in Lancashire. Lower middle-class background, a brother serving as a medic in the army, dad a shopkeeper, Mum a hospital receptionist in Burnley. For no reason that anyone can see, Khan the younger decided to join ISIS in Afghanistan, got on a flight, was arrested the minute he set foot in the country, was sent back to Britain, arrested, charged, convicted, jailed. Tom checked and yes, he was still languishing in jail. He was not the Antwerp Bomber. Tom's stomach rumbled.

He had one more name to check and for a moment he was undecided. There was nothing wrong with eating. He wasn't very old. Maybe he could allow himself a croissant and a coffee from the deli van. It wasn't a crime. True, the stump of his leg was killing him and the walk would aggravate the pain but food was food. It was only breakfast after all and he was working hard making the world a safer place.

'I'm going to the deli van', he announced. Claire looked up and smiled mirthlessly. But at least it was a smile, he supposed. 'Shall I bring you back a surprise?', he asked but she shook her head. He left before her bad humour returned. In the lift he thought about the fact that he had not logged off his computer as per departmental instructions. But what did it matter? The only person who would know was Claire.

***

'Are you sitting down', asked Mark. Liz raised an eyebrow.

'You can see that I am sitting down, Mark.'

'Well listen to this. Shannen and Gavin Singleton?'

'Yes?'

'Dead. Both murdered last night.'

'You are joking', she said slowly.

'Not joking. Stabbed in their flats.'

Liz didn't speak for a moment or two.

'I'm going to tell the others', said Mark

The mood was solemn at the briefing.

'This proves that we are on the right track but it was a contingency we didn't plan for. It suggests that somebody is talking out of class so to speak. The murders are going to be investigated separately from our work but there can be little doubt that they were killed because of our questioning – this can't be a coincidence. We'll be kept up to date with that investigation but I expect that there will be repercussions, probably for me.'

The DI looked gaunt and worried as if she had already been under the cosh that morning, which was likely to have been the case.

'In the meantime, we carry on as normal.'

There had been talk of Pieter and the Belgian detectives going back to Europe but that seemed likely to be put on hold now that some tangible progress was being made. They had become a good team, working well together, but until the scale of the problems they faced became clear, their futures in Britain were uncertain.

***

The flight was uneventful and the flight attendant saw to his every need. In the few hours he spent aloft he managed to eat well and to sleep. He wanted a joint or maybe something stronger but he couldn't quite summon up the nerve to ask. There was plenty of booze available but it was not offered to him. He presumed that the attendant had been briefed on Muslim sensibilities towards alcohol. This was a much more luxurious way of doing things than he was used to – he supposed that decadent was the word – and he could see the irony of travelling in an American-built private jet. This symbolised everything he had come to despise. Had he not been on board and if the equipment needed had been available to him, he might have fancied shooting it down.

The luxury would be curtailed when he got to the desert. He hoped that living the hard life of the ascetic would reinvigorate him and make him fall in love with the difficult path he had chosen. Perhaps time in the desert would toughen him up. In truth he'd lived a comfortable life before purposely 'falling off the radar' for the sake of Jihad. His trip to Afghanistan in 2011 had been a shock to him. He had felt mildly heroic until he'd actually got there and spent time living in the mountains. It had not suited him at all; he was a soft westerner used to sleeping in a proper bed, watching TV and going to Pizza Hut with his mates. If he was honest with himself, it had taken some time before his desire to contribute to the holy war had returned. Where other young idealists had been captivated by the mountains, he had seen hardship. Some breathed in lungs full of fresh, pure air. He had choked on dust.

Not everyone was suited to hard fighting in the mountains. Nevertheless he felt as though he had found his own battleground and one on which he could be far more effective than any number of hidden gunmen.

It had been all too easy to go back to Britain and fall into a routine, but after a few months he had made the final decision to give himself to the cause and had disappeared for good. At that point the idea of being a suicide bomber had been nothing more than an abstract thought.

A Toyota Land Cruiser was waiting for him, along with an unsmiling driver and, he supposed, a sort of armed chaperone. The men wore western clothes but were unmistakably North African in appearance. Neither spoke. He was getting used to the silent treatment, but he didn't yet know if it denoted respect or distrust. For some time after Antwerp he had considered himself to be something of a celebrity terrorist, but that feeling had waned somewhat especially after Ingrid's sickening murder. That was when the rot had set in, when he had truly begun to question his commitment.

Ironically, it also marked a time when there was no turning back for him.

The heat was unbearable. He felt that to breathe this roasting air might sear his lungs like barbecued steak, and he hurried over to his transport.

His hosts climbed into the front of the wagon and he climbed into the back. The dusty exterior belied a sparkling interior replete with leather and climate control. The car was no battle wagon. Did these men know who he was or what he was expected to do? Did they think they were in the presence of a hotshot or did they see yet another foolish martyr? Nothing in their demeanour gave him any clues. When he felt depressed and full of doubts, as he was feeling now, he had often wondered about the different levels of commitment shown by his fellow Jihadists. Some died and some lived. Who decided?

The desert swept by in a blur of yellows and browns. He was resolutely unimpressed. Nothing about it made him picture himself in tribal garb, clutching an AK47 and smiling defiantly for the camera.

Some got caught up in the romance of it all, but he did not. He saw himself as an urban guerrilla, somewhat more sophisticated than a hills man. The AK47 was a clumsy, ugly thing that a monkey could use and which could only really kill small numbers of people. He had to remind himself that he was a strategic weapon, a nuclear bomb rather than a grunt with a bayonet.

The quality of the road got worse and worse the further they got from the little aerodrome. They drove through a shanty village with dead-eyed peasants sitting at the roadside. He felt nothing for their plight... was he liberating them from something? If so, then what? *Did they know what he was doing to help them? Did they care? What were their views on Jihad?* There was something totally unpitying about what he was doing and not just in the context of the thousands he intended to kill. It was the knowledge that he had to give so much – everything, in fact – whilst others merely talked about war and lived off the state.

The big car crashed through a pothole, reminding him of where he was. He was insulated against the desert sun and the smells and the dust. At the minute he was travelling through desolation and near misery in a speeding cocoon of decadence, cut off from the struggle he was engaged in.

His thoughts strayed back to the inequalities of Jihad. The ones who died, as he was expected to, became martyrs. But who remembered their names on earth and was some special part of Paradise put aside for them? The famous ones lived on and made speeches, rallied the troops and recruited more suicide bombers and gunmen. It was an unfair division of labour or, more accurately, an unfair division of sacrifice. Even their enemies, despite having no equivalent to the suicide bomber, expected their generals to accept a certain amount of personal risk. Perhaps the clerics and the planners saw their sacrifice as having to defer their own entry to Paradise. He wasn't sympathetic.

To his left, a range of craggy brown hills, to his right flowing dunes, waves of sand that moved with glacial slowness but never settled to a flat calm. A few shrubs fought for life but otherwise the place could hardly have been more sterile. Every so often he spotted the hulk of a car or truck, rusting at the side of the road. The Arabs were not known for their driving finesse and here was the evidence of their carelessness. He felt silly as he compared that with his own carefully orchestrated introduction to motoring, sitting as a terrified teen behind the wheel of a Nissan Micra. These men probably couldn't parallel park but in the open spaces of Libya it hardly mattered. A comical image of a little Japanese car, liveried as the *Jihadi School of Motoring* entered, then exited, his head.

The sun was high in the sky when they stopped, and his newly restored reserves of Islamic fervour were immediately swept away by the wall of heat that met him as he stepped down from the truck. He looked around in awe as beads of sweat formed on his brow. The desert was perfectly flat as far as the eye could see but only flat in detail. Underfoot it was ridged and hard like concrete. No trees grew, no houses had been built and no animals ventured forth. This wasn't a place for life and yet here they were with every intention of living.

Some way over to his left, a beige saloon car sat on four flat tyres. Ahead was another Land Cruiser, a flat-bed truck of a type he didn't recognise and a Bedouin tent. The truck carried several oil drums and these were held in place with broad canvas straps. He stood for a moment as one man unloaded his bag and the other ushered him towards the single tent. Khan felt out of his depth. He wanted to leave this terrible place. He wanted to go back to his flat in Germany and smoke a joint and do a shift in the bookshop with its literary garbage neatly stacked on dusty shelves. He wanted boredom and routine, a proper bed. He had asked for nothing like this.

When he entered the tent, he stood and let his eyes adjust to the gloom. He could smell spices or drugs or... it was something he didn't recognise. Eventually he could make out the shape of two men sitting on rugs. They gestured to him to sit and made him welcome. Both men wore traditional robes and beards. They oozed confident authority and he was not afraid anymore. How had they taken away his fear, he wondered?

It was customary to talk about anything other than the business in hand and that is what they did for some time. They spoke in perfect English and after a few minutes of talking about the heat, about the difficulty in getting water, the forthcoming Olympic games, and the suitability of Japanese cars for the rigours of desert travel, Khan began to wonder if he had stepped into the wrong tent.

Eventually the older man – his beard was streaked with grey – nodded his head a few times. This was a signal that the conversation would move on.

'You have come here to make a bomb?', he said. Khan wasn't quite sure that was the case but he agreed nevertheless. The younger man spoke next.

'Tonight, we will be packing up and moving. You will get used to this. We are Bedou and no one expects us to put down roots. But the reason we keep moving is to make things difficult for the American satellites. We never know when they are watching us so we must seem innocent at all times.'

'Maybe they can hear us talking now', said the older man with a wry grin. 'They might have heard me talking about Mr Trump's hair or Mrs Clinton's sour face.' Both men laughed and Khan began to feel at ease. They passed him a pipe and he inhaled deeply. The world seemed to go a little bit fuzzy at the edges whilst their voices remained clear.

'Tomorrow someone else will be joining us. He is the man who will be directing you. We are merely your hosts. We have a driver for the truck and a few men who act as sentries. They are armed but not with rifles. Rifles you can see from the sky. We will look after you and ask no questions.'

The older man chuckled and said, 'although we already know what you are up to…'

***

The German police had photographs from the crime scene and collected any skin samples, dust samples and fingerprints they could harvest from the flat.

They were utterly bemused by the murder until two details were revealed to them. The first came from the caretaker who spoke about Ingrid's visitors or sub-tenants. The second came from their own database which revealed her as a sympathiser for the defunct *Baader-Meinhof* gang. She had done well to avoid prison in the 1970s and 80s, mainly due to the intervention of a top Berlin lawyer, funded by no-one knew who.

The caretaker's observations were of more immediate interest.

'She was always bringing young men back to her flat', he said. The detective asked if she was having sex with them and the caretaker laughed.

'She wasn't much to look at. She wasn't young and attractive you know.' He was asked if one of these men might have killed her.

'I suppose so. She owned a bookshop. You don't usually get killed for that.' He managed a chuckle but the detective didn't even smile in return. 'The last one she had here was an Indian or something like that. Stayed for a while. I think he worked in her shop sometimes.'

'Okay. Can I have a look at your CCTV?'

'Don't have it. No need. I told the owners there's never any trouble.' There was a hint of pride in his voice. The detective looked annoyed.

'Maybe you should get it? What do you think? You've just had a murder.'

They were frustrated by the lack of CCTV footage, a serious omission in these days of increased vigilance and mass information gathering. When a simple mobile phone was betraying its owner at every turn, positively haemorrhaging personal information, it seemed incredible that a major crime could have been committed which left behind almost no trace of the perpetrator. Back at the station, they added details of the murder and their one potential suspect to the ever-expanding Interpol database. As ever, they had no idea if the information would be of any use.

***

Tom brought his croissant and coffee back to his desk and set them down next to his monitor. He could tell from the look on her face that Claire was rueing her decision to forgo his offer of sustenance but he said nothing. She had failed to seize the moment.

He was about to tuck in when Andrew entered their office and shut the door behind him. The look on his face was grim and was all the more noticeable because he was a man given to moments of vacuous jollity.

'Just had a phone call from Perth. The people they were investigating – they used the words scrotes, oddly enough – have been found murdered.'

'My God', said Tom. Claire didn't speak.

'It can't really be a coincidence. They don't think so anyway. So, someone up there is leaking information. Until I get further guidance on this, we will have to be very circumspect about what we share with them. I suppose we would have to say that anything that might put another individual at risk has to remain within these four walls. Anything of a more general nature we can share, but just be careful.'

'How does this affect what we are doing?', asked Tom.

'I don't know yet. For now, just carry on. This matter is already being dealt with at Cabinet level. They will be informed, and they can make the decisions, if any need to be made.' Andrew paused and looked at his subordinates with almost comical seriousness. 'Not a word of this to anyone. We keep this between the three of us.'

When he had left Tom looked over at Claire for her reaction but her head was bent and she was working at her computer as though she was unaffected by the news. He decided not to push her for an opinion. Perhaps this was how she dealt with things, by getting on with work, by trying harder than ever before. He knew almost nothing about her and certainly nothing about how her brain worked.

Dismayed by the news he'd been given, he took a bite of his croissant. It was really good.

***

'Every now and again they send a drone over', said the younger man. He and Khan were standing together surveying the unending desert.

'Does it attack?', asked The Bomber, trying to sound unconcerned. He remembered the American gunships patrolling the skies over Afghanistan. He had felt fear and the others, some of them veterans of the long war against the USSR, laughed at his concern. Fear had returned at the mention of this latest weapon.

'They *can* attack but often they just carry out reconnaissance. Nothing to worry about so long as you look innocent.' He looked at the Westerner trying to gauge his mood. Like the rest of them he was filled with enthusiasm and devoid of guile.

'How long have you been a Jihadi?', he asked.

'Me? I am not a Jihadi. I am a Bedou. I live in the desert and make my living whatever way I can. Politics has no interest for me. I have no master. I don't live and die for a cause. My loyalties are to myself, my family, my clan and so on. There are no borders for me – none that I recognise anyway.'

'You don't believe in the cause?'

'I am sympathetic but no more than that. I am being paid to offer assistance but we have given ourselves over to many paymasters over the years.'

'You would sell us out to the Americans?'

'No. Not that.'

They watched as a tiny convoy slipped off the distant highway and began heading in their direction.

'We'll be going in a minute or two', said the man.

'Who are these people?', asked Khan. The idea of betrayal was uppermost in his mind now.

'You'll see. All part of the unique service we offer. I think you will be impressed. We are keeping you safe.'

They stood in silence as the peculiar convoy made its way towards them. After a few moments he could make out the shapes of the vehicles and his mouth dropped open. He shot a glance at the Arab, noticed his broad grin and then returned his gaze to the convoy.

Two dusty Land Cruisers and a flatbed truck. The Toyotas looked identical to their own vehicles. The flatbed was the same old-fashioned thing they had and, now that it was closer, he could see the same arrangement of oil barrels on the back.

'What do you think?', asked the Bedou. 'Decoys. We move on and these stay here. There is another set of identical vehicles in another part of the desert. We confound our enemies in this way.'

'Deception', said Khan in awe.

'That is the word. A useful tool for us. It is something that the British were very good at. Helped them win the war. They had whole armies of tanks and soldiers which didn't exist. The Germans fell for it. It worked then and it works now.'

The tiny cavalcade pulled up and the drivers descended from their cabs. Some time was spent – wasted – in greetings and small talk but eventually they got to work putting up their tent.

'Time to go my friend', said the Arab.

***

Chapter Ten

Tom wiped a crumb away from the corner of his mouth and noticed that his computer had been logged off. He said nothing but instead tried to recall the sequence of events leading up to his departure for the deli van. Failing to log off was a security breach but he wasn't the first and nor would he be the last. He personally wouldn't squeal on anyone for that offence but there were plenty who would. He cast a furtive glance around the office as if he was being watched, which was a silly, paranoid idea. Tom sipped from his coffee as he tried to think this through. *Was he in trouble?*

A few years ago there had been a fella called Gordon in the office. He was tall with a bizarre grey streak running through his hair which he probably wished was attributable to a bullet scar but which was just a slight genetic abnormality. Gordon played the whole laconic, world-weary bit and gave tiny tasks an importance they didn't deserve, as if everything was an imposition but that he would deal with it for the sake of harmony. He took the world's troubles on his shoulders even if the troubles in question didn't really exist. Tom had considered him to be a bit of a knob, although he was never sure how his colleagues viewed him. He was certainly tolerated with good humour. More good humour than he deserved. Gordon was nothing special, just a sort of internal courier with additional clerical duties, but he certainly knew how to act important.

But things ended badly for Gordon when, one rainy day in December, he was summoned to his supervisor's office and an entire list of blunders and indiscretions was revealed to him, giving him no option but to resign. It was a shame really. He should have been told about each mistake as soon as they were discovered and given a chance to rectify them. Instead, a case was built against him, which, when made suitably robust, was presented as a *fait accompli*. Gordon was royally stiffed. The poor man probably deserved better, but a decision to remove him had been made some time before the appropriate evidence had been collected to bring it about. Tom wondered if the same thing was happening to him. Failing to log off might just be the latest in a line of misdemeanours which was being aggregated with a view to dismissal. He could be 'doing a Gordon' in other words.

He sighed long and hard. Claire did not look up but tapped away steadily at her keyboard. *Had Andrew's little speech been an indication that everything was okay?* He knew that was not necessarily the case; if they were stitching him up then they had to carry on as if everything was normal before the final act. More reassuring was the fact that he was still working on this most important of cases. If he was that indiscreet then surely he would have been pulled by now. Nevertheless, he was certain that he had not logged off.

'Did anyone come in while I was out?', he asked Claire. She looked up. Her face was pale. He assumed she was succumbing to flu or something similar.

'Andy came in but went out again.'

'No one else? Not Wendy or Matt?'

She shook her head but then relented suddenly.

'Wendy. Very briefly.'

Tom nodded. He'd found his culprit. She wouldn't just log him off and say nothing. His failure would have been passed on. The bitch.

'Someone logged me off', he said tonelessly. He felt a sick dread in the pit of his stomach.

'You're supposed to log off if you leave your computer', said Claire without looking up.

'Yeah, I know but I forgot. It must have been Wendy. She'll drop me right in…'

'It was me.'

'You?'

She looked up.

'I saw her spying on your monitor so I logged you off in case she came back.'

'Oh.' Although her words didn't quite ring true, he was glad that she'd taken that precaution on his behalf. 'Thank you', he spluttered.

'It's okay.'

Tom sat still for a few moments before deciding that he was not in trouble. *Since when have I been so paranoid*, he wondered? He spent a few more moments thinking about the investigation and about the recent murders. *I wouldn't like to be a copper in Perth right now.* Then he logged back on to continue his work.

It took a few moments before his screen came back to life and a few more until he found the files he had been perusing. He swallowed hard and for the second time that morning his blood ran cold. The fourth file was missing! He put a hand to his mouth, not in shock but in a facsimile of concentration, making sure not to touch any keys. He remembered a joke or a sketch, something like *step away from the equipment* – and without physically doing so that was his next action… or inaction. There was a key he could press to get back his recent searches or the files he'd been using. Press the wrong one and he'd lose the file forever. Press the right one and he could carry on as normal. Whichever he did, he now knew that someone had tampered with his machine.

There was an additional problem. He couldn't tell anyone what had happened, nor could he ask for technical advice. It was his carelessness which had enabled someone to sabotage his work. Tom shot a glance at Claire. Although he didn't suspect her, he assumed she knew who had done this. Unless it was done remotely.

He rubbed his eyes. He was beginning to think he needed glasses. With some trepidation he pressed a key. Nothing happened. The file did not reappear. Tom nodded, taking in this new information at the same time as he assessed the developing situation. He could remember the name he'd been studying: Mohammed Ifran Khan. Things weren't so bad. He logged back into the database, entered the name and waited.

There was no Mohammed Ifran Khan listed. There had been last time he checked, but no longer.

'What the fuck?', he muttered. He glanced at Claire but she was engrossed in something. She'd barely spoken today.

Tom retyped the name and checked the spelling before pressing enter. Nothing. He went through the list of names from the beginning. No one by the name of Mohammed Ifran Khan was listed. He was about to speak when Claire beat him to it.

'Got him!'

He came round to her desk at once.

'No photo but here he is. Stopped by the British Army in Afghanistan. In the back of a Nissan 4x4. A sniffer dog picked up traces of explosives but there was little else to go on. A man named Mohammed Iqbal Khan was questioned for some time at the roadside but then he and the others were released.'

'How do you know it's him?'

'Of the four names you gave me, two are dead, one is in prison. He's the only one.'

Tom had his doubts but also had nothing better to go on, especially since his own suspect had ceased to exist, either actually or electronically.

'Okay, Claire. Let's go with that. What do we do now?'

'Find the man who questioned him and see what he can tell us. He might also be able to describe him for us.'

'We know who he is?'

'His name is right here. Lance-Corporal Jack Sullivan. We have his army number and his regiment. Piece of piss to find him.'

This revelation seemed to have brightened her mood somewhat. He wanted to flatter her ego a little.

'Good work. Now we're getting somewhere.'

'Yep. We just need to find him.'

***

'What are you thinking?', asked Mark. He and Liz were in the canteen, sitting across from each other at a Formica table. The air was thick with the smell of frying oil, despite an abortive attempt to introduce a healthy eating regime a few years previously. Hard-working coppers didn't want fruit and veg before their shift or at any time during it. Liz rubbed her cheek and spoke quietly, fearing that she would be overheard.

'I'm thinking about Shannen and Gavin. I know they were scrotes but they didn't deserve that.'

'No one will mourn their passing but it's going to create a massive stink. I mean someone has told the story to someone else who wanted them killed. There is no point even thinking otherwise. This is going to come back and bite us on the arse.' He hacked at a chewy sausage with his knife. 'It wasn't me by the way. I haven't spoken to anyone about it apart from you and the rest of the team.'

'Me neither. But someone has. Someone we know. This is someone we are working with.'

'Unless it is someone down in London.'

'MI5 or whoever? No way.'

'Why not?'

'They are strictly vetted for those jobs.'

'So are we Liz.'

She took a sip of bitter tea and said nothing.

'One of the Belgians?', she said at last. Her voice lacked commitment.

'God knows. The thing is, there is no one that I actually think could do it. Marc, Eddy and Pieter are all sound guys. They are trusted by their own governments to do this, that's why they're here.'

'They might have let slip something.'

'They might but to who? They are hardly boasting about their work to the locals over a few pints every night. The chances of them accidentally spilling the beans is pretty small.'

'The DI?', suggested Liz.

'Well, if you don't mind, I'll let you put that one to her. It is not something I particularly want to put forward.'

'Fine. I feel like there isn't much more we can do.'

'We will wait for orders from above', said Mark with resignation. 'There are other crimes…'

***

He looked over at the mountains. Sheer distance had purged them of colour and yet finally he was beginning to feel something for the purported romance of his location. He had also begun to admire the silent, watchful men who'd been given the task of keeping him safe. No names were used and they were mercenaries of course, but he trusted them implicitly and looked upon their expertise with awe. They were real men and he didn't use the term lightly. These two, he thought, could survive a nuclear war and continue living amidst the carnage. They seemed to need practically nothing. Even the older man – he must have been in his sixties – was lean and fit like an athlete, although his skin was burned almost black by the sun and in that respect, he resembled a mariner with a lifetime at sea.

Men like these didn't retire of course. They worked, lived, roamed and then one day they died and their bodies were eaten up by the desert which had served them so well. He should have objected to their lack of religious fervour. They were Muslims but cared not for the war against the infidel. Instead he took comfort from their total lack of zealotry. In a sense, and it sounded a bit silly when he thought about it, they were easy to like. Plus, someone had paid them well enough to ensure their loyalty. That latter quality was never in doubt. Their commitment to the limited task they'd been given was total. They had committed themselves, and that was that. This was a point of honour for them, an unbreakable agreement.

Maybe one day, when this was all over, he would return and see them again... He cast the thought away at once. That would be a mistake. Things would not be the same again. They would have moved on, found a new temporary paymaster and would be working for them as efficiently as they were now doing for him. They wouldn't betray him in future but they wouldn't help either. Even this realisation was a comfort to him. He knew exactly where he stood with them. They couldn't let him down because they made no promises of undying support in the first place.

He marvelled at their relationship. It was perfect for the circumstances.

The sun was falling below the horizon now, infusing the air with shards of yellow and red. The heat haze that had partially obscured everything around them had dissipated and a cool breeze came from the south. There had been a time during the day when his clothes had been saturated with sweat and he had suffered terribly. He'd been miserable and cross with himself until the two Arabs had taken him inside and plied him with a litre of water. Ah, the restorative powers of water! It was the difference between life and death, never more so than out here in the desert. Out here, water was everything. There were no taps in the desert. The sun stole the water but the Bedou always knew how to make it last or find more. Thirst and anthrax were the big killers.

The Bomber sighed happily. Death seemed a distant prospect now. Inside the tent, the Arabs chatted and played games, laughing uproariously like men of any nation. He was still an outsider but that sort of fitted in with the arrangement they had... in fact it was vital. And yet he did not feel isolated by this. He turned to face the old truck and the two Land Cruisers, feeling a sudden affection for them. They gave him a sense of security, despite the fact that one of them carried the materials required to make a bomb. How strangely his life was turning out.

When he gazed at the sky, seeing wisps of white turning to grey, he thought about the American satellites high above and wondered what they made of it all. *Were they being watched? Did it actually matter?*

His idyll was short-lived however, for, coming from the north, he spotted a car racing across the desert, heading directly for them. This, he knew, was his new master and he wasn't eager to meet him.

***

'Here we go', said Tom. He scanned the details on his computer screen and relayed selected highlights to Claire who listened intently, her previous ill humour miraculously gone.

'He's left the army now but... Tours of duty in Iraq and Afghanistan. Infantry... blah, blah, blah... from Stafford. Last known address Bob Geldof Way.'

'Bob Geldof Way? You just made that up', said Claire.

'Nope. Bob Geldof Way. That's what it says. Probably named after someone', he suggested. Claire rolled her eyes at his attempt at humour.

'So, if that's our man then we need to ring him and get him in here. We can send rail tickets and he can get them from the station on his debit card. Andy can authorise it.'

'Or we could go out to see him?', said Claire.

'You're joking aren't you? Have you ever been to Stafford? They still eat their young out there.'

'Have you been?'

'No.'

'Then how do... never mind. Let's get in touch.'

Claire began her enquiries but quickly drew a blank, getting a phone number for the address only to find that Jack Sullivan no longer lived there. In fact, no member of the Sullivan family did.

Undaunted, she carried on. Eventually, she obtained a phone number for his mother and got through at once. She was encouraged.

Claire used a standard subterfuge to avoid any awkward questions.

'Mrs Sullivan? My name is Claire and I am ringing from the National Census. Do you have time to answer a few questions?'

Mrs Sullivan confirmed her identity and also agreed to answer questions. She seemed fairly guileless, perhaps even gullible, the sort of person who might buy anything if asked in the right way. Claire gave Tom the thumbs up sign as she continued.

She ran through a series of questions, the answers to which were of no interest to her. They were mere scene setters to build trust.

'And how long have you lived at that address?'

'Oh, let me see... about three and half years.'

Claire pretended to type this information into her keyboard.

'Okay and your date of birth is...'

'Twenty-sixth of the ninth, sixty', answered Mrs Sullivan. Seemingly it did not occur to her to ask why the Census, holder of details for everyone in the United Kingdom, did not already have these details to hand.

'Now we have you down as being the only resident at that address. Is that still the case?', asked Claire, taking a bit of a punt.

'Yes. Just me.'

She knew from experience that people were often reticent when it came to admitting to the presence of partners especially if having a partner interfered with entitlement to benefits. She didn't actually care if the woman was telling the truth about this, but by subtle increments, she was getting nearer to the real reason for her call. She felt a little buzz of excitement which transmitted itself to her body language. Claire was itching to find Jack Sullivan now.

'You're being very helpful Mrs Sullivan. Just a few more questions. Did I mention that we send you a free pen for helping us?'

'Er... no, you didn't.' She sounded rightly unexcited by news of a new writing implement. Tom, knowing that they had no such pens, frowned at this. It was an embellishment too far in his view considering the woman was about to spill in any case.

'Now, you have a son called Jack who no longer lives with you, is that right?'

'Yes.'

'And you don't have any other children?', she asked. It was another leap in the dark.

'I have three other children. Two girls and a boy.'

'Okay...', said Claire, adding details to her imaginary database. It was something of a gaffe on her part to suggest that Jack was an only child but it hadn't put Mrs Sullivan off her stride.

'Do you have an address for Jack?'

'No. Sorry.'

Claire frowned. She had come this far but all her fake enquiries had been in vain if the woman didn't even know where her bloody son lived.

'You're not in touch with Jack?'

'He rings now and again but I don't know where he lives or anything. He has a caravan and he moves about finding work here and there.'

Claire pulled a face and shook her head at Tom who listened in from his desk opposite.

'So, a touring caravan... Where was he last?'

'Oh... Northumberland. He was on a farm but I don't have an address. He's not there now, I can tell you that much.'

'No clues about where he went? North or south?'

'Nope.'

Claire had had bigger setbacks than this; her work could lead her into blind alleys and dead ends. Sometimes there was no suitable outcome. Sometimes she had to admit defeat.

'Ah. You must have a mobile number for him?', she said.

'It's blocked. I don't know how he does that or even why he does it. He can ring me but I can't ring him.'

'What about your other children, do they have a means of getting in touch with him? Or do any of them know where he is at the minute?'

'I doubt it', said Mrs Sullivan. Claire thought she detected a note of something like boredom or frustration now.

'Last thing. Definitely the last thing. Can I have the addresses for your children or even telephone numbers.'

There was a pause. Jack's mother was finally getting suspicious.

'Who did you say you are?'

'My name is Claire and I work for the National…'

'Well, I'm surprised that you don't have all these details already.'

'The Census only works because of the cooperation of people like you', said Claire. Flattery usually worked.

'Hmm. It's just you don't seem to have any details at all. My family hasn't just landed here from the Moon.' At this point Claire might have described Mrs Sullivan's attitude as being that of mild exasperation. She didn't really blame her if that was the case. The artifice was crumbling too quickly under the sheer weight of lies she had told. The golden rule of lying was to keep it simple, hence the use of her real name, but she had dragged the whole story round the houses by now, stretched it until it was ready to snap.

'It's fine if you feel unable to help. You have been very helpful and given us a lot of your time. It really is appreciated…' She heard Mrs Sullivan sigh with heavy resignation.

'Your best bet is my son Matthew. He is in the RAF but I have a mobile number for you.' She paused again. 'I shouldn't really give it out…'

'You can ring me back on this number if you are unsure…'

'No. It's fine.' Claire scribbled down the number, thanked Mrs Sullivan yet again and hung up.

Tom had watched the whole process.

'Well done', he said. 'How do you know that this fella is actually going to be able to help us?'

'I don't but as far as I can see he's the only person we have who knows what our bomber even looks like. The image he has of him probably isn't very clear and it is likely to be out of date but it is better than nothing, which is what we have otherwise.'

'He has parents and friends and siblings…'

'But he has done a great job of covering his tracks so far.'

'True. Okay. Let's find Jack Sullivan and see what he can tell us about the Antwerp bomber.'

Claire smiled, but her smile was cut short as Andy burst into the office.

'Get your coats. We're off to the Cabinet Office Briefing Rooms.'

***

The man called himself 'The Tiger' which seemed both pointless and fanciful. Khan thought he might struggle to engage this man in conversation for a number of reasons, chief being, how did he address him? *Mr Tiger? Mr The Tiger? Tiger? Tiger, sir?* Bloody ridiculous. He didn't resemble a tiger, nor did he resemble someone with even a few of a tiger's attributes. The Tiger was thin – weedy might have been a better word – with a grey beard and grey hair, both of which belied his relative youth. He wore designer glasses like a true desert warrior, and a pair of Nike Air *somethings* protruded from beneath his robes. It was an idiotic ensemble.

The Tiger might have been more at home working in his father's pharmacy or manning the reception desk at a garden centre. Khan hoped that some great strategic genius was contained within the unpromising frame he was faced with.

They sat at the fire, each man cross-legged. The flames leapt on a bed of glowing orange embers, but the wood – dried over a period of years – burned cleanly and almost without smoke. Sitting around in this way felt like an act, something to give their discussions a sense of drama, as if blowing up a city wasn't dramatic enough. The whole scenario was preposterous. He found himself wondering what someone like The Tiger would have done had it not been for the Jihad? But he was trapped now. His entire future was bound to these strange men.

The Arabs – men whose company he truly enjoyed – were nowhere to be seen. He presumed they were in the tent, chatting, smoking, playing games in a routine as timeless as the desert itself.

The Tiger wore a pistol on a belt alongside a curved dagger which looked purely ceremonial. Now, he could imagine one of the nameless Arabs having a dagger like this, knowing how to use it and not being afraid to do so either, but it didn't really go with the Nike Air *thingies* and the designer specs. The pistol looked like an old Walther from the Second World War.

Finally, after a long, drawn-out, and frankly tedious period of contemplative silence, they got down to business.

'You know why you are here?'

It was a stupid question, chosen for melodrama rather than because it furthered their plans in any way. The Tiger might have been repeating the words in a Hollywood script.

'Yes', said The Bomber.

'Good. The truth is we have been losing ground. It is time to strike a blow against the infidel to prove that the fight goes on. They can never win this war but they can't admit this. They can't admit that whatever action they take against us we will still eventually win. But they know it all the same. Their politicians hide behind statistics and point at maps and make great statements which don't tell the true story at all.'

The Bomber inclined his head, hoping to give the impression that he was fascinated by this rhetoric. *Was it indoctrination or just a stirring speech? Or was it merely the verbal outpourings of a deluded man who saw himself as a great fighter?* He was inclined to the latter view, but indulged his new master with all the reverence he could muster. Nevertheless, he was being told things he already knew.

'We are like a Cobra', said the man. He was staring at Khan intently now. 'Cut off the head of the cobra and another ten heads grow in its place.'

Khan might have found it funny had his opposite number not been quite so serious. He was a parody of a war leader. The Bomber wanted to get to his feet, kick the fire out and shout at him. *A fucking cobra? If you cut the head off a cobra you have a dead snake, not one which grows ten new heads!*

Metaphorically, he sat on his hands and let his new mystical leader take him on his journey through the fantastic realms of nonsense until perhaps he would get to the point. *What a pompous little arse*, he thought.

'They think they are safe in their cities. They think that they can plan against us. They think that they can capture a piece of desert and claim to be winning the war *they* chose to fight. But we must prove that that is not the case.'

The Bomber was well aware that both sides used whatever measure of success suited them best at any particular moment. When ISIS captured a Syrian town, they proclaimed another battle won. Likewise, when the west re-captured the same town they made the same claim. He said nothing. There was nothing to be gained from aggravating this man, The Tiger. He just hoped that there was something more concrete to his musing than this. Did he have a plan?

'I have a plan', he said. He jumped when a spark shot out of the fire. Khan pretended not to notice and gazed at the blue-black sky, marvelling at the sheer number of stars it held. One of the stars moved at speed and blinked. It was a plane of course. Khan wondered if it was a reconnaissance aircraft.

The spark had burnt a tiny hole in the fabric upper of his trainer and he was annoyed now, not just at the damage but at the fact that his speech had been undermined by a silly act of nature.

'The plan is to take eight dirty bombs to London and plant them at eight strategic points. The bombs will detonate and put the centre of London out of operation for years to come.'

The Bomber scratched his ear. For some reason he felt he already knew this.

'That is a good plan', he said. It was a laughable plan unless this clown was able to put some flesh on the bones.

'One dirty bomb would not do enough damage, that is why we are having eight. Casualties from this attack will be lower than you might expect. The conventional explosives required to detonate the bombs will kill more people than the radiation. However, our aim is to produce fear and to put London out of action. It is a city which thrives on tourism, and it is a financial centre. But who would visit or invest if they think that the place is riven with insidious radiation? The clean-up operation will take weeks or months and will put the entire city centre out of operation. But it will also show that we can strike how we want and when we want. We are showing the world that there is no defence against us. London will become like a grave. Even when the immediate danger has passed, people will keep away. People are terrified of radiation. They know about the associated health risks – cancer being chief amongst these – and put these to the forefront of their minds.

'They think that the bombs dropped on Hiroshima and Nagasaki caused genetic illness through several generations of inhabitants and that it continues to this day. No one is interested in knowing that the reported genetic abnormalities had gone after just one generation. No one really thinks about the fact that both cities are thriving hubs of business. You say 'Nagasaki' and people think about the mushroom cloud, about acres of rubble, terrified children with radiation burns, sitting, crying, mourning the loss of parents. They think about the next generation being born without eyes or with limbs missing. The truth? Nearly half a million people live in Nagasaki today.'

Khan blinked, suddenly alive to the potential of the attack he was going to carry out.

'Why do I tell you this? Because the truth doesn't matter. It's what people think that does the damage, and we are assisted in our quest by the media and by Hollywood. The media will spread the fear. Whatever they say becomes true and they want fear because it sells. They can sell papers or put advertisements between the news bulletins. So, on one hand they are telling you about the dangers of going near London and the risks of death and illness and on the other they are selling you deodorant and panty liners and food supplements for your cat.

'It is ridiculous. Secretly they love war. Did you know this? They love war. The Americans love it because they can sell useless weapons to terrified allies. The British love it because fighting wars is all they are good at. The Germans love it because it shows the world that they have changed and can be trusted with a few guns and tanks and that they are responsible partners in defence. The French love it for the same reasons, so long as they can be seen to be making the decision for themselves and are not at the behest of the Americans. The Australians love it because they will do anything to kiss the asses of the Americans. They all have their reasons. Fear provides jobs and keeps the wheels of industry turning. All the technology they have produced comes from the military.

'But the truly marvellous thing about all this is… we are still winning. They can talk about victory but they can't produce it. We *will have* an Islamic State. If not today or tomorrow, then someday.'

The rhetoric was fine. It was great, in fact, but The Tiger was short on detail.

'Eight bombs though…', Khan said, doubtfully

'The bombs will be constructed and put into the metal liners of the street bins. We will have a fake council truck driving round emptying the bins as normal but they will replace the usual liners with our new versions of the same and when they are all in place… BOOM!'

He laughed. The Bomber allowed himself a chuckle. There was one aspect of the plan which he particularly liked – it didn't sound as if it would be necessary for him to die after all.

'And you my friend will be on that fake team of council workers. Furthermore, you will press the button. And the best bit? The start of your journey to Paradise will be on film.' The Tiger smiled like an idiot.

'What do you mean?'

'The internet will have a live broadcast of the explosion that kills you. They will be able to watch you standing there, then pressing the button and being vaporised. They will see it all. They will know that we cannot be beaten. And you? You get to sit at the top table in Paradise.'

***

The DI came out of her office and gathered together her little task force.

'It seems prudent to break up this task force since we appear to have a leak. Maybe not an intentional leak but there is one. Somehow our investigation, whilst providing superficial success, seems to have caused or contributed to the deaths of two local citizens.'

She cleared her throat. Her words sounded like they were drawn from an official press release.

'You can probably guess that a fair amount of crap is going to fall on us – on me really. I have to be seen to have taken immediate action. Don't be surprised if you are interviewed on the matter. Personally, I don't think that anyone had intentionally created this problem, but the problem remains nevertheless. This sounds like a farewell speech – I suppose it is – but I want to thank you all for your efforts and of our friends from across the Channel. I hope you settle back into your old routines after all the assistance you have given us over here. That's it. You all now have a couple of days' leave and we'll be in touch about what happens next.'

She gave the smile of a very worried officer and left them again.

Liz looked at Mark.

'So that's it', she said. 'Fancy a drink?'

'Nothing better to do', he said.

***

Chapter Eleven

'You look worried', commented Claire. She and Tom had gone to the pub after work. Neither was driving.

'It's nothing.'

'Go on, tell me what's up?'

'Seriously, it's nothing. Besides you have looked rather worried yourself these past few days and you have not told me why.'

'Okay. Here's why', she said settling her head on a cradle made from her entwined fingers. 'Life. Sometimes life gets on top of me.'

'Fair enough. We all feel that way sometimes.'

'Precisely. So, what ails you?'

'Okay. If you must know. This thing we are working on – it sucks.'

'How so?', she said looking perplexed.

'Whatever we are doing it just feels wrong. I can't help thinking that we are barking up the wrong tree. We are going after the wrong man, and at some point we are going to get pulled up rather sharply. We won't have a leg to stand on.'

'Is that a pun? Because you are missing a foot?'

'No. It is a metaphor or a simile or one of those things. In fact, it's probably just a cliché but you know what I mean.

It is not a reference to my disability.' He desisted when he had managed to make Claire blush.

'I'm sorry. It was stupid thing to say. I shouldn't poke fun…'

'No, it's fine. I'm not actually that bothered. I just think that we are going to get hauled over the coals for this.'

'The meeting went well today. The PM seemed pleased.'

'Did you see the looks Sir Maurice Gilmore was giving us? I think he thought we were bloody mad.'

'We were only reporting the facts.' Claire gave half a shrug. 'It went well. Really.'

'If you say so.'

The pub was hot and loud. Tom hated it. He knew that it was frequented by other intelligence agents and for that reason he hated it even more. He couldn't bear the buzzwords and the hushed conversations. They were such an insular bunch that every conversation ended up being about work simply because those outside the intelligence community could never hear about their day-to-day business. It bored Tom.

In his mind, he played back events of the day where they had found themselves in the presence of the PM.

The Cabinet Offices Briefing Room (COBR) had once been given the acronym COBRA, for obvious reasons, although this terminology had recently fallen out of favour for reasons which were less obvious. The rooms in question were not underground bunkers or anything so uncomfortable but they did have sophisticated communication links with other friendly governments. The composition of the staff present at meetings varied according to the nature of the emergency. This meeting had been hosted by the PM herself and, unsurprisingly, included the chiefs of the three armed services and of the emergency services, as well as a handful of government ministers. The atmosphere had been an odd mix of tension and exaggerated *savoir faire*. Very British… or French.

Andrew had done most of the talking. Tom was rather impressed by the fact that the PM knew his first name, almost as though she knew *him*. Perhaps she did; his boss undoubtedly moved in different circles to the wounded ex-sergeant. Andrew was well-spoken, urbane and a bit of a toff. The phrase *well-connected* probably summed it up. Tom, by comparison, wasn't any of those things.

He cleared his throat in the manner of someone about to deliver a best man speech, but from there on his tone was sombre.

'The MV Odessa is lost. We think she was essentially 'knocked out', communications, engines and so on, and left for dead. Another ship pulled alongside and off-loaded a cargo of nuclear waste and then sailed for Tripoli. We assume that Odessa was sent to the bottom with her crew, apart from the one who facilitated the take-over and subsequent theft. A search continues for wreckage et cetera but that is really not our concern.

'The Israelis sent a special forces team into Tripoli to take back the waste – or rather to put it out of commission – but it had gone. They withdrew empty handed.'

Gilmore interrupted at this point.

'Are these pirates aware of the Israeli raid?', he asked.

'I presume so, sir. They won't know that it was an Israeli team, although they might suspect that. The Israelis are the most skilled soldiers in the region. Whoever is behind this will obviously be aware that their crime is being investigated.'

Gilmore nodded.

'The location of the waste is not known to us but it may still be in Libya. If you want to hide something then where better? Miles of inhospitable desert. Our suspicions are that the stolen material is going to be used to make a so-called dirty bomb. I believe that you have all been briefed on the risks and limitations associated with these weapons?' Heads nodded. If anyone was unsure of how a dirty bomb worked or what it did then they weren't ready to admit it.

Andrew felt a moment of panic when he looked at the faces all turned in his direction. These were some of the most powerful people in the country. These were the people who scuttled in and out of 10 Downing Street, with a little faux-anxious wave to the press. The moment passed and he continued.

'There is a strong thread of opinion which thinks that the target for this bomb is London. Britain is still seen as the United States' closest military ally. More so than France. More so than Germany. It's perception which counts in the eyes of ISIS. They like propaganda victories, as well as causing economic and physical damage. That is pretty standard for terrorist groups generally and they are no different. Symbolism is important. IS is a very modern terror group, very much operating with one eye on the media. For some of their leaders they are creating news as part and parcel of their campaign.

'That is one part of our investigation into the current threat. The second part follows on from what I was saying about media manipulation and symbolism. The last big terrorist outrage was, of course, the Antwerp bombing. This fell into our laps due to the fact that a sample of DNA was found on a marijuana cigarette smoked byThe Bomber, which linked him to a small-time drug dealer called Shannen Cassidy in Perth, Scotland. With the assistance of the police up there we were able to partly establishThe Bomber's identity. We are tracking down his associates and trying to find out more about him.

'The reason that this has become so important is that we think he will be selected to operate the dirty bombs.'

'Seems like a lot of supposition', said Gilmore. Andrew looked at the man as he replied, taking in the expensively tailored suit and hand-made shirts. Gilmore didn't buy 'off-the-peg' and unlike some middle-aged men in his position he actually made an expensive suit look expensive.

'To an extent you are right of course, but we have to draw up various possibilities and give each of these a weighting according to likelihood, based on a number of factors and the most up-to-date intelligence we have. We build a sort of profile – which sounds a bit fanciful – but it gives us a number of scenarios which we can at least prepare for. What we do is a bit like an old-fashioned weather forecast, and sometimes we get it wrong... but our enemies don't tell us what they are up to or what they hope to achieve, so we have to second guess. By doing so we have arrived at the likelihood that the Antwerp Bomber, who is currently their biggest star, will pull off an even bigger attack than the last one. Using him is symbolic. We don't know what he looks like but in every other respect he is the poster boy for IS, and when we look at the prestige targets in Europe – and this will be a European attack for there is no way that this bomb or bombs can be transported undetected to the US – we have London, Paris and Berlin.

'The biggest of these is London. The one most associated with the war against IS is London. The one which creates the biggest headlines if subject to an attack of this ambition is London.'

'But this could be pie in the sky?', asked Gilmore. He was astute but a pain in the arse too.

'If you are suggesting we might be wrong then, yes, I would agree. But my job is to brief you on things that might happen. To a large extent terrorist groups set their own agenda. We don't fight them on a conventional field of battle where there is some mutual understanding of timescale between the two protagonists. We simply have to assess the threat and be prepared if we can.'

'Thank you, Andrew.' It was the PM who spoke. She turned to the heads of the three armed forces. 'Can we do anything while these bombs are being prepared or stored in Libya?'

It was the head of the RAF who spoke.

'That would be the ideal, Prime Minister. Much better to tackle the threat in someone else's country than our own. If this bomb-making material is there and if we can find it then we might use drones to negate the threat, followed up by a special forces operation on the ground to deal with the hazardous materials that have been taken. It might be a British operation or even a joint operation with the US or Israelis. We have some contingency plans and some of our forces are on standby in the region.'

Tom shot Claire a look. Neither party had been asked to make any contribution. This was not a source of regret...

The workings of the pub, the noise, the smells brought him back to the present. Looking back on it, Tom guessed that it had gone well.

'In the context of knowing almost nothing I suppose we looked like true professionals.'

'These people aren't stupid. There is guesswork involved in what they do.'

'I suppose so.' Tom had opted for a whisky. In his mind it was the best drink for this situation. It was warm and calming, inherently relaxing. 'I thought it got a bit sticky when it came to talking about our mole.'

'Not our concern', said Claire, hurriedly. 'That's something for the cops in Scotland to deal with.'

'Wouldn't want to be them.'

'No.'

Tom caught a glimpse of his reflection on the huge mirror behind the bar. Between a bottle of vodka and another of Pernod, he looked pale and tired. The last few days had taken their toll.

'For a while I thought it was Wendy, you know?'

'Thought what was Wendy?', asked Claire suspiciously.

'The mole. Sounds ridiculous – mole – but I thought it was her.'

Claire was taken aback and seemed to take refuge behind her glass of wine as she drank.

'Do you still think that?', she asked.

They were joined by another customer, a tall black man wearing a smart raincoat. He looked like a solicitor. As he ordered his drink, their conversation became rather more circumspect, sterile, without names or details.

'No. I suppose it is just my innate dislike of the woman. I also don't trust her. She dropped me in it once.'

'You told me', said Claire quickly as if to cut him off before he spoke about the same old thing again.

'That day, when I didn't log off my computer…'

'Yes.'

'Well you know those things we were looking at?'

'Yes.'

'One of them had gone.'

'How do you mean?', asked Claire without apparent interest.

'I mean it wasn't there. It wasn't on the computer and it had been deleted from the database.'

Claire said nothing.

'Don't you think that is strange?'

'I suppose so.' She said the words as if he was being nothing more than an annoyance. The man in the overcoat moved away.

'But how could something like that happen?'

'A computer glitch? Human error?'

'Sabotage?'

'Is this why you thought Wendy was up to no good?'

'I always think she is up to no good, but yes, I suppose so. But I have to admit I wouldn't have had her down as an out and out traitor, just a bit sly. She's not a traitor as in someone betraying her country.'

'But you just said that…'

'I know but I don't really believe it. Anyway, why would anyone do it?'

'You're talking yourself out of it now.'

'Yes. I don't think anyone is an actual traitor. But someone has said something they shouldn't have said. Accidental.'

They lapsed into silence for a while but he was surprised when Claire opted to continue the conversation.

'If it was her, I mean if she was a traitor, what would you do?'

'What anyone would do.', he replied, guardedly.

'What?', she persisted.

'I'd report her at once. To Andy. What else could I do? Are you saying that you think she is a traitor?'

Her response was an enigmatic shrug, positively French in its ambiguity.

The bar began to fill with the late tea time crowd and Tom felt his confidence evaporate, realising that he and Claire had nothing in common. She seemed to have clammed up, and the atmosphere between the two deteriorated. Tom had experienced this phenomenon before on various social events with work colleagues when it had gradually become apparent that, outside of work, he had nothing in common with the people with whom he was expected to make small talk. He was astonished on occasion to see how the two sexes reverted to some sort of clichéd type; the men talking about cars, the women talking about babies and weddings. He supposed he was being sexist or racist or typist. He never expressed his reservations, the fear of being hauled up for some breach of professional etiquette greater than anything he had faced in the army, where no one had seemed to give a damn.

Civvy street was full of hidden dangers, sort of cultural booby traps that saw a casual remark turned into an investigation into one's conduct. Some people were all too ready to take offence and some actually sought instances to grab offence where none had been attempted or intended. Badinage became some sort of -ism with severe complications for the would-be joker. Of course, he knew it would eventually creep into the armed forces, taking the edge off the humour which kept troops sane in or out of the heat of battle.

There had been times – not many, but a few – where he had missed the army. It was black and white. There were no shades. Every task was performed in a particular way and everyone knew when to speak and when to shut up. There were no meetings or meetings about meetings; you were told what to do and you did it.

'What are you thinking about?', asked Claire.

He shook away his reverie. The whisky was just starting to hit the spot.

'Nothing much. Well actually I was thinking about the fact that we barely know each other. Times like this you can easily run out of things to talk about.'

'Isn't that the point?'

'The point of what?', he asked dumbly.

'A date?'

He risked her wrath by saying, 'a date? Is that what this is?'

She rolled her eyes.

'Well, what would you call it?'

'An after-work drink', he said plainly.

'Okay but you don't just go for a drink after work with anybody', she countered.

'Do you want us to be romantically involved?'

'Well, don't you? And who says 'romantically involved' by the way? You sound like Stephen Fry.'

Tom let it go. He was glad that the conversation had picked up again and that there was a sense of togetherness even if it meant something different to each of them. It wasn't the whisky that made her seem attractive to him – she already had been – but it didn't diminish that attraction either. When she was on good form – and that didn't mean tipsy – she was funny, tender and alluring. When she wasn't, he just kept out of her way. Not for the first time he noticed her clear complexion and her even, white teeth. She looked as good as many other women only managed when they were plastered in make-up or airbrushed on the front pages of vogue.

He finished his drink.

'I'd better get off', he said. 'Got to wash the cat. Takes ages to blow dry him.'

'I thought it was a she?'

'Never been sure. Truth be told I don't have a cat.'

'Then stay for another.'

He was tempted but he had to be strong. He reminded himself that office romances never worked out and he still had huge reservations about Claire anyway. That was the only way that these secretive types ever met anyone, but it wasn't ideal. After all who wanted to spend cosy nights talking about intelligence matters? Dead letter boxes, live letter boxes, encryption, surveillance... yawn.

'No. Seriously. It's a very exciting episode of 'Turn My Shitty House Into Something I Can Sell To A Mug.' This woman lives in the middle of a council estate in Leeds...'

'That's not a TV programme', she said.

'It ought to be', he said.

'I'll buy the next round if you stay.'

'Now before I agree to anything, does that mean that you pay for and go and get the drinks? Or just pay for?'

'Pay for...'

'Right I'm off. It's not the money, it's the standing at the bar waving a tenner at some bimbo who isn't even looking at you...'

'Alright, alright. Both. What do you want?'

'Treble Whisky.'

'You twat.' But she stood and pushed her way through to the bar, while Tom, his spirits bolstered by... spirits... sat thinking that his day wasn't ending too badly for once. He looked at his fellow drinkers and decided that other people had it worse than him. The missing foot pained him and the prosthetic couldn't quite prevent him from having a limp, but he wasn't fat yet, nor was he bald. When he combined these facts with the company of an attractive woman, easily the best looker in the pub, then things weren't too bad. He had a job, a place to live and a small pension. *Would he swap those to get his foot back?* He wasn't actually sure.

Claire returned from the bar looking slightly irritated and Tom was able to remind himself why he was so eager for her to go instead of him. Buying drinks at peak times could bring about a sort of *every man for himself* frenzy, where manners were cast to one side in the name of getting served. Good manners were bedfellows of disaster in these circumstances.

'Thanks', he said as she set the drink in front of him. 'This saves me going to the bar for the next three rounds.'

'I chickened out and got you a double.'

'Oh. Two rounds then. Why did you chicken out? You thought I couldn't handle it?'

'I wasn't sure if there was such a thing as a treble. I didn't want to look silly.'

'There *is* such a thing but I know how you feel. Cheers', he said, holding up his glass. 'So, about this date', he said. 'Are you intending to be out all night?'

'Probably not. But I'm in no hurry to get going. I've already washed my cat, you see.'

'Is that a euphemism?'

For a second, he thought he had overstepped the mark but she laughed, sending relief flooding his body like endorphins. But for that moment, which began as he finished his inappropriate comment and ended when she began to laugh, he felt like a fugitive on the cusp of discovery. A sick dread had washed through him. It wasn't something he could attribute to the possibility of upsetting his hot date and he didn't think it was down to the alcohol deadening his senses and heightening his natural human paranoia – it was something more profound than that. Maybe the events of the past few days had caught up with him. People had been killed and there was a definite risk of many more joining them if they – he and Claire – messed up.

'Do you have a sense of dread?', he asked.

'Dread about what?'

'About what we are doing? We have to be on the ball with this.'

But Claire seemed very blasé about the work on this occasion, when normally that was his role. *She was the true professional and he was just a chancer who'd stumbled upon a good job which he really didn't deserve.* Tom didn't really want to talk about it and yet he was plagued by doubts.

'It's just a job', she said after a sip of wine. 'You of all people should know that. I'm surprised that it isn't you saying these things to me. You are 'Mr Couldn't Give A Damn', the hard-bitten ex-soldier who's seen it all.'

'Is that how you see me?', he said astonished.

'I reckon.'

'I was in the Intelligence Corps.'

'That's the army.'

'It is but it is the more… intelligent… end of the army, hence the name.'

'Ho hum. Does your foot hurt?'

'Only the missing one.'

'No one's told the nerves that the foot has gone?'

'Something like that. Have I told you this already?'

'It's a commonly reported phenomenon.'

She broke the next short silence with a question.

'What I just said about you – the soldier bit – that's what I don't understand. I always think that soldiers must take everything very seriously because they are dealing in life and death and because they take orders without question. They act robotically almost without conscience. And yet you just seem to take the piss.'

'Is that what you think?'

'Yes. You make fun of everything, to the point that I can't actually imagine you being able to take an order or to even do what you are told.'

'I think you are wrong about soldiers. That is where the confusion lies. Soldiers always take the piss. They joke about everything. That's how they cope. They moan and complain but they get on and do whatever needs to be done. They don't make a big deal about it or say that they 'want to make a difference'. Soldiers aren't robots either. They have to make decisions without having a meeting to get support for all their suggestions. That's why I can't stand all the po-faced crap that is spoken at work.'

'Oh', she said inadequately.

'When the mortar bomb landed on the roof of the ops room in Afghanistan I thought I was going to die. It felt like the entire thing was lying on top of me. I could barely hear or see. I didn't know if anyone was even going to look for me or if they would find me before I ran out of oxygen. I thought that everyone else in the room had been killed; I didn't actually see how it could be otherwise. And now I find it hard to take life too seriously.'

'Was anyone else killed?'

'No. A miracle. I was the only casualty. I lost a lot of blood and by the time they got to me I was unconscious. But I am here to tell the tale. Just don't expect me to be bothered when the photocopier doesn't work, or someone runs out of tea bags.'

At the far end of the bar someone set off the jukebox playing some eighties power ballad, precisely the sort of music Tom hated most. He hated it more than rap. Although distant, it still made conversation difficult. Claire downed her drink.

'Get 'em in, big boy', she said with uncharacteristic bonhomie.

'You're a bit drunk', said Tom.

'And you're not, so get them in.'

He stood and gently prized open a path to the bar, which was still his least favourite activity on a night out. The place had filled with swaggering revellers power drinking on empty stomachs, guts spilling over belts, slip-on shoes squelching crusty carpet as music pulsed like a huge musical heart around which every other action took place. Tom's vision of hell was realised in its grotesque glory. This, he supposed, was what a bad trip might be like. Although he made it to the bar, the wounded veteran angle didn't help him; his injury was too well disguised, he coped too well. And yet that bloody stump pained him terribly, especially when he was overheating as was now the case.

He returned with two drinks, vowing that these would be their last. The journey to the bar had effectively killed off his good spirits but he was gentlemanly enough not to complain or to suggest that they curtail their night.

'I don't know anything about you', he said as he sat.

'Nothing to know.' Claire had to raise her voice over the din. Her eyes held a watery glaze as her brain slowly detached itself from her mouth. The slur was there but held in check for the meantime. Despite her modest claim, she began to tell Tom all about herself. 'I went to a nice girl's school in Hertfordshire. Very posh. Turned out nice young ladies. Then off to uni to study languages, then an interview for this job, and the rest isn't history.'

'Isn't history?'

'So, what about you?'

'Joined the Intelligence Corps straight after school. Tours in Afghanistan and Iraq. Foot blown off in a mortar attack. Back to civvy street. Got an interview for this job and here I am. I have gone through it before.'

They chatted semi-drunkenly before Claire suggested that they retire to her place.

'For coffee?', asked Tom.

'Maybe after if you want…'

Chapter Twelve

Today he would be taken to the place where the bombs were being tested but his mind was not focussed on that at all. There was something so stupid about dying needlessly, especially when he considered the fact that those who planned his death had no intention of following suit until the time of their natural death. Bin Laden had only died because the Yankees had found him and killed him, otherwise he would still be alive today.

He sat by himself, a coffee cup held in both hands, watching the unmoving, never-changing, ever-changing desert. Had the Arabs of ancient times believed that the world ended on the horizon as their European contemporaries did? He had no sense of that here, only that the world went on forever. You could live here and think that New York, London, the Taj Mahal, the Amazon River, Mount Everest were mythical places, the lands of fairy tales and dreams. You could live here and learn nothing but never miss that lack of education or even wonder about anything more than the sand and the stars.

The sun rose but spread its warmth slowly. The night had been cold and his blankets had slipped from his shoulders with each sleeping turn he had made. He awoke for the last time feeling tired and depressed. Jihad was easier when you had a proper bed and decent food. He wasn't convinced that these rough desert dwellers had food hygiene certificates – some of their cooking practices seemed rather unwholesome – but he had no option but to eat what was put in front of him. Before giving his heart and soul to the Jihad he had enjoyed regular forays to McDonalds. He missed their chicken burgers mostly.

In a sense he could see the desert's beauty but it held nothing of real interest for him. Maybe if he stayed long enough…

Behind him, the rest of them snored like drunks. He had certainly grown to like the Arabs. Permitted to live, he might even have missed them when the time came to leave, but as things stood, he wasn't going to be around to miss anything. His thoughts came back to death, the feeling of being cheated. He was being used, feted for something that he could have done without dying in the process, and yet when he thought of an alternative – one that he could actually bring to the attention of his bosses – he drew a blank, for he knew that they were fixated on his glorious demise.

His death was central to their plans. The dramatic end to his life was a demonstration of their collective determination to overthrow the West, that they simply could not be stopped.

Could he fake it? It would be hard if the event was being filmed as some sort of live TV spectacular! It made him angry now. He wasn't quite ready for Paradise and there had been times recently when ill-formed and unworthy doubts had momentarily flickered in his mind. They were so vague that he couldn't ascertain what these doubts related to but they left him feeling sick and depressed.

Naturally, he tried not to think that way, but, like an ache, the same old thoughts came back time and again. *And if he died and there was no Paradise?* Obviously, he wouldn't know about it. Anger rose in him like bile. These thoughts couldn't be his but they felt like a betrayal of Allah nevertheless. The Qur'an told him that Paradise existed but, in this desert, he saw precious little religious study going on to reaffirm his faith,

The Bomber felt profoundly empty as these thoughts circled around his consciousness like vultures. He wanted to escape, and yet he was stranded both physically and spiritually. How could such a thing happen? Hadn't he done more than enough for the cause already? The desert was his prison and his devotion to the cause of Islam was the spiritual warder that kept him there. He didn't know how to say he wanted out, and besides, what might they do to him if his newly discovered weakness was known to them? For all he knew they might behead him as an example to others, as if he was a deserter from an army.

They were merciless. Was backing out from Jihad a greater crime than being an infidel? He was quite sure that those who would sit in judgement wouldn't have their names on the waiting list of volunteers to take his place. Anger, fear and despair coiled inside him. He'd plant the bombs but did he really have to die in the process?

The Bomber continued to sit like a man at peace with the strange planet he lived on, and yet he was assailed by doubts.

The sun had detached itself from the horizon by the time he heard the sounds of men waking and preparing for the day ahead. Already he'd begun to understand the ways of the desert; it would be some time before the night's chill had burned off, but when it did his mood would lift.

Booted feet crunched on the hard-packed sand, but he kept his gaze fixed on some point in the distance, letting his mind settle for the day ahead.

'You think it is beautiful?', came the voice. He recognised it as that of the older Arab and he turned to him as he answered.

'I suppose I do. It is growing on me. You must love it?'

'I know nothing else. I never thought about it.'

'Today we look at the bomb. A demonstration.'

The Arab seemed unmoved by this information, almost as though he didn't want to know, which may well have been the case.

'I have seen all sorts of things in my time here. I try to see everything and nothing. It is better for me that way. I am loyal to no one and everyone.'

'A strange life?', suggested The Bomber.

'Not for me. I know nothing else. Your life would seem strange to me.'

He looked askance at the young man for a moment and then sat next to him folding his legs under himself like a man half his age. Together they watched the sun climb into the sky by tiny increments. The Bomber had never felt so calm in the company of a virtual stranger. He somehow exuded wisdom and confidence as if he might actually outlive the desert itself.

'You are troubled', said the Arab. It wasn't an opinion and he wasn't necessarily offering a solution. His words were a statement of fact. The Bomber's nod was almost imperceptible but the accompanying sigh wracked his body.

'They expect me to die', he said. 'I have to go up with the bomb.'

'It isn't something I would choose for my own children. Nor for myself.' The Arab spoke plainly but The Bomber wanted to hear more.

'What should I do?'

'You don't want to die?'

'No. The people who plan my death carry on living.'

'I suppose that is their role. Your role is something else.'

'I will get my reward in Paradise'. He offered the words through a mask of pain.

'Is that not enough?'

'I don't know. I could still plant these bombs and live. There is no real need for me to die.'

'You know they won't accept this from you?'

'I know. Nothing less than my death will do. It is all part of it. They love their martyrs. They want everyone – the entire world – to see me die. I have to show that I think my sacrifice is worth the horror of dying. I will symbolise the rightness of the cause.'

'Why you and not someone else?'

Khan had nothing to lose by telling the truth.

'A bomb went off in Antwerp', he said. He had no idea if the Arab knew about things outside of the confined world he inhabited.

'I saw it on the internet.' The Arab smiled for he knew that no one expected an old man of the desert to use the internet, or even to know of its existence. 'I get it on my phone in certain places.'

'Oh. Well that was me. I planted the bomb.'

The Arab nodded without comment.

'I was supposed to die then but I planted the bomb and left. Does it shock you that I did such a thing?'

'I see all sorts of things happening here. But I don't think you should be telling me about it.'

'Because we pay for your loyalty?'

'Not for that reason. You can depend on our loyalty and discretion even after the work is complete, but I am sure that your masters want as few people as possible to know. This is a dangerous world for anyone but especially for you.'

'But what do you think about the fact that I killed so many people?'

'You seek my approval?'

'I'm not sure. I will plant the bombs they want me to plant. I believe in the cause for which I am fighting but I just don't want to die.'

'You reach Paradise before those who give you your orders.'

'Supposing Paradise doesn't exist?'

'Is that what you think? If you believe that then you shouldn't waste your time with the Jihad. Without Paradise the whole reason for having a holy war collapses. The entire religion collapses. Why would you die for that? Why would you fight for that?'

'Do you believe in Paradise?'

'I am a Muslim.'

'Ha. That doesn't quite answer my question.'

'I suppose I do believe. I could be proved wrong, but in the meantime, I might as well think that Paradise is waiting for me. I don't intend on going to hell. But for me religion is partly just a force of habit or a label that I carry around. It is expected that we all have a religion even if it isn't Islam. Most of the time I don't even think about Islam and I don't study the Qur'an.'

'Have you never studied it?'

'I have… but a long time ago.'

Khan smiled.

'I don't know where I am going, if anywhere', he said wistfully.

'Your masters pay me and my loyalty therefore is to them. But I will not tell them what you have told me. But you mustn't expect me to help you if you are trying to escape from this situation. I am saying this so that you understand the situation and not because I want to sound harsh. It may be that there is no escape possible and the crime you have already committed means that you can't turn yourself in to those you have offended.'

'I am trapped', said Khan.

'Either way, you face your enemies, or risk making new ones. I can't say which would be worse. But we should change the subject now.'

The Tiger was approaching. He greeted them effusively and gave them their orders for the day, which consisted of having breakfast and then taking the truck out to a different patch of desert.

'Twenty miles', said The Tiger. 'We set it off and then drive away. We know it works but this is just confirmation.' But The Bomber had no interest in watching this latest device going off.

***

They rang the police in Dunstable and explained the situation, hoping that an officer could be sent round to ask Bill Sullivan if he knew the whereabouts of his brother. They undertook to do so but couldn't guarantee when that would happen.

'So, we wait?', said Tom.

'We wait.' Claire tapped at her keyboard but then stopped abruptly. 'Did you enjoy last night?'

'Yes. It was fine, yes', he replied, guiltily. Even as he said the words, he knew his response fell short of what Claire might have hoped for. A stony silence followed. She might have been typing with greater force now but he wasn't sure. Each key stroke sounded like a karate chop.

There was no apparent reason for her enmity if you looked at his actions in the context of a man acting with courtesy and respect towards a woman with whom he had to work. And yet, as they continued their research, the atmosphere seemed to grow steadily more oppressive, leavened with ill-will and threats yet to be voiced. Tom began to wonder if he would ever get the measure of this woman even as someone he could work with. The previous night he had told her more about himself and about how he ticked than he had ever told anyone, and yet now he almost felt that in his candour he had betrayed himself. *Was that even possible*, he wondered? Could disloyalty extend to oneself?

Tom was relieved when the phone rang, a return call from the police in Dunstable. There was no preamble and the address was given over without fuss.

Tom held the address up and waved it like a flag of surrender.

'That's where he is?', said Claire sourly.

'That's where he *was*', he corrected.

'Okay', she said, uncertainly. She was still peeved. Last night he had dropped her off at her flat, consumed the requisite coffee, made his excuses and left. One of two emotions took hold of her at that moment, or possibly some subtle blend of both, but when he left her, she was disappointed or angry. His head was hurting from the effects of the alcohol and his foot hurt from walking too much. And that was why he left rather than take her up on the rather obvious offer she was making. She was attractive, available and clearly willing, but he foresaw complications in his future that he wanted to avoid. He couldn't get to grips with her personality either which, inexplicably, grated on his nerves.

She was about to say something more when Andy came in asking for an update, which was delivered in concise form by Tom.

'Visit or a phone call?', he asked.

'Not sure. We've only just got this.'

'It's an address in Northumbria', said Claire, pointedly. 'It must be three hundred miles away.' Her tone was curt, possibly designed to make Tom look bumbling in front of his boss. When he thought about it, she had acted in this way before, portraying herself as a paradigm of efficiency at his expense. Bootlicking in this manner was alien to Tom, but he understood that ambitious people often behaved in this way. He did feel the sting of betrayal, however. After all, she had been allocated to him as support, not the other way round. This was essentially his job, not hers.

'Phone call?', suggested Tom. He didn't care enough to feel chastened by Claire's words and didn't fancy driving three hundred miles in her company.

'That sounds right. One other thing. We've had a message through from Interpol – just a routine thing really – but there has been a murder in Essen in Germany. Their suspect is an Asian man. Almost no details at all.' Andy glimpsed at his note a second time. 'A young, Asian man.' He looked at the doubting faces of his two subordinates. 'Could be our man. Antwerp to Essen can be done in less than three hours. The woman he killed was a suspected member of Baader-Meinhof if that has any bearing. Some sort of old boy network? Honour among terrorists?'

'Baader-Meinhof has been defunct for twenty years', said Claire.

'Lots of people retire from a job and keep their hand in. Why not this woman? Maybe she missed the thrill of living dangerously. She wanted a bit of excitement? Well anyway, it may or may not be him, but at least you know.'

When he had gone, Claire spoke.

'About last night… I don't know what went wrong.'

'Nothing went wrong. I wasn't feeling so hot and maybe a relationship with someone at work isn't a good idea. I mean, my God, you're an attractive woman and everything, but who wants to work in an office with two love birds? Who wants to witness their tiffs, or their adoring gazes across the bank of desks? It's bad news.'

'So, you don't even fancy me?', she said with a certain hurt persistence. Tom guessed that no answer was going to work.

'I didn't say that but the rest is true. Listen, most relationships eventually go sour until you meet that person you want to marry, or whatever, and even then there are no guarantees. But what I am getting at is, when that happens to us and we have to keep working together in a tiny office? It would be a bloody nightmare.'

Her cheeks were flushed with, he presumed, humiliation and even as he uttered these words of rejection, he had call to question his sanity. He'd never get a similar offer from such a good-looking woman again.

And yet he knew it was the right thing to do. He hadn't wanted to hurt her feelings but this show of affection had been foisted upon him. He was beginning to worry where his rejection of her was going to lead. *Was the woman even sane?*

'Can we talk about it later?', she asked. Tom agreed but didn't make any promises about when 'later' might actually be. Above all, he wanted to avoid a scene in the office and his vague reply seemed to have done the trick. She gave a curt nod and looked away. It occurred to him then that her – dare he call it an infatuation? – didn't even make sense when she could have had any man she wanted with the click of her fingers. Matt, for instance, the humourless arse in the office next door, would have sold one of his moobs to go out with her. She was as beautiful as Tom was plain.

She could even have gone out with a man who still had two feet!

'I'm going to ring this farm in Northumberland', he said. He was assailed by a sick sense of dread.

***

They watched as the old truck drove beyond their impromptu viewing point and halted. The driver and his two assistants jumped down and with some trepidation removed the metal container from the back, laying it in the sand with great care as if it might explode.

'We will have eight of these', said The Tiger. 'They are the exact size to fit into a bin in central London. Someone stole one for us, measured it and sent us the dimensions, in case you are wondering. The bombs will be placed in position in the morning, first thing, and when we are ready and there are plenty of people about, we, or rather you, will detonate them. It will be watched by millions of people.'

The thought of it made him feel bilious but he managed a polite smile.

'Won't the explosion destroy the camera?', he ventured.

'Maybe but it won't matter. The images will be sent already. It might look even better if it ends so suddenly. This is going to shock the world. This will be in the public domain before the censors have a chance to get at it. You will be the most famous person on Earth.'

'In Paradise?'

'Yes, that too', said The Tiger. He didn't like being corrected but he couldn't really say much against his martyr when he needed perhaps to stiffen his resolve. He was keen to harness the younger man's dedication, for there might be difficult times ahead. Did he carry doubts? Was there a look of fear in his eyes? It wasn't the fear of failure he was seeing but something else, and it worried him.

He handed Khan the remote control, a small box which looked like a device for changing channels on a TV. The Bomber turned it over in puzzlement, for on closer inspection it looked *exactly* like a remote for a TV.

Intercepting his perplexity, The Tiger explained.

'We can't give you an old-fashioned detonator if you are to move unhindered through London. You must have something innocuous in your possession.'

'A remote control for a television? Who carries one of those around with them?'

The Tiger was angry now.

'We struggled to find a mobile phone big enough for the electronics. You are not going to be searched anyway. You just need something small to carry around, something that fits in a jacket pocket.'

Khan nodded. It still seemed ridiculous to him but there was no point in further argument. Besides, within himself he had crossed some sort of mental threshold after which his heart simply wasn't in the fight any longer. It all hinged upon the necessity for him to die. The Tiger was very keen that he should die, to the point that the bombing might have seemed a little bit flat had he not done so in such a graphic way.

He could suggest that they swap places, why shouldn't that excellently named fighter live up to his name? What better way to die than as *a tiger*? The fear of suggesting such a thing was momentarily greater than the fear of death. The only plan he had come up with was to go to London, detonate the bomb and not die in the process. There was another alternative. He thought of virtually nothing else, so various scenarios had come to him. *What about he went to London and then didn't detonate the bomb? What then? Go on the run? Hand himself in? Tell the authorities before the bomb went off, foil the plot, get the others arrested?*

He dragged himself back to the here and now. The Arabs had laid the bomb on the ground and were walking back towards the spectators, chatting like two mates on their way back from a football match. One of them drove the truck. It bumped and careered on the rutted sand. Khan could hear the suspension groaning rhythmically like an old spring mattress. He felt empty again, neither happy nor sad. He caught the older Arab looking at him with concern but didn't quite make eye contact.

'So, you have to imagine that eight of these bombs are placed in strategic points in central London. Imagine the infidel going about their business, buying their American goods, getting copies of things they already have. The women with their short skirts and low-cut tops.' He saw two of the Arabs giving each other lascivious glances, they were obviously less easily offended than their temporary employer. The Tiger acted like a magician or a travelling salesman displaying his wares to a disbelieving audience. A sharp wind tugged at his gown, revealing his preposterous American trainers. Khan thought the situation absurd.

After a brief hiatus during which they looked dumbly at the bin, The Tiger smiled and said, 'over to you.'

Khan pulled a face, pressed the button and braced himself. He continued to brace himself for the following few moments during which the bomb resolutely failed to explode.

The hiatus continued embarrassingly.

There is a problem with bombs which fail to explode and it is the same as that faced by the parents of mildly disappointed children whose best, most expensive firework has failed to race skywards at the appropriate moment.

'Press again.'

Khan turned to look at his boss.

'Press again', he said with growing impatience.

'I have. I have pressed it', he said.

The Tiger snatched the control from Khan and pressed the button, his face creased with anger. He swore in another language. Khan shot a glance at the two Arabs who had befriended him but their faces were blank. They were survivors, businessmen. Nothing cracked their imperturbable facades. Somehow, they had managed to entirely divorce themselves from proceedings.

Now they all looked accusingly at the bomb, willing it to go off and yet it sat there full of metallic defiance, quite unbendingly resisting the chemical reaction its function required.

The obvious question was, *what do we do now?* and yet no one dared to say it partly for fear of upsetting The Tiger and partly because they knew the answer. They would have to leave it. No one could be expected to approach the bomb, and even if someone was fool enough to do so, what could they do with an unexploded bomb?

A breeze got up, lifting the topmost layer of sand and sending it into eddying swirls like ghostly dogs chasing their tails.

The Arabs looked to the skies.

'There is a storm coming', said the oldest one. 'We need to pack away the tent and stay inside the vehicles. His authority was such that the drivers immediately acted upon his words. The tent came down in thirty seconds and the possessions held inside were crudely tucked away in a similar amount of time. Throughout, The Tiger stood there fuming. This was the moment of his greatest humiliation.

The last strips of blue sky were snipped away by the rolling cloud mass. The Arab walked over to his employer and suggested that they should drive away from the bomb, if not the storm. The Tiger, still seething, agreed sourly. A few large, warm drops of rain had fallen as they mounted their vehicles, and within seconds they had pulled away

The Bomber wondered what this failure meant for him and his mission. If he went to London with eight bombs that didn't explode then he would live to fight another day... or maybe live to find another means of getting to Paradise. If he went to London with one bomb of eight which didn't explode then that might work in his favour, so long as he was standing next to that one when the others went off. The thought pleased him immensely. He could turn that into a survival plan. Thank Allah The Tiger couldn't read his mind.

They had bumped along for a hundred yards or so when the bomb finally relented with an explosion that shook the air and rattled their transport as it was engulfed in a shock wave. They kept driving even as tiny metal shards fell like rain. Khan realised that they had been much too close to the bomb in the first place, and the tiny shred of faith he had in The Tiger, that ridiculous man, was gone in an instant. They could all have been killed had they not moved off. But their tiny convoy stopped and The Tiger dismounted in a rage. He swore and jumped and waved a fist at the air. The words were a mystery to The Bomber but the meaning was clear enough.

He couldn't help taking comfort from the fact that, if these bombs were faulty in their design or manufacture, his mission might still be cancelled. But he would still be left with a problem even if that did occur. With all his metaphorical bridges burned, what was he going to do next?

***

'A US satellite has picked up a bomb explosion in the desert near Tripoli', said Andrew. 'Might be worth looking into.' Tom was tempted to look at the atlas he had bought but it remained in a desk drawer.

'We have a possible destination for Jack Sullivan.'

'Okay. Where?'

'The very far north of Scotland.'

'That's pretty imprecise', said Andrew.

'It is better than we had previously.'

'That's true. Just remind me why we need to see him.'

Tom opened his mouth to speak but Claire got in there ahead of him, with an eagerness neither man had expected.

'He bumped in Mohammed Khan in Afghanistan when he was a soldier out there. He knows what he looks like.'

Andrew pursed his lips, unsure about chasing after this retired soldier.

'His appearance may well have changed in the interim and it could be that he isn't too familiar with Asians... what I mean is that he might not be able to tell one from another.' The words sounded wrong, like something racist, certainly something which should have remained unsaid.

'We haven't got anything better', said Tom, supporting his colleague, although he harboured doubts of his own.

'Okay, what about our pals in Perth?', suggested Andrew. He lingered in the no-man's land between their office and the bigger room outside.

'Perth is quite a way south if you look at it on a map', said Tom. 'Besides they have problems of their own after the leak. We don't want anything more leaked out. And as far as I can figure out Scotland only has about three police officers on duty at any one time.'

'An exaggeration?', suggested Andy.

'Only a slight one.'

'Right, listen. Get a plane up there, hire a car and get hotels – whatever it takes. Just get up there and find him... but it had better do some good.'

Claire began to make the arrangements as soon as their boss had left the office. She seemed mutely excited by the prospect of their time away and Tom found this disturbing. They weren't having a dirty weekend – it was work and he hoped she fully realised this.

'Where exactly are we going?', he asked. 'I don't mean to sound like a party pooper but the North of Scotland? That's a huge area!'

'Fly to Aberdeen, hire a car, travel along the north coast and go to John O'Groats.'

'And we'll find this man?'

'Maybe.'

'Maybe?'

'The far North is what we have been told. Well, you can't get much farther north than that, can you?'

'It doesn't follow that he is there. We don't know what he looks like', he said, at which point Claire produced a pair of small black and white photographs of their man.

'Like this', she said.

'Ah.'

***

A squall hit as they crossed the short section of tarmac to board the plane, acclimating them to the weather they might encounter in Scotland. They had carry-on luggage only.

The flight to Aberdeen was brief and uneventful. They didn't get adjoining seats and Tom didn't care; his well of small talk was running dry. The food on offer was basic and Tom had a coffee and a tiny muffin which wouldn't have sated the appetite of a small child. He daydreamed for much of the time, thinking about the life he wanted and about the impossibility of ever having it. A cottage in the country, with a small garden and plenty of local walks for the dog? No chance. A dog to walk in the country? No chance of that either, certainly not while he lived in a flat in Pimlico. A nice car? Pointless while he lived in London, and besides, what constituted a nice car anyway? His male colleagues, and some of the females, aspired to BMW ownership and that fact alone made him aspire to something else, although he knew not what. He supposed he wanted children, but what then of the car and the house in the country? Who could afford all of these things working for the intelligence services?

On occasions like these he tried, in a purely secular sense, to count his blessings, and doing so usually cheered him, he supposed. He was seated next to a youngish man who wore the uniform of a surf dude: leather bracelets, Converse and Superdry. He was tanned and his blond hair sat on his head like a sea of pale golden bubbles. Tom wondered how he was going to fare in Aberdeen, a city which he wasn't expecting to be overly balmy.

So, perhaps he didn't have this young man's apparently carefree existence, where the biggest worry he had was where to catch the next wave, but he had enough going for him to feel fairly content. For one thing he had a flat, which although tiny, had a mortgage which he could at least manage. For another thing he had a job with supposed prospects. Neither of these things were to be sniffed at.

And yet he wasn't content. Not really. No matter how many times he told himself that he should be, and however many times he reminded himself of the bomb explosion which could have, but didn't, take his life, he felt that there was something missing. He sighed as he pushed the cup and the wrapper from his muffin around on the fold-down tray before him.

Tom and Claire picked up a blue Ford Focus from the car hire. Claire drove. Despite his injury, Tom could drive but it caused him pain on long journeys and so he always gave someone else the chance to take the wheel if possible.

'Buckle up and let's go', said Claire, chirpily. Tom did not share her enthusiasm but he did as ordered. Claire was a decent driver and, in that respect, he felt relaxed in her company; quite how the conversation would pan out was another matter. And as for sleeping arrangements…

'Is the hotel booked?', he asked.

'We don't know where we are going to end up, so no it isn't.'

Tom was wary of impromptu hotel visits having had a few bad experiences in the past. For instance, as a young soldier he had gone with mates to Blackpool, his first, and to date only, visit to Lancashire's great resort. Their weekend dash had left no time for prior booking of accommodation and when they arrived, they were given the full Joseph and Mary treatment. Eventually, having viewed a few barns and mangers, they found a B and B run by one of the town's fair maidens who greeted them suspiciously on her doorstep, arms crossed, a frown so deep that her make-up cracked and a tight perm that affected the flow of blood to her head. Tom had explained who they were, that they were on a weekend's leave and that they wanted a room, but she had taken one look at their dress sense and short hair and decided they were homosexuals.

Suspicion was written across her face like contours on a map.

She looked at Tom and then at his two mates. Her fleshy body still blocked the doorway.

'Are you all int 'th'army?', she asked, peering at them like suspects. Tom didn't know what she was talking about and wondered if she was from somewhere foreign like Lithuania or Bulgaria.

'Pardon?' He was transfixed by her ugliness. Never before had he seen someone who looked like a pantomime dame in their normal day-to-day business. She was a sort of powdered witch.

'Are you all int 'th'army?', she said again. One of his mates piped up with a translation and beamed his understanding.

'Sorry, yeah we're all in the army.'

At last she was satisfied and obviously held the army in high enough regard to permit them to stay in her B and B. She stood to one side and once they were in the hall, she led them upstairs. He could remember the stair carpet well, its lustrous orange seared into his retinas, its sponginess redolent of a mattress. This sponginess could only have been possible if previous iterations of stair carpet had not been lifted as the replacement was laid, resulting in the originals being trapped beneath, like layers of skin. In another hundred years the mass of stair carpet would make entry to the house impossible.

Things hadn't improved when they had got upstairs to the room they would have to share. A single bed lay along one wall and a double sat behind a curtain in one corner. The room had an elderly armchair in another corner, an ancient television of the sort Noah had on his ark, mounted to the wall, and next to that lay a mystery room behind a concertina door. The three soldiers looked at each other with something like comic horror when she had left.

'What's in there?' asked one and carefully they pulled the door across and peered inside. It was a toilet.

'That'll be nice if you're trying to watch Coronation Street and someone is right next to the TV having a dump', commented Tom.

***

'You've gone quiet', she said, stirring him from his reverie.

'Looking at the scenery', he lied. The lie did prompt him to do just that and he allowed his gaze to follow the hills that lined his route north. A thick grey mist hung over the country, a greyness that was reflected back onto the ground, infecting even the grass with a drab hue that matched his mood. He worried anew that Claire might really turn against him if he didn't meet her expectations in some regard. He was slightly frightened of her and that knowledge frightened him still further. He worried that rejection might lead her to invent a version of events in which his character was painted rather blackly. She might, strictly for purposes of revenge, say that he had tried it on with her, and when things like that were said, where did it end? It worried him greatly. He might have told himself that he was being irrational and yet this scenario did not seem irrational to him at all. Tom strongly suspected that Claire was not used to being spurned.

They hit the dual carriageway and she sank her foot to the floor until they were twenty over the speed limit. He said nothing; it was her licence at risk not his. Their occupation gave them no immunity from prosecution; James Bond might have got away with it but only because he was fictional. Tom found his mind wandering as they drove, the muted rumble of the wheels having a soporific effect that didn't quite induce sleep but made him rather relaxed. A few days away with an attractive woman wasn't the greatest ordeal of his life he supposed but he might have to take care that she understood fully the nature of their relationship. Not for the first time he wondered if there was something wrong with him, especially when he looked at her in profile, taking in the perfectly formed nose, the beautifully cut hair tucked behind her ears – ears that themselves were perfect. Yet his reservations remained like a lump in a chair that you can't avoid sitting in, or a dirty mark on your TV screen that won't come off and gives your favourite actress an extra eyebrow when she comes on screen.

He was thinking about the fact that she didn't bombard him with questions and idle chat when she began to do exactly that. Some people didn't like silences. Some people feared them. Some people felt embarrassed by them and thought it was their duty to make sure they didn't take hold. Claire was one or all of those people.

'It's beautiful up here', she said. Tom agreed. Instantly, he was on his guard against sounding like he might be enjoying their adventure. 'So we are looking for a caravan. It would be helpful if we knew what sort and so on.'

'The car is a Mitsubishi Shogun short wheelbase, metallic blue, LJ55MSJ and the caravan is a Westlake Kestrel.'

'Oh. A Kestrel eh? When I see a caravan trundling along at forty miles an hour on a B road with a two-mile queue of traffic behind it, I am always reminded of a magnificent bird of prey soaring high above the mountains, catching the thermals as it patrols majestically. Have you ever noticed these big camper vans driven by pensioners are always called Marauders or Intruders or something like that? They're not really doing either of those things – marauding or intruding. A better name would be *chintzy bungalow* on wheels. A friend of my dad has a big motorhome called a Buccaneer. What has a motorised bungalow got to do with swashbuckling pirates?'

Claire smiled at his gentle diatribe and he was, despite his misgivings about her, secretly pleased that he could amuse her. There was something comforting in being able to make someone laugh, he had always thought, his problem being that when he tried to do so at work he had always come across as rather a lightweight to his po-faced colleagues. Especially humourless Matt.

'Do we know why he has taken off in his caravan?', he asked Claire. He waited for his answer as she powered past a caravan; not the one they sought, although the possibility passed through both their minds. She pulled in rather sharply but kept accelerating.

'By all accounts he just wants to be a free spirit for a while.'

'He wants to find himself?'

'That's ironic. It is actually *us* who want to find *him*.'

'True. If he can't find himself what chance do we have?'

The hills gave way to mountains, some still with a hint of snow on their peaks, more like a dusting of icing sugar. Grey clouds shifted through the valleys, amorphous sharks navigating a course towards their prey. Occasional glimpses of sun sent bursts of light onto the mountainsides, bringing colour – purples, yellows and greens – where there had been mere swathes of monochrome. He could see Scotland as a land of adventure, ripe for rich tales of kidnapping, deceit and intrigue. This was a land where spies could land and hide out, a place for enemies and friends to keep out of sight. Sullivan had chosen well.

For a time, they got stuck behind a pensioner couple in their Nissan Note and Claire's cool driving persona began to evaporate until she shouted, 'speed up you tossers.'

Tom looked at her, mildly shocked and then risked taking her to task.

'We'll be old someday', he said.

'So?'

'We'll be driving slowly because our reactions aren't what they used to be.'

'And?', she snapped, her annoyance clear. He could have stopped there but he didn't.

'Well, when that happens, we will want people to be patient with us.' He had purposely adopted a rather patronising tone.

Claire said nothing at first and they drove along slowly, with just the rumble of the tyres to fill the void.

Then she said, 'stop being so fucking reasonable', to which Tom made no reply. After another silence and then the inevitable moment of overtaking, he dared to speak again.

'We can't just drive around until we find him?', said Tom.

'Well, I had thought we would head for John O'Groats and work our way backwards.'

'Even if we see him on the way up there?', said Tom facetiously.

'Obviously not', said Claire.

The plan sounded wholly unworkable. It relied totally on luck. It was stupid and yet he knew that it was impossible to argue with her.

Chapter Thirteen

Herv Ankoplar stood on the balcony of his office and looked over the city. He smoked and drank coffee, knowing that one of them would probably kill him someday, but he wasn't a man who looked forward to growing old after a lifetime spent in the service of his country. Retirement seemed like an entirely horrific prospect to him. Unmarried and childless, why would he bother to get out of bed if not to smite the enemies of Israel? He drew on his cigarette and pondered the future, taking comfort from the fact that he still had three years left with the possibility of a few extras added on. His life had involved the removal of his country's enemies, in the early years fighting them in the deserts, and latterly wherever the need arose.

He still thought of himself as a warrior. and even in periods of relative peace the course of the war was plain to him at all times. He neither foresaw an end to the conflict, nor a time when men like him wouldn't be needed. Okay, so he no longer wore a uniform and he didn't often carry a gun, but he still battled away behind the scenes with only a tiny number of people knowing what he actually did for a living. His men were spies, dissemblers, thugs, thieves, saboteurs and agents, but they acted in the name of Israel.

The sun was high in the sky, its heat on his arms. He closed his eyes and just listened to the traffic, the shouts from the nearby traders, the café chit-chat, the noises of a bustling city. It gave him comfort to know that the war he fought made it possible for this normal sort of life to continue. He'd lit another cigarette when his deputy called him through.

'A phone call, Herv. The Americans.'

He rolled his eyes. *The Americans – they who must be obeyed.* They liked to have the Israelis in their pockets and bankrolled them to some extent but the truth was that in a hostile world where anti semitism was not just surviving but flourishing, it was good to know that America was there in the background. The World's Policeman kept a paternal eye on its embattled Middle Eastern friend. During the first Gulf War, when Saddam Hussein had sent his ancient missiles hurtling down on Israeli cities, at a time when Israel had taken no interest in the dictator's war, the US sent batteries of Patriot missiles to bring them down. In so doing they had shown their support for their Jewish allies and also kept them out of the fighting. That the IDF could probably have shifted Saddam's ragbag army by itself mattered not. It was more important to keep them neutral for the sake of the weirdly assembled and relatively ineffective Arab alliance that had been cobbled together. Military sense gave way to diplomacy.

It didn't do to keep the Americans waiting, so he made the effort to return to his desk.

'Herv Ankoplar', he said.

The American on the other line was one of the more unassuming CIA men, one who, although they had never met, he trusted implicitly. Bill Morgan, to use their own vernacular, wasn't a phoney.

'Hi Herv', he began. 'Some big news I thought I would share with you. Our satellites have picked up a bomb blast in the desert to the south of Tripoli. Nothing too major but no signs of nearby troops, just three civilian vehicles; a truck and two SUVs.'

'Strange.'

'Strange indeed. Our thinking is that it is something to do with the missing nuclear stuff. It all sort of ties together. We're looking at taking a sample of air from the area, basically detecting, or not detecting, radioactivity.'

'How will you do that?'

'Possibly a drone or get some boots on the ground.'

'Okay and the vehicles?'

'They drove into Tripoli itself and we have lost them but we will keep looking until we find them again. They won't be hard to deal with but we need a bit of evidence before we act. We've gotta be careful with this one. Lots of people could get very upset with us if we mess up. The President is very keen for us to look squeaky clean in the Middle East.'

Herv knew that this latter statement meant not getting caught.

'Anything you'd like us to do?'

'Keep your guys on standby. Inform your boss.'

***

They came to a standstill on the outskirts of the city and the old Russian truck, designed for rugged dependability in the wastes of the Russian interior, began to overheat. When he was informed of this latest calamity, an incensed Tiger stepped down from the air-conditioned cocoon of the Land Cruiser and stormed over to the offending vehicle. The Bomber, who always travelled separately and in the second SUV, watched as he blustered and remonstrated with the Arab driver. The latter held his hands up, his meaning clear – it wasn't his fault – which was undoubtedly true. Finished there, he stormed over to the second vehicle and Khan lowered the window, feeling a blast of heat on his face as he did so.

'Their fucking useless truck is breaking down', he raged. Khan was tempted to make a comment about buying something better from the Americans perhaps, which would sound rather facetious of course, but he wasn't sure how much he cared any longer. He had lost faith in the whole project including the self-styled large cat who called himself The Tiger, and although it might be possible to recharge his faith in the Jihad if his life could be assured, he wasn't completely committed any more. It was not like Antwerp. That had been a halcyon period. He recognised it as such now and the thought of greater glories seemed unlikely. Khan was unaccountably depressed. Maybe, he reasoned, it was the heat.

He stepped down from his own vehicle as if to assess the damage and provide a solution. He knew nothing about such things but said, 'get them to pull over into the shade and switch the engine off. I will stay here and you can carry on.'

The Tiger looked at him with surprise. His solution was not a radical one but benefitted from extreme simplicity and, with a look of weary acceptance, The Tiger nodded his head. He scribbled an address on a piece of paper and stuffed it ungraciously into Khan's hand.

Seconds later he had driven off down a side street that avoided the worst of the hold up; his driver knew the city well. The Bomber was surprised to find himself alone with the two Arabs and the truck driver, the latter a man apart. The driver wandered off to find a café and Khan waited next to the Land Cruiser.

'We are safe here', said the younger Arab. 'The Yankees will have picked up that explosion. They will be looking for us but they can't pick out one truck in the middle of Tripoli.'

'This is why the decoys are useful. If they blow one of those to pieces, they will assume that the matter is finished.' It was the older man who spoke. 'They use drones these days. They won't even bother to check if they have hit the correct target. There is nothing to make them think that there is more than one truck.'

The younger man had retrieved three cans of Coke from the Land Cruiser.

'A present from the infidel', he joked. Khan was parched and cracked open the red and white can without compunction, draining it in two gulps. 'It is not against the teachings of Islam to drink Coca-Cola', said the Arab with a wink. Khan looked at him, unsure how to respond, unsure if he was being baited, but the man looked utterly guileless.

'Lots of things are not against the teaching of Islam', said the older man absently. Khan looked at him for further meaning but he was obviously not going to say more. They continued to wait under the burning sun and by the time the truck's driver returned the vehicle had cooled, and the traffic which had caused their delay had thinned.

'We can catch up with the boss', said the younger Arab. He managed to imbue the word 'boss' with utter disrespect. Khan smiled.

'Where is this place?', he asked.

'It is a hotel. Very plush. You will enjoy it after your time in the desert. He used to think that we would sleep outside on the concrete but we told him that we weren't immune to the charms of a proper bed. He is an idiot. His knowledge of the Arabs comes from watching Ali Baba and the Forty Thieves.'

The older man shot him a look to tell him that he had overstepped the mark.

The drive was a short one, the chaotic traffic more manageable now that the day was wearing on. The fumes that had swirled and billowed had taken their leave of earth and were swarming upwards. The air became fresher as a result.

The hotel was as described, built to accommodate wealthy westerners and staffed by obsequious Arabs in ridiculously ornate uniforms who bowed and scraped, scraped and bowed, always hoping for tips. In place of concrete there was marble, in place of teak, walnut, in place of silver, gold. It was obscene but oddly comforting too. He gazed around him in awe thinking that here was the sort of thing that symbolised the reasons for having the Jihad, and yet...

It was almost too obvious to think about. The hypocrisy was stunning. How did The Tiger reconcile war with this almost infantile obsession with his own comfort? Khan, for the first time, began to wonder who his sponsor actually was. Where did the money come from for this hotel stay? It might well be the case that he was a wealthy Saudi; they loved to fight a comfortable Jihad.

The concierge managed to hide his distaste for the scruffy men in his midst – perhaps the sudden appearance of desert Arabs was a commonplace event – and rang through to their host's suite. He smiled and asked them if they would like a coffee as they waited. They declined and a minute later The Tiger appeared, wearing a tan suit, blue shirt and gleaming brown loafers. Had it not been for the colour of his skin he might have been some sort of preppy American businessman, selling electric fans or refrigerators. He played the part well, whatever he was supposed to be. He looked washed and thoroughly cleansed of the desert, like a man who had never set foot in such a forbidding place.

He smiled effusively and then collected their room keys.

'I have booked you in. Come in. Make yourselves comfortable and tonight we will discuss our business over dinner.' He acted as if he owned the hotel. Perhaps he did.

***

'I've never been to Scotland', said Claire. Tom thought she sounded proud of the fact and added one of his own.

'I've never been to Spain', he said.

Without crashing, she fired off a glance of consternation.

'So?'

'I was just saying. Most people have been to Spain and I have not.' Had it been his intention to kill the conversation stone dead then he had succeeded. Either way, she did not follow up her first observation with another and they continued to drive in silence. The road was long, greyly damp, twisting and practically devoid of other traffic. Tom thought about a dozen different things but kept returning to one thing in particular. It troubled him that he was not attracted to Claire.

Why? He tried to think it through logically. He knew that his previous theories were wrong. It wasn't just because they had to work together. It wasn't because she was too enthusiastic about her work. It wasn't even anything to do with her privileged background which contrasted so starkly with his own. They were, at best, excuses rather than reasons. Tom tried to put them to one side in his mind so that they wouldn't cloud the reasoning process he was going through. He made a clicking noise with his tongue and laid his head back until it touched the head restraint, and then it came to him. The problem was that they had nothing in common. They could go to bed, have a night of passion – he wasn't averse to that at all – but the problem came afterwards when they had to make small talk and whisper sweet nothings in each other's ears. That was the bit he simply couldn't imagine himself doing successfully. She thought she was too good for him. She was privately educated and all the rest – horses, hockey, university – whilst he was an ex-sergeant, educated at a comp.

He thought too about that second date and about her expectations. She would grow bored easily and become demanding. Eventually they would spend less and less time together until she drifted off with some other sap. He feared that by this stage he might truly have fallen for her and that the pain of rejection might kill him. All in all, it was just easier to avoid the whole thing. There was no possible happy-ever-after, and it was that he perhaps wanted more than anything else. If she couldn't provide it, then what was the point? They could not survive together, and when he thought about it further, he couldn't really imagine her being able to maintain a stable relationship with anyone. She was moody, high maintenance. She had obviously been spoilt as a child and that had made her demanding. Or maybe she had been neglected. The end result was often the same thing: a constant need for reassurance and attention.

He tried to find things about her to dislike, but she didn't have a fat arse, or a flat chest, or discoloured teeth. She was perfect like a model but not so tall. She was witty and charming. She spoke well and with intelligence. But she drove him nuts.

'There is a sign for John O'Groats', she said tonelessly. They turned off and headed for the end of the world.

***

He had changed his shirt but wore the same suit. The rest were dressed in fresh clean linen. Everyone looked scrubbed. It could have been a gathering of old friends.

They ate lamb and chatted amiably, and only when they had reached the coffee course did they return to serious business. Khan was surprised that The Tiger included the Arabs in his planning but it soon became clear that he was not finished with them; they were still integral to his plan.

He didn't bother to keep his voice down.

'I have been onto, what we shall call, my technical department, and I am assured that the problems we had can be addressed easily and sorted out.'

Khan smiled indulgently even though his heart sank at the prospect of completing his mission.

'The equipment we need is being prepared both here and in the country of intended use. We have a garage workshop which is converting a truck into a replica of a council vehicle, correct in every detail. We have a man who is reconnoitring the area and selecting locations for us. Eight locations. The necessary electronics are being worked on and we will have a back-up set in readiness. We are sorting out accommodation, the video equipment and making sure that the whole enterprise can be viewed on the internet.'

His eyes gleamed as he spoke. His earlier annoyance had gone now that the plan was back on track. The Tiger stopped speaking as a waiter came to collect their plates and began again as the man retreated. The air was cool and a staff member resplendent in a red frock coat opened a series of

French doors onto a veranda. It might have been romantic had it not been for the fact that he was in the presence of men who were more or less plotting his death.

'We have flights arranged for you to take you back and a car to pick you up. No surveillance. No one knows you exist. No one is expecting this.' He turned to the Arabs now. 'You my friends must ensure that our equipment is ready to be flown out and that the decoys remain in place until you hear news of our mission's completion. At that point you will find that the remainder of your payment has been deposited. Very soon the world will be a very different place.'

***

The first Reaper was targeted towards two Arab encampments, one to the South of Tripoli and one to the south east. It spent an hour 'looking' for signs of life, be that movement, smoke, or heat signatures. The lieutenant operating the UAV watched his screen intently, fascinated by the little pastoral scene. He'd spent operational time in the desert before being posted to a tiny, secret air base which operated only drones, and now, even looking down in two dimensions, the sounds and smells of that wilderness seemed to come back to him. Next to him sat another drone pilot. The second Reaper was under his command.

He recognised the Russian built truck, ex-army, crudely painted red by its new civilian owners. Dozens of these decrepit things – gifts from Moscow – remained behind, pressed into service by backstreet hauliers, carrying livestock, passengers, weapons and probably drugs. The two SUVs he recognised as Toyota Land Cruisers, not new by any means but in good condition. They were the ideal desert vehicle. They could go anywhere and unless you were a total mechanical ignoramus they never broke down. The tent was a typical Bedouin home, ornate but made to last. In themselves they were not suspicious but they formed the basis of his brief – he'd been told to look for this combination.

He felt the presence of his immediate superior standing over one shoulder but concentrated on 'flying' the drone.

'Anything?', asked Captain Poole.

'Nope. No signs of life but it matches the description perfectly.'

'How much time have you left over the target?'

'About ten hours sir.'

'Move on to the other one and give it a good look over. Is there anything else in the neighbourhood? Anything at all?'

'Not a thing, sir.'

'Hmmm. Keep looking, lieutenant.'

It was an eight and half minute flight to the next target. The desert in between was sterile and featureless, an unending plain of hard-packed sand. The drone eventually flew into a valley with dunes on either side, but this it cleared in a minute or so, emerging into a continuation of the previous plain. He climbed now, opening the vista as he did so, and levelled off once he spotted the tiny caravan of vehicles on the horizon. His suspicions were raised as he noted that it was virtually identical in composition to the previous encampment; two SUVs, an elderly Russian truck painted red and a traditional tent. It seemed like a set up.

He made the drone circle, its array of instruments searching for the usual signs of life but he knew that the encampment was a dummy. After a few minutes had passed he sensed Captain Poole over his shoulder.

'Nothing, sir. Not a thing.'

Poole grunted.

'Radioactivity?'

'No radioactivity, sir. But this camp is virtually identical to the previous one we looked at. One of the SUVs is a different make – it's a Nissan instead of a Toyota – but everything else is the same, right down to the tent.'

'Okay lieutenant. Give it another few minutes but I am sending an armed drone in to wipe them off the face of the earth. We have SEALs on the way to check out the wreckage. Dropped in, hiking out and picked up by navy helicopters. We'll be done in two hours. We're just waiting on your word, lieutenant.'

***

The campsite was divided into two parts, one for caravans and statics and the other for tents. The two were separated by a low hedge, bent over the years by the prevailing wind. It resembled a series of ragged, broken-backed skeletons more than a hedge.

A brisk wind came in from the sea but the sun shone from a cloudless sky.

'Photographer's weather', said Tom, joking. Claire stared at him blankly

'We might as well start at reception', she said. Tom disagreed but didn't bother to argue. Discretion might have been better since they had no overt authority to ask about a customer's private details. There were ways and means of course, but these were things that Tom preferred to avoid, especially if he ended up skirting around the edges of legality. He wasn't exactly a spy but he opted for complete anonymity where possible.

They pulled the hire car over to the squat redbrick and cream plaster building that doubled as a reception, bar and restaurant. The car park was potholed. Most of the parking bays were obscured, the white lines having lifted away after years of weather-beaten neglect, but they pulled in next to a red Mazda MX5 and got out.

'Nice', said Claire.

In the reception area they were greeted by no-one... but upon ringing the brass bell a very smiley lady of early middle-age came out to greet them. She spoke with an English accent – somewhere down south – and listened attentively.

'Hi. We're looking for Jack Sullivan', said Claire.

The woman smiled again and Tom thought he saw a flicker of… he didn't know what… cross her features. Was it, recognition, doubt, fear?

'I don't know the name…'

'Could you check your register for us?', said Claire. Her tone was curt. Tom knew that this was the least effective way to elicit someone's cooperation and sure enough the previously helpful lady at reception closed up.

'I don't really give away details of our guests', she said.

'We just need to know if he is here.'

'Are you the police?'

Claire had blown it. Had he not known better Tom might have supposed that she was deliberately sabotaging her own enquiry.

'I'm sorry. No, we are not in the police. We work for the government down in London and we are conducting an investigation which concerns national security.' Tom knew that everything she had said was true and yet even to him it sounded distinctly dubious. The woman, smile gone now, looked at him and then consulted her book, making sure that only she could see what was written on the pages. He thought he might have made a breakthrough and watched the woman's face intently as she searched for the name.

When finally, she met his gaze, she was smiling. It was an attractive smile on an attractive face. Tom prepared himself for the good news, hoping that Claire would be able to contrast her handling of the situation with his. The subtle approach always worked. A little charm went a long way.

'No', she said, still smiling. 'No one of that name.'

Bollocks.

He didn't bother to ask if she was sure. Her tone of voice had closed down the chance of further enquiries. He sensed that Claire was going to say something else and quickly intervened.

'Thank you very much for checking. Can I leave you my card? It is very important that he gets in touch with us. We think he is up here somewhere. He has a caravan – a tourer – and a 4x4.'

She took the card, glanced at it without really seeing and said, 'I'll let him know.'

'But you said…', stammered Claire.

'If he turns up. I'll let him know, if he turns up', she corrected.

They thanked her a second time and left, making the short journey to the hire car. Inside, Tom spoke.

'She's lying.'

'Yep.'

'So, we could drive away and then come back on foot.'

'We could try a few other places first', suggested Claire

'Why would we do that if we know he's here?'

'Just to make it more realistic… I mean to confirm what we think we already know.'

Tom gave a puzzled shrug. Claire started the engine.

***

Captain Hopps took up station, next to the pilot of the recce drone. He shifted his head from one side to the other, flexing the taut muscles. He'd slept badly and even a long hot shower hadn't released the tension he felt. The ground crew were preparing his drone for flight and he awaited their confirmation before he started the engines. The flight of Reapers would be transiting out over the same area, seeking out the two Arab encampments and wiping them out prior to the insertion of a SEAL team that would check the wreckage for evidence of bombs or bomb-making ancillaries.

He spoke to the young lieutenant next to him and was acknowledged politely, although his fellow drone pilot did not take his eyes off the screen in front of him. His team took up their seats to his right. Each was a drone pilot.

'It's all yours. No signs of life at all.'

'Roger.'

'Both camps are virtually identical.'

'One's a decoy?', suggested the captain.

'That would be my guess. I'll put it in my report.'

'Makes no difference. I'm going to blast them both to high heaven anyway.'

The lieutenant kept the recce drone loitering as its companion took off from the short desert strip. Armed with Hellfire missiles it needed a longer take-off run than the recce drone but it and the other drones on the flight would quickly dispatch the two targets once over the battlefield. The advantage of such a weapon system was that no aircrew came into danger during its operation. The slight disadvantage was the chance that control could be lost. The UAVs also had a very high accident rate and were regarded with suspicion by the crews of manned aircraft who feared personal obsolescence.

In fifty-eight minutes, the UAVs swapped places. Then Hopps' drone fired its missiles and the captain watched with satisfaction as the vehicles erupted in flame. Although he was a professional airman, the thought that he was merely engaged in the most realistic computer game ever devised did not elude him. Flying an F16, as he had once done on operations in Iraq, had a greater cachet, but this was a much more refined and comfortable way of dishing out death. The killing itself – there was none in this mission – gave him little satisfaction, but knowing that a job was well done certainly did.

In the adjacent seat, the lieutenant was bringing his own aircraft back to base. Hopps turned away from the blazing encampment and led the accompanying drones towards the second target. Within minutes he had achieved the same thing again, burning ruins as evidence. In his headphones he had the navy helicopter pilot giving him flight data as he sped inland to drop off the SEAL party.

He reached for his can of Coke, a back up to the coffee he habitually drank, and thought about what war had become. How long would it be until he was no longer required at all? How long before the drones picked their own targets, prepared themselves for missions and carried them out without conscious intervention from their mortal, human masters?

'Terminator', he said, referring to the popular film. Next to him the lieutenant nodded. He had often made that same cultural connection himself.

***

The hotel was better than some he had stayed in and he was undismayed to find that he and Claire had separate rooms. Reception was manned – personed – by a blonde-haired woman of fuller figure and indeterminate age, forced to wear an entirely tartan uniform which made her look and feel like a Harris Tweed bean bag. Despite this handicap she was cheery and efficient and unlike some others of her profession she didn't pretend to give a shit about the reason for their stay. Hers was a refreshing lack of inquisitiveness. She didn't implore them to have a nice day, simply because it was beyond her powers to make it so and because there were other people in her life about whom she genuinely cared.

The lobby had plenty of dark wood and brass, lush rugs and the obligatory stag's head but elsewhere it was clear that some amount of renovation was required. In places the wallpaper bulged where plaster had come away from underneath, and in others it bore the long white scars and black marks of careless use. The stair carpet was worn in the centre and pristine at the edges and there was an air of slight neglect, maybe a smell or maybe a threatening creak of a floorboard. Nevertheless, it had charm.

'What do you think of the place?', he asked her over dinner. Her previous bad mood had gone now and she smiled at him.

'I like it. It would make a nice spot for a romantic liaison', she said.

Tom managed not to look alarmed.

'I like places like this', she continued. 'You can imagine a rich history, can't you? Secret meetings. Who knows what sort of deals have been done here? There is something special about the coast and about either end of the country. The wildness and the enormous expanse of sea beyond. Adventure, intrigue.'

'Caravans', added Tom, facetiously.

'Spoiling the mood there, thank you very much.'

'Sorry. I just remember a holiday to Cornwall and there being caravans as far as the eye could see. It felt like everyone had one and they were all converging on the same spot. Admittedly Cornwall is beautiful once you get there.'

'Spies and smugglers.'

'And missing soldiers.'

She looked at Tom seriously and asked, 'do you think he has deliberately gone off the radar?'

'Jack Sullivan? I don't know. Who can say what has made him go off in his caravan?'

'It might be something like PTSD?'

'It might be, but not every soldier ends up with that. He might want to organise his life, or he might just be avoiding some woman he has managed to impregnate with a child he doesn't want to take responsibility for. I wouldn't always give someone the benefit of the doubt.'

'I think he is hiding from something.'

'Maybe, but we don't have any information about something he might be hiding from. There is nothing to suggest that he is on the run.'

'Well, tomorrow we will have better luck. We'll have a full day to explore and find him.'

'I thought we were going back tonight to look for him?'

'Is there any point?'

Tom was perplexed by her attitude.

'If we think he might actually be there, then yes, we need to go back.' Claire's normally incisive brain seemed sluggish of late. He might have used the word 'dopey', to describe her. Clarity of thought was her forte and yet she was forgetting the facts of their mission even as they occurred.

It was seven o'clock before they returned to the car and drove back to the campsite.

***

Chapter Fourteen

Jack was jet-washing one of the firm's static caravans when Penny tracked him down. She saw the cloud of spray before she saw him and homed in at once.

He stopped what he was doing as she approached, glad of the break, glad of the company, despite his overall yearning for tranquillity and solitude.

'Two people have been looking for you', she said. 'A man and a woman. Young, smartly dressed. The man had a limp.'

'A limp what?'

'I'm not joking Jack.'

'No one knows I am here', he said, puzzled.

'Well *they* did. They asked for you by name, knew what sort of car you had and everything.'

'Seriously, no one knows. Not even my mum knows I'm here.'

'You must have told someone.'

'I might have mentioned that I was heading up north but that could take me anywhere.'

'Then they were lucky.'

'The thing is, what did they want?'

'They wouldn't say. Well, they said they were from the government and he showed me some sort of ID card but it could have been anything. He said something about security but I didn't tell them you were here.'

'Why not?', he asked.

'Why not? You must be in trouble! I'm not going to drop you in it!'

'I'm not in trouble', he said earnestly.

'You have come up here, and no one knows where you are, and you're not in trouble? Pull the other one.'

'Honestly. I'm not in trouble. I just want some peace and quiet.'

'Well, who are these people then?'

'No idea.'

'They managed to find you when no one knows where you are. What does that tell you?'

'That they are moderately determined. Maybe they are from a solicitor's office trying to give me a huge cheque left to me by a recently deceased auntie.'

'They said they were from the government.'

'Okay, not that then.'

Penny was looking at him with a mixture of suspicion and fear. She was far more worried about the appearance of these two strangers than he was.

'You don't believe me, do you?', he said.

'Well, I...'

'Hold on a minute. I know why this has spooked you.'

'Really?', she said.

'*You* are hiding from someone. If someone can find me, then you are worried that someone can find you. I'm right, aren't I?' He knew from the look on her face that he was. 'Come inside and tell me about it.'

She shook her head.

'I was just looking out for you', she explained.

'I know and I appreciate it.'

'He left this card', she said, handing it over. Jack spent a moment or two inspecting the simple business card. A name and a mobile number.

'Tom Black? Doesn't ring any bells.'

'Are you going to ring?'

'Later, maybe'

'Be careful', she warned. He knew that she wouldn't accept his explanation of events, so he agreed to her request. After she had gone, he continued cleaning the caravan.

***

Widely regarded as the best of the US Special Forces, with capabilities comparable to those of the British SAS, the SEALS, drawn from the US Navy, were the obvious choice for this mission.

Two teams of four sat in the bowels of the vast Sea Stallion helicopter and listened to their final briefing. Each team was lightly equipped with rifles, basic survival equipment, food, water and one hand-held monitor per four men, held in the possession of the team medic for no other reason than it looked like the sort of thing he might use. The monitor was a more sophisticated and much more compact version of what had once been termed a Geiger Counter. Technological miniaturisation reaches every aspect of our lives.

Wearing full NBC suits, the team held their respirators, ready to mask up as soon as they approached the LZ. The suits were uncomfortable, the charcoal-impregnated fabric further increasing their already raised body temperatures. But the suits would do their job, protecting the troops from nuclear, biological and chemical hazards by effectively sealing their bodies off from the outside world.

The suit was least effective against radiation, the hazard they potentially faced, but to send them in wearing standard uniform was deemed unconscionable. The US military establishment understood only too well that their troops had to feel as if they'd been equipped to give them every possible chance of survival. It wasn't a purely altruistic move; it simply made the troops in question operate more efficiently.

The plan was simple. The helicopter would drop off one team at the first target site and then proceed to the second site to drop off the next team. It would then return to the first site, pick up the team who should have completed their work and then repeat the process for the second team taking both back to the aircraft carrier. It was the sort of thing they had trained for relentlessly and therefore quite straightforward.

Minutes later, the giant helicopter was sitting on deck beneath the blurred disc of its rotor, waiting for permission to take off.

The troops inside felt no fear. In and out. Utterly simple. They remained impassive as the Sea Stallion lifted from the deck and then peeled away from the carrier. At just one hundred feet above sea level it wouldn't be bothering any shore-based radar.

They swept over the coast well to the east of Tripoli and then gradually altered course for the first target. The remains of the encampment came into view minutes later, information that was relayed to the SEAL team commander by the loadmaster/gunner. All eight men masked up dutifully, checking the fit of their own and then their buddy's mask.

Team One prepared itself for a swift exit and were gone almost as soon as the Sea Stallion's wheels touched down. On the command of the loadmaster they lifted away in a swirling storm of sand.

The SEALs lay in all round defence for a minute or so after the sounds of the enormous aircraft had died away, each sense attuning itself to the sounds, smells and sights of the desert through the heavy rubber masks they wore.

Sealed off from the outside world, none of them detected the overpowering smell of burnt rubber and fuel which permeated the air. Silence reigned. The team leader – a petty officer – tapped the butt of his rifle, signalling that his men should rise and begin the task they had been briefed for. No words were necessary. Words could bring death. Words wasted energy. Words could bring confusion to carefully scripted and choreographed missions.

Rising one by one in near silence to emerge from the sand like corpses disinterring themselves, they began their stealthy approach to the target, spreading out as they did so. The bulky NBC suits made their outlines indistinct as though the men themselves had become blurred.

As they closed on their objective, each man instinctively kept watch behind for enemies. But they were utterly alone.

The old Russian truck, a Ural, had lost its coating of red paint in the fire created by the Hellfire missile, exposing the blackened desert yellow given to it by the factory in distant Russia. The cab was partially detached from the chassis, and the engine, sitting far to the front, was wrecked, torn open by the missile which had hit. The two SUVs were similarly damaged. One still burned but the other merely smoked, its chassis almost touching the sand since the tyres had been blown out. Pieces of debris crunched underfoot. The team medic, monitor in hand, kept a wary eye out for signs of life but also signs of radiation. When the team leader looked his way, he shook his head.

The still-burning SUV crackled and popped as various components reached some critical temperature. The men backed away but continued their cautious patrol through the encampment. The tent was a series of rags, its ornate decoration still visible in tattered pennants that flapped like dying serpents. When they had made a complete pass through the encampment they turned and went back again over the same route.

'If anyone was here, they're dead now', called the team leader, his voice muffled. The need for silence was gone – they were quite alone. 'What about radioactivity, doc?'

The medic looked down at the monitor, although he already knew the answer.

'Nothing. Not a thing.'

'There was no bomb', said the petty fficer.

'Nope. This was the decoy by the looks of things.'

They began to close in on one another, shortening the line until they were in a huddle.

'So, what do we think, boys?' He pulled off his respirator and grinned. His face was sweat-shiny. His team followed suit.

'This wasn't it. There are no bodies and there are no personal belongings in the tent. It was an empty tent. Just for show.'

'Okay, we sit here and wait for our transport back.'

A simple job done, they now waited for the tell-tale clatter of the Sea Stallion's huge rotors.

'Here she comes', said the petty officer as the helicopter loomed over the horizon. It came in fast and low. The men turned their backs to the downdraught until the machine had landed, and then without further instruction they piled on board. They lifted off immediately and headed off to pick up the second team.

***

Herv snatched the phone receiver as he dabbed his brow with a handkerchief. His Slavic ancestry made him ill-suited to the hot climate of Israel. In a sense he had gotten used to it but the heat still depressed his spirits.

'Ankoplar', he barked with unintentional volume.

'Herv, it is your favourite CIA man here.'

'Bill. It is average to hear from you. My American cousin, that is what the Brits call you.'

The American laughed.

'The big news is that we have destroyed two desert encampments that we think might be connected to the dirty bomb.'

'Good. Efficient as ever, Bill.'

'Now, the trouble is that we think these were decoys.'

'Ah. And that means…'

'Well Herv, that probably means that the bomb or bombs are on their way to the proposed target.'

'And you still think London?'

'That is the consensus of opinion. The grounds for thinking that are shaky. There was murder in Germany carried out by an Asian on a former associate of the Baader-Meinhof gang. We are putting two and two together and assuming that is our man. Tenuous, I know. But, as ever, we have to make our plans based on what we know, or what we think we know.'

'You have told London?'

'Not me personally but someone has. Since we know that they are heading that way we should be able to intercept the stuff. I'd like to think so anyway. We have warned all the European governments and we know that this weapon is likely to be used against a big target. Really it has to be a city – it's the only type of target that makes sense.'

'Bill, does this stuff leak radiation? I mean can it be detected if it was in a container say?', asked Herv.

'I'd have to check but I think it depends on how it is carried. Presumably when it is being transported from the power plants it is encased in something that stops the radiation… if that wasn't the case they'd never get anyone to move it. But if these people have already put it into bombs then who knows? It is something that I wouldn't want to transport but how much information do they give the poor foot sloggers who have to do that job?'

'Next question, Bill. How do you think they will get it to Britain if that is where they are headed?'

'Not by plane. Certainly nothing that is chartered. So, it has to be a ship.'

'That'll take a long time.' He consulted a map on his wall. 'Even if they set off from somewhere like Algiers it is still a long trip.'

'How else could they do it?'

'Vehicle?'

'They still have to get it on a ship to get it to Europe and then they have a long drive to Calais, say, to get it through the tunnel.'

'How long can our allies stay on high alert waiting for this stuff to come through?'

'Until it is found. What option have they got?'

'But you know how these things work. There is a scare, everybody flaps and then they get over it. Even governments do it.'

'Except yours, Herv. You are always ready for anything.'

'Well, that's sort of what I am driving at. Why not bring the bomb to Tel Aviv?'

'Because you would catch them, Herv. You could search every truck, plane, ship, pram and scooter if you had to. They know this. They need a soft target, one which will shake the world to its core if attacked.'

'You're saying that Tel Aviv isn't a good enough target?'

'I'm saying London is a better one.'

***

Tom felt the phone vibrate in his pocket and, with difficulty, extracted it. He didn't recognise the number but answered immediately.

'Tom Black', he answered. Claire looked straight ahead and drove.

'It's Jack Sullivan. You have come looking for me but I don't know who you are or what you want.'

'Mr Sullivan. We need your help. You served in Afghanistan with the army…'

When Sullivan made no response, he carried on as if the man on the other end of the phone had verified that statement.

' …and you encountered a man called Mohammed Khan.'

'Did I?'

'It is written up in the regimental log for that tour.'

'You expect me to remember that? It's years ago.'

'No, we don't but we need you to help us identify him. We think he is involved in something but no one has any idea what he looks like.' Claire had found a place to pull over and was listening intently to the exchange.

'Involved in what?'

'Something big. I don't really want to discuss it on the phone. Can we meet you?'

'How do I know I can trust you?'

'Have you any reason not to? Is there someone after you?'

Jack thought about this for a moment. Was there any requirement for this degree of caution?

'Okay. You already know where I am. Come to the bar.'

'Is that where we can find you? When we spoke to the receptionist earlier she…'

'She was just looking out for me. She must have thought you looked dodgy.'

Tom laughed.

'Fine, we'll be there in a few minutes.'

Jack rubbed his face and looked at the phone as if it had more secrets to deliver. He had to admit that he was intrigued. It felt as if there was one final adventure for him before he settled down to whatever life fate held in store. As he made his way to the bar, he recalled the time when he had finally left the army, handing in his uniform and ID card, and then receiving the letters giving details of his deferred pension and his reserve liability. He had been sent a red book with his record of service detailed inside, and that was it. And yet it had always felt like unfinished business; the army couldn't just let him go with all that service and training behind him, could it? *Was that really it?* He could kill a man at three hundred metres with a rifle, although he wasn't sure that he ever actually had, and yet that skill was being discarded with such uncaring ease.

One last adventure. Was this it?

Despite Black's reassurance he took precautions, including asking Penny to remain behind in the bar as he talked. If he was to be abducted or in some other way harmed, he wanted a witness. He also brought his phone with him in case he needed to call for help. Who he planned to call wasn't clear to him, but it gave him a sense of wellbeing to know that he could.

He ordered a glass of pure orange, wanting to keep a clear head, and took a seat near the door. That was his third precaution – he would keep himself between his visitors and the only viable escape route available to him. But the truth was that he knew no danger awaited him and that his mood had been affected by Penny's paranoia. Talking of which, she looked decidedly sheepish as two strangers entered the room and asked her where the man she'd told them wasn't here was sitting. She pointed vaguely but such was the paucity of bar customers that Jack was easy to pick out. They had already walked past him to get to the bar.

His first impressions were that they were on the level. Oddly, he trusted them at once. They sat but the male rose again at once to buy drinks. He offered Jack a beer but the latter held up his glass to show that there was no need. The female showed him her ID and explained in vague terms that she worked for the security services. Jack tried not to look impressed but already he was wondering how he might turn their requirements to his advantage. There was more to life than mere patriotism, they needed him and not the other way around.

The man returned with a glass of beer and an orange juice. Jack felt like telling them that there was no chance of getting caught drink-driving up here but he desisted. He didn't care what they did or if they got caught.

'Thank you for agreeing to meet us. Your name came up when we started looking for this man, Mohammed Khan, on our database. We think he is a terrorist and that he might be involved in a bomb plot. The problem is that no one knows much about him.'

'Including me', said Jack honestly.

'It might seem that way but there is no one else who has ever even seen him.'

'Well obviously some people have seen him', said the female. 'But you are the only person we can trace who has any idea what he looks like.'

'You know this was years ago, don't you?'

'Yes.'

'I may have had dealings with him but I really don't remember the incident at all. We stopped loads of people every day. We made notes about who we stopped but this is just a name. It could be anyone.'

'You're all we've got.'

'Sounds a bit dramatic, that. If I am all you've got, then you've got nothing. These people all look the same apart from anything else.' He took a drink from his glass. 'What do you want me to do?' He genuinely felt that he would be of little or no assistance to them but at the same time he didn't want to miss out on the strange adventure they seemed to offer.

Tom and Claire exchanged a look and then the latter said, 'we want you to come to London with us.'

***

Liz and Mark hadn't seen each other for four days when they were called into the DI's office. Liz had been working in another station and Mark had taken a few days leave and gone climbing with friends near Pitlochry just to clear his head. The tension and physical effort of scaling a rock wall provided the perfect antidote to the strains of work. With time to think he had been able to reassure himself that he had not inadvertently said anything which might have led to the deaths of Shannen or Gavin. He was sure that responsibility lay elsewhere. The problem with that apparent certainty was that the finger of blame had to point at Liz instead. He didn't want to believe it could have been her. She would never have said anything on purpose. *Could she have said something by accident?* Well, he couldn't even imagine that.

The DI seemed fairly relaxed. *Had things worked out okay after the pressure she had been under?*

'This business that you were working on hasn't exactly gone away but it is not our concern any longer. I have spoken to the Chief Constable about you both and he is happy that neither of you did anything to compromise the operation. That is my view and now that is his view. Having said that I doubt if it was one of the other officers working with you who said anything – by that I mean the ones who came over from Europe – and so the assumption is that perhaps one of the constables drafted in to help with the CCTV footage must have said something. There isn't going to be an investigation for one simple reason; Shannen and Gavin were both involved in the drugs trade. That brings with it considerable danger. A deal went wrong, or they owed someone money or they sold some bad gear or whatever. Someone killed them both. We are looking for the murderer but that is all.'

Liz and Mark nodded.

'Last thing. Play this down. If possible, say nothing. If that isn't possible then just play it down. Shrug it off. Whatever it takes. For everyone's sake we want this to go away. The press will be happy to call it gang-related, drug-related, whatever they decide to make up but they are not going to suspect the truth.'

She looked at her two officers for a brief moment and then asked if there were any questions. There were none.

***

They met once again in the COBR. The atmosphere was tense. Raymond Garvin, minister without portfolio, was holding court, and everyone else listened. Garvin's particular blend of expertise was quite unique and even his enemies agreed that every once in a while he was exactly the right man for the job. This was one such occasion. Garvin was pugnacious, determined, insightful and displayed a startling clarity of thought that astounded those in his presence. He got to the root of any problem given to him. He had the gift of being able, not only to explain what was happening, but to suggest what should be done about it.

To counter that list of attributes there was an even longer list of seeming deficiencies, including impatience, a lack of empathy, a touch of sexism and the inability to accommodate views which clashed with his own. Some saw the latter as a strength, depending upon whether or not was their opinion with which he was disagreeing. Meetings that included Garvin were always to the point, finished quickly and generally came with a solution to the problem being discussed. At that point he left it to his superiors to decide if they adopted his solution or not.

For many however, the biggest problem with Ray Garvin was that in those moments where his expertise was *not* required, he could seem like an interfering 'pain in the arse' and had often been described in that way.

A former special forces soldier, diplomat, businessman, security consultant and latterly MP, his skills crossed boundaries where other MPs faltered and foundered. Now in his late fifties he dressed well but not in regimental fashion; he still liked to blend in. He had many contacts and his contacts had their contacts. He wielded influence. He knew everyone who mattered and made a point of befriending those whose time had yet to come.

'The problem you have is a recurring one. When our security services foil a bomb plot or some other terrorist act, no one gets to hear about it and they gain no credit for what they have achieved. The public only get to know about their failures and yet without failure there can be no success.'

That last comment caused a few brows to crease.

'If you succeed at everything you succeed at nothing', he said hoping in vain that this might further explain his original idea. 'Without losers there are no winners.'

The PM interrupted sensing that the meeting might get mired in verbiage.

'You mean that to succeed is to not fail?', she said.

'Yes, Prime Minister. That is what I mean. Something like breathing isn't classed as success because it is something you do all the time. Winning a game of cards *is* success because you *don't* do it all the time.'

There were a few nods round the table and he felt encouraged.

'So how does this insight help us, Ray?', asked the PM.

'Naturally, we must gather our resources so that we have the correct people on standby for the emergency when it happens, but…' He held up a finger for emphasis. 'If we fail then we must quickly put that failure into context. We have to give some details about all the plots we have prevented. Not in great detail of course but something.'

'But we plan to succeed?' said another voice. He ignored the hint of mockery.

'Yes. We need detection equipment at ports and airports. We need increased surveillance in the capital and if that means getting the army in then we do that.'

'The army aren't trained for that', said another dissenting voice.

'Some of them are. In fact, some of them are ideal for this type of task and I'll give you another advantage of using the army – you don't have to pay them overtime. If you put them on a rooftop with a rifle and a pair of binoculars they will stay here until they are relieved.'

John Cranston MP, not a fan of Garvin but like him an ex-soldier, nodded his agreement.

'Swamp the capital', he murmured.

'We don't know what he looks like, what he intends to do, when he is due, or if he is really coming', said another dissenting voice.

Garvin looked down the long table at the speaker, an ex-PE teacher called Caroline Burns, and a rising star. She had a reputation for being prickly and tending towards militant feminism. Garvin knew that and was guarded in his response, especially since she spoke the truth and did so directly – rather as he would.

'All of that is true Ms Burns, which is why we need a multi-level response. Firstly, we must try to intercept the material as it comes into Britain. We need discreet, properly-equipped and properly-trained teams at each port and airport but we must accept that they might fail, or that they will be bypassed. And if that happens, we must have the city staked out. If he gets through, we must track him down relentlessly before he plants his device if possible, or as he does so. But we still might fail to do that and so we must have EOD on standby and troops trained and equipped for a swift clear up.'

'When?', asked the PM. Her tone was that of someone who had listened carefully.

'Now, and it all must stay in place until the threat has been dealt with or has passed.'

'It might cause panic', said Burns.

'As will a bomb going off in the centre of London. Which would you rather have? But I accept your point. For a variety of reasons discretion is vital but that is certainly one of them.'

'Does the army have suitably trained troops?', asked the PM.

'We lack men and the very best equipment but we can provide the cover that is being proposed. Plenty of our soldiers have surveillance training and they are all trained to deal with nuclear weapons. And it must be remembered that the sorts of device we are talking about are just conventional bombs which distribute radioactive material over a large area. Despite the insidious effects of radiation this bomb poses a much smaller threat than a proper nuclear weapon.'

'So, it can be cleaned up?', asked the PM.

'Yes, it can. The more personnel we have the better. Perhaps the RAF could spare us some of their personnel? The waste would have to be swept up really and then disposed of. We would use teams and give them a limited amount of exposure before replacing them, rather in the way that a radiologist limits his or her exposure to X-rays. The problem might be restoring public confidence in the affected area. The press will sensationalise this and make things ten times worse. A section of the public will almost certainly believe that they have been attacked with a nuclear weapon rather than a dirty bomb.'

Burns asked another question, holding her pen aloft as she spoke.

'How do we know that the target is London? Why not Birmingham or Manchester. Or Edinburgh?'

'We don't, Ms Burns but where would you choose? You are going to detonate a bomb in a British city to cause maximum disruption and shock effect. Do you go for a provincial city with a relatively small population where your actions might attract plenty of attention thus hindering your escape, or do you go to the capital, where you can disappear into a sea of seven million souls with the chance of bringing the country to a standstill? If he sets a bomb off in Birmingham, then some people might not even realise that this has happened in the UK. The effect would be much reduced if they think we are talking about Birmingham, Alabama. But if it goes off in London, one of the most famous cities in the world and formerly the capital of a huge empire, then no such mistakes will be made.'

'Is there any extra equipment that we require, General?', asked the PM, turning to the head of the army.

'Possibly, Prime Minister. Once I get working on this then it will become clear where our shortages lie.'

'Whatever you need, General... Can the Americans help us?'

'Yes, probably, or maybe even the Czechs. They used to have great expertise in this field.'

The PM nodded and said, 'well unless there are any questions, I suggest that we get started. We will reconvene on Tuesday.'

Chapter Fifteen

May

The next time Khan met The Tiger was in a house in Winchester, far enough from London to be off the radar but close enough to it to launch the attack. The house was in a middle-class area; three storeys, neat lawns, gazebos, barbeques, Volvos and conservatories. People here voted Conservative and read the Daily Mail, including the three Indian families in the street. The local school was the third best in the area.

The terrorists hid in plain sight, as they finalised their plans. They did not suspect that anyone was looking for them but if and when a search did begin, they wouldn't look here. They simultaneously stood out and blended in. They were two young men of Asian origin but this wasn't a place where bad people lived. Terrorism happened on TV and nowhere else…

'When?', said Khan.

'In a few days. The timetable is of our making. When we are ready, we strike. If we have to wait, then we wait. No one hurries us along. No one knows anything about us. They aren't looking for us and they aren't expecting a bomb.'

'They are alert to the danger. There are more police than usual.'

'They are always alert to the danger and the reason there are more police is because you are looking for them. There are the same number of police officers on the streets but now you see them whereas before you took no notice. Your senses are heightened.'

'Where are the bombs?'

'They are on their way. Some are coming in by plane, some by ship, some through the tunnel. We need eight bombs but we are bringing in sixteen.'

'You told me none of this before.'

The Tiger passed Khan a joint and indicated that he should smoke.

'It will relax you', he said soothingly.

'Why didn't you tell me?'

'You didn't need to know before. Now you do. Don't see this as an insult. This is just security. Having sixteen bombs means that we can afford for some to be intercepted and we still have plenty left.'

'There is more chance of them getting detected.'

'We had to weigh that up. Anyway, all you need to worry about is getting your eight bombs through and planting them.'

'And the rest of the stuff – the truck and the video equipment?'

'It is all prepared. We have a driver on standby. The truck is ready. We just need to load the bombs and then take it out. The driver knows his route. When he drops you at the last of the bins then you stay behind and he drives away. You set up the video link. Shortly afterwards we give you a signal and you press the button and make history.'

Khan felt his head swim anew with the enormity of his sacrifice; he was just days from death.

He took a deep faltering breath and then looked around the room as though answers to his problems were printed on the wall paper.

'You must take courage.' He pointed to the unlit cigarette. 'Smoke', he said. 'This is a great journey you have undertaken, the most important of your life, but your destination is in view and you just need the strength to keep walking.'

The Bomber was tired of this superficial profundity. It was the sort of thing that lonely people put on Facebook hoping that the rest of the Facebook world would 'like' it.

'I feel like I am being hunted', he said unhappily.

The Tiger laughed like a patronising uncle, although the two men were close in age.

'You aren't being hunted. No one knows who you are, or why you are here.'

'I can't even go to the shop.'

'Yes, you can. You aren't going to be challenged about your identity if you simply ask for a paper. This is a country simply going about its business, unaware of the catastrophe which lies ahead. This is why we will win. We cannot be beaten. We are phantoms. You can't kill a ghost.'

***

The Special Reconnaissance Regiment was raised to perform surveillance duties, replacing its *ad hoc* predecessor, 14 Intelligence Company and freeing up the SAS and SBS for other roles. The old 14 Int, as it was known, had performed, and perfected, its intelligence gathering role during the long-running campaign in Northern Ireland and a core of troops from that period had helped establish the new regiment, which for the first time had its own uniform distinctions.

The new unit was much bigger and an official part of the British Army, which in time it would have its own traditions and list of battle honours, unlike the near mythical 14 Int.

The SRR was part of a changing order of battle. Armour was being phased out, the infantry cut back in favour of troops who could fight the terrorist at his own game. In the event of a conventional war this change of emphasis might be a dire problem but for the present they fulfilled the country's most urgent need. In the first instance two companies were briefed for deployment in the capital. Their training was first rate, better than many rival organisations, and all that was required was the fine tuning for an urban deployment. Both company commanders were given an ops room in the police station nearest to their intended deployment. They had permanent comms with their ground troops. The unit's commanding officer – a lieutenant colonel – was patched in from the regiment's regular base. To complete the communications net they were also linked to the COBR.

The range of equipment available to them was extensive. In addition to the usual service weapons they had access to listening equipment, thermal imaging and high-powered photography. They worked to different sets of rules for different theatres. Working in the UK required a stricter code than that for a deployment to the Middle East. Rules of Engagement were important, especially if anything came to court, which was always a possibility.

In the event of a contact, they would hand over to either armed police or possibly SAS troops, unless it proved impossible to do so. Of course, faced with an armed man they would shoot after giving the appropriate warning, but their primary task in this case was to spot or locate the terrorist who was bringing a bomb to London. The intelligence picture was far from complete but new information, once received, would be passed on instantly.

Soldiers of 11 Explosive Ordnance Disposal (EOD) Regiment were also being briefed for a new mission. Ten bomb disposal teams were being discreetly drafted into London and housed in existing barracks, sometimes those of the Army Reserve, awaiting their potential deployment. They too understood their roles perfectly and most personnel had recent experience in Afghanistan and on attachment to other armies and, in some cases, police forces.

Their expertise was world class. The techniques and equipment they used had also been tested in the long campaign in Northern Ireland when twenty-three bomb disposal officers had lost their lives. The bomb had been one of the main terrorist weapons, getting more and more sophisticated as the years wore on, and their knowledge base was the most extensive in the world. To supplement their bravery (the unit had earned a huge number of gallantry awards) they used remote technology as often as possible. The 'Wheelbarrow' robot had become a familiar sight on television news as it rolled out to deal with an IRA device. It was synonymous with 'The Troubles'.

The EOD regiment came from the Royal Logistic Corps, descendants of the Royal Army Ordnance Corps, and they operated under the call sign 'Felix', the origins of which have become lost but which may have related to Felix the Cat and the fact that a cat supposedly had nine lives. The bomb disposal officers were a mix of commissioned officers, usually captains, and senior NCOs or warrant officers.

The remainder of the discrete armed force drafted into the capital consisted mainly of infantry snipers from nearby battalions. Their task was obvious but the nature of their actual position less so. A small task force had been established to rent suitable surveillance and sniping positions in the city, from where the entire area could be watched. Inevitably there would be blank spots but a series of flats had been hastily pressed into action and sniper/surveillance teams inserted in civilian clothes, with rifles in hockey bags and holdalls filled with various bulky items of military hardware.

The location of each flat was recorded on a map, the object being to ring the city centre. As a back-up, quick response groups were added to supplement those provided by the police.

And once all that had been done, all they could do was wait.

***

They paid Jack's site fees for a month and took him back on the plane to London with them. Tom was curious to know what made the man tick but Claire seemed to feel that their job was done, that merely finding him had brought them much closer to a resolution of the problem faced by an unwitting country. Jack himself was willing enough but his doubts about personal suitability seemed well founded, although he was playing these down now that he had agreed to help them. Tom wasn't too surprised when he asked how they were going to pay him for his time. It wasn't a contingency he had looked at but he knew that there was a way of doing it, the equivalent of raiding the petty cash.

On the plane they barely spoke to one another, each alone with their thoughts and worries. The ex-soldier had adapted to his new situation with relative ease, perhaps flattered by the attention. Nevertheless, he seemed a good sort, calm, reliable, fairly unobtrusive. Quite what use he was going to be was another matter. Tom wondered if, somehow, he had been railroaded into taking Jack Sullivan along for the ride. He didn't want to suggest anything of the sort, especially if it meant admitting that they were wasting his time and their own... but his doubts remained.

Every so often his thoughts strayed of their own accord, back to the computer record which had gone missing. There was nothing he could say about it without getting in trouble for his own carelessness, which was in fact a breach of security. But yet he knew that that record had been there and that it had subsequently been deleted. It still surprised him that it could be removed with such ease. He had suspected that Wendy had been responsible, simply because she had come into the office in his absence. And why had she gone in, when she had no business to be there at all? However, he came back to the same question over and over again, no matter which angle he came at the problem from. Why? Why would someone with the highest security clearance do such a thing?

And had she been in the office at all? He only had Claire's word for it. Could it be Matt? Matt was a flabby nerd, boring, objectionable but was he a traitor? Every man had his price but the thought that plodding Matt had been bought by a foreign power or by a terrorist group was too much of a stretch. Things like that were common enough in the films but incredibly rare in real life. Reality, as ever, was dull.

Jack – their prize – was going to be put up in one of the surveillance flats and the intention was to keep him on standby, should their suspect appear. Tom wasn't quite sure how this was going to work. The whole plan seemed based on a fabric of utter horseshit.

They made their way to the flat and introductions were made. His companions for the next few days were two soldiers from the SRR. They viewed Jack with extreme suspicion even though he was introduced as an ex-soldier. These were men who viewed everyone with suspicion… He wasn't sure if that was typical of the breed, for he had never met any troops from that particular unit before, but special forces were loath to accommodate lesser mortals into their plans at the best of times. The fact that he wasn't even a serving soldier put him a long way down the pecking order. Immediately he felt unloved.

Jack looked around him at the furnished flat.

'I've slept in worse places than this', he said. The two soldiers looked at him with near total disregard. He got the message straight away. From then on, he made himself comfortable, reading and watching TV. It began to feel as if he wasn't quite engaged in the war in terror, that he was a mere spectator, whose presence was grudgingly accepted and nothing more. To be tolerated wasn't terribly exciting or encouraging. Tom departed but promised to be back in touch.

Jack had brought a week's worth of clothes, a wash kit and a few books. His phone remained in his possession but he had been cautioned about its use; he could be contacted and that was the limit. There would be no Facebook entries beginning with the words, 'guess what has happened to me', with the tacit suggestion that his little electronic friends enquire after the mystery events which had overtaken him. He had been sternly reminded that he'd once, many years ago, signed the Official Secrets Act and that once signed one was never free from its conditions. This felt like the first time that he'd ever actually been in possession of an *official secret*. Nothing he'd learnt before couldn't be found on the internet.

His room had once belonged to a child and had been hastily re-painted when the property went onto the rental market. The outlines of a *My Little Pony* border shone dimly through the magnolia paint and there was more than a hint of pink visible through the hasty brush strokes that had been used to transform the room from child's bedroom to functional second bedroom for the successful young city dweller. It was an utterly underwhelming place to spend time. The living room had a television set but this remained switched off so that the surveillance troops' work would be undisturbed. Instead, he watched the elderly portable set in his bedroom.

He vaguely understood the function of some of the kit they had arrayed next to a large living room window. A sizable object resembling a shallow wok was part of a listening device and they seemed to have a variety of recording equipment at their feet, some of which clearly was not yet in use. The soldiers took it in turns to use binoculars and a tripod mounted scope to watch the street below. Jack didn't interfere or take any interest in what they were doing. He was amused to discover just how much he really didn't *care* about what they were doing. Disinterest was a two-way street; he wasn't going to spend any time reminiscing about aspects of service life with his new buddies. This was purely a place for him to live so that he was close to the action if required and he formed no part of their brief at all.

Already he was bored but then he remembered that boredom was central to everything in the army. It was not so much that the army marched on its stomach as that it existed for its capacity to handle inactivity. He recognised and accepted the fact that inactivity was going to be the name of the game for him. If he was ever required, then it was going to be for a very short space of time, probably a moment of near total confusion and controlled panic. He was required to identify someone that he had seen briefly several years ago, a face that he hadn't particularly taken note of. Back then, he could never have known that this would happen or he might have paid more attention. Inactivity made him think back to those days with a fondness that he hadn't always felt. The passage of time had blotted out the frustrations and discomfort, the annoyances and the moments of tension. Fear had not been a constant, but he had known it, and yet now he was unable to replicate the gut-twisting emotion of coming under fire, the quickening of the pulse, the drying of the mouth, the feeling that you wanted to curl up into the smallest ball you could make from your body.

He lay on the bed and stared at the ceiling, trying to project those thoughts on the plain white surface of the bedroom: the RPG rounds, the bullets, the screams. It had been real once, but now it seemed no more personal than something seen in a Hollywood film. Jack wondered if the soldiers in the next room had experienced the same things as him. He supposed they had but they had moved on to greater trials, reached higher standards, taken greater risks, such that ordinary men like him were of no interest.

Thoughts still nagged at him. *Was he supposed to feel something? Was he supposed to care? Was anyone supposed to care about him?* The whole experience was so utterly unreal. *What was his purpose?*

When he closed his eyes, he could just about conjure up an image of Afghanistan. He remembered a corporal whose nerve went, could picture him being led away after a patrol that was cut short. *What was the man's name?* They had never seen him again and his name was... well, it had seemed as if he had been deleted from the regimental records. He ran a hand across his face and felt his thumb grate against the stubble which grew there. These were events which had lain untouched in his head for years and yet now they began to emerge like dust lifting off an old armchair being used for the first time in a decade. They aroused his curiosity and yet he had made no conscious effort to submerge them. They were part of him but he had convinced himself not to live in the past.

Although he knew where his medals were, he didn't feel the need to put them on at every suitable opportunity. The various veteran's groups and regimental associations, both actual and virtual, all had to make do without his patronage. Jack did not delve into the veteran nick-nack market either, although there were T-shirts, badges, mugs and amusing gifts galore. All that he had retained from his army service was a few good habits and painful joints.

***

The Tiger looked at his phone with horror but quickly recovered his composure before any change in his demeanour could be spotted. His bomber was staring out of the window.

But he quickly assessed the situation, his mind working with lightning speed and coming to a rapid decision. He prided himself on this ability, the ability to think on his feet, and saw himself as incisive and courageous. It was this ability which made him a leader rather than a foot soldier. This was why he wasn't a suicide bomber – he was irreplaceable. Anyone could blow themselves up but not everyone could plan and problem solve – that was his gift as he saw it.

But still the text had come as a shock. It was a line of communication that was for the direst of emergencies only but things didn't get any direr than this. Khan was still staring out of the window, oblivious, and it was that fact which might have given him the inspiration he needed; his soldier, this disposable man, would remain oblivious to the new threat. There was no point in telling him that their plot had been discovered and there was every point in ignoring the apparent problem which this posed. The bombs would either be planted or they wouldn't, that much was Allah's will in any case. Khan could embark upon his mission, unknowing of the scrutiny given over to the centre of London and one of two things would happen. Either he would be caught and his mission curtailed, or he would evade capture and successfully plant the bombs. In the first instance, The Tiger would suffer a disappointment but live to fight another day and in the second he would know that he had staged a great victory... and live to fight another day. Khan was replaceable. *Did he know this?*

And the London bomb was only the first in a series of attacks which he personally deemed to be in the pre-planning stage. So, Khan would be entering the lion's den but that didn't mean he would be caught. The British assumed that an attack on London was imminent but they always thought that and they still had no idea when or where the attack would occur. Furthermore, they wouldn't be expecting eight bombs so they might find one and leave the rest... He was perfectly satisfied that nothing had changed. All of this reasoning had been done in a moment and The Bomber hadn't even diverted his gaze from the street outside, although it did make him wonder if it was now better to go sooner – perhaps before their enemies were fully prepared – or to wait until the first wave of alertness had subsided. He was beginning to think that the first course of action would be best.

'We can bring things forward', he said. The sound of his voice made The Bomber jump, stirring him from some sort of reverie. He continued to gaze out of the window.

'Why?'

'We are ready to go. The truck driver is ready, the bombs are ready. Everyone is briefed. We are ready a little bit sooner than we anticipated so why hang about?'

It sounded so reasonable but he wasn't the one who had to die. He made no comment. The Tiger – self-styled guerrilla leader – would do what he wanted.

The suggestion continued to sit there like a newly added item of furniture. It was in the room like an entity, a sort of awkward object that no one liked but which was hard to ignore. He wanted to stand up and walk out, leaving The Tiger standing there in open-mouthed shock. In fact, he had run through that exact scenario a number of times recently, with some slight variations but with an unchanging core idea. What prevented him from carrying it out was the fact that he had nowhere to go to, at least not yet. He had begun to hate The Tiger and to resent him. He hated the way he looked and the way he spoke. He hated the stupid clothes her wore which made him look like some sort of Harvard graduate with a degree in Business Administration, all paid for by a doting father who expected his terrorist son to take over the family business. He hated the plans which he made for other people and the fact that other people died when he continued to live. There was glory for him but he pretended to pass it on, sending it upwards to Paradise. He was a hypocrite.

'Tomorrow. Why don't we do it tomorrow? I can set the wheels in motion and tomorrow you can take out the centre of London.' He made it sound like an activity at a children's party. Inwardly Khan cringed.

In secret he had made plans for his escape. They were not exactly advanced and he had no faith that they would work but they offered him a slim hope of continuing life.

He thought about how bringing the attack forward would affect his own plans. In theory, of course, he had no need for plans, his life was no more than a few grains of sand lingering in an egg timer, but his level of commitment had definitely changed, or more precisely, dropped. He sensed The Tiger watching him, waiting for an answer he didn't want to give.

'Okay', he said.

The Tiger smiled with delight.

'I will make the arrangements', he said eagerly. He didn't quite rub his hands together but nearly. He was childish enough. Khan could see an excited, watery blaze in his eyes as adrenaline coursed through his limp, flabby frame. He resembled a contestant on a reality TV show, more than a military strategist. Khan hated him. The thought that he could kill him with ease and the thought that no one would mourn his passing, or even discover he had died, crossed through his mind. In fact, it crossed through his mind more than once, pausing, as if hoping to be picked up and put into practice. He had killed before and although he had found that act distasteful, he had done it and not been caught. Now the need for such an act was greater than ever. Otherwise, this time tomorrow he could be dead, he who could offer so much...

He stood now and moved away from the window into the hall where The Tiger stood excitedly talking into his phone and past him into the bedroom he was using. More than anything he wanted peace, quiet and time to think. The bed seemed to groan as he lowered himself onto it but he found himself strangely at peace as options opened up to him. Suddenly death seemed like just one possible course. Now there were others. He could pick. Khan lay there, closed his eyes and ordered his thoughts.

***

Tom and Claire moved from their office into another better equipped room in the COBR complex. They were joined by a tense looking Andy who supervised and gave guidance on how the flow of intelligence should be used and disseminated to those whose job it was to coordinate the country's response to the latest threat. There was a definite change in tempo, a sense of hitherto missing urgency, a feeling that great events were unfolding. Tom also sensed that everyone wanted a slice of the action now that things were reaching their climax. People he had never seen before were bustling about, coming in and out, poking their noses in and asking questions that had been answered ten times previously. These were the hangers on, coming in at the last minute and hoping that some shred of credit might land at their feet.

Their appearance did not surprise him at all, more shocking would have been a non-appearance. He was well used to the phenomenon and half-expected to be edged out of the way now that the final act was due to be played out. In one sense it was encouraging, for he knew that these previously unseen people who would claim to have been beavering away behind the scenes must have smelt success otherwise they would have kept their distance. Tom could think of at least one other occasion in which they had arisen like Lazarus only to find themselves associated with an operation that had gone terribly wrong and in which an innocent man had been gunned down on a train. Admittedly, the victim hadn't bought a ticket but that wasn't enough to justify his death. When the full horror of the mistake had become apparent these additional staff had tried to melt away but such was the suddenness of the man's demise that they had no choice but to stand and take their share of the blame. Oddly enough they had kept their jobs and one or two had been promoted. That was how things went. Tom, who had played no part in any aspect of the operation, felt himself cocooned in a blanket of self-righteous glee. The feeling hadn't lasted. There was always another balls-up around the corner.

For now, he was beginning to reappraise Andy, wondering if he was the sort of boss who would allocate credit to the correct people, namely he and Claire. He wondered anew if Andy was gay and if this had implications for his promotion prospects. Probably not these days but once it would have been viewed as potentially too compromising. And even as he was pondering this, he began to wonder about Claire's contribution to the operation.

There was nothing he could say about her and he didn't even feel the slightest need to cast doubt on her work, and yet those same doubts resurfaced like a bath toy emerging from a thin sea of soap suds. Time might prove her instincts correct – maybe Jack Sullivan held the key to success – but a lot of what she had done recently seemed decidedly dubious.

Particularly, he wondered how Jack Sullivan might actually be able to help and of course he hadn't forgotten about the stuff which she claimed had been deleted by Wendy. Why hadn't she stopped her? Why had she compounded his error with one of her own by letting it happen?

He supposed that one way or another it would be over soon, although he also acknowledged the fact that the attack might never come, leaving them hanging on forever in a state of heightened security from which they could never deviate. He wasn't sure what would actually happen but not that. It might be relatively inexpensive to ring the centre of London with elite troops but it wasn't free and it wasn't sensible either. At some point they would have to act or be re-assigned.

There would either be a flap or there wouldn't… It would go live or it would pass and they would all be stood down. That's how it was. If it happened, he was very likely to be a bystander. He was brought back to the present by Andy.

'Okay, we are starting to get some pictures through from the surveillance officers', he said in reference to the undercover police patrolling the streets. They were equipped with cameras and mics, all carefully concealed but giving a constant stream of information that could be analysed, evaluated, acted upon or ignored. There seemed scant chance of them happening upon The Bomber, but that wasn't the point – they were doing something. They were being proactive, to use the current bullshit phrase. If the authorities didn't take these measures, then they could be accused of letting the terrorists move about at will.

Avoiding blame, no matter how ridiculous the situation, was more important than any small likelihood of success. That was the game they played. He supposed that Jack Sullivan was being raised from his pit to scan the multiple screens which fed the information back to the decision-makers, including Andy. If their mission was a notable success the press would seek to quickly establish the details of the operation, making it up if they needed to, unless of course the security services scored the greatest success of all which was to foil a plot and leave behind no indication that anything untoward had actually occurred. That was often how it panned out.

A bank of screens came to life, each offering a different view of central London from the perspective of an overcoat or shirt collar. Occasional updates came through but otherwise radio silence was maintained. Tom leaned back in his chair to watch the city's unknowing populace hurrying about from work to lunch and from lunch back to work. All life was there in glorious 2D, the glowering mothers with prams, the teenagers with chip-fat acne, the merchant bankers full of importance, invincible, deeply in love with themselves. There was no such thing as an ordinary person. The word 'average' was inapplicable. Polish builders vied for pavement space with doctors and dentists, architects and solicitors. They were a morass but each fascinating in their own way. They each had their own story to tell but these they had set to one side as they hurried about their business: screwing over the poor, trusting bank customer, pulling teeth, diagnosing bad breath, suing rich people or building walls.

The novelty of this unregulated people-watching spree would eventually wear off for Tom but for now he was drawn into this multiplex cinema of lunchtime life.

All races were in evidence, every social class, and every bad habit from texting on the move to nose-picking was there, revealed in gritty detail and pored over by soon-to-be sleep-dulled eyes. It was almost a cliché: the Japanese tourists with their American rucksacks, the Americans with their Japanese cameras, the French with their onions...

Tom watched in astonishment as the officer passed two men, seemingly of Pakistani descent, having a blazing row in the street. The policeman walked past and then turned, keeping them in the picture, literally in the frame. He didn't speak. The two men jabbed fingers in chests and spat with anger but the reason for their disagreement was unknown. One was dressed in a longish robe over which he wore a grey jerkin and the other was more western in his appearance, jeans and shirt. The undercover officer watched them for a while and then turned away. Neither was The Bomber.

Tom wondered if the cop had received information from Jack Sullivan. He would find out later. But this was just the start. There were days of this to go and it would soon be stultifying in its desperate sameness.

The undercover cops moved through the crowds, blending in, but they didn't exactly know what they were looking for and London was such a melting pot that men of Asian appearance were common. They could rule out women, he supposed, and white Europeans and Japanese, Koreans,

Chinese, but still the whole thing was a game of chance. It was better than doing nothing but only just.

He moved away from the bank of screens, his interest waning. He looked over at Claire and saw that she had also lost interest. She had returned to her desk and had begun tapping keys on her computer, engrossed. Of late, her attempts to seduce him had also waned and he was glad. Not even the notion of rejection impinged upon his relief, even if he couldn't pinpoint the reasons for his wariness.

In one sense he should have liked her, she ticked all the boxes in terms of looks, intelligence, wit and so on. But there was something else, or rather there wasn't something else… He was still baffled.

Events had begun to settle into a dull routine when Andy was called out of the office. When he returned just moments later, he looked distressed.

Andy, whatever his shortcomings, never looked distressed.

'Tom, I need a word', he said pointedly. 'Outside.'

The comment was addressed to Tom and definitely not Claire but he obediently rose and followed Andy from the office. He fired a quick glance at Claire but she was intent on her work and tapping away at her keyboard.

Andy closed the door behind him and led his subordinate away.

'Are you sitting comfortably?', said Andy although it was clear that neither man was.

'Metaphorically speaking, yes.'

'The Met. are coming for Claire.'

'What?'

'She's being arrested. She has been tipping off someone in ISIS about our operation. That's all I know at the minute.'

'She's on the computer now…'

'Her access has been stopped. She'll be finding this out around about now.' Tom stood, unable to speak, unable to process the information he had received. 'Here they come', said Andy nodding down the corridor to the double doors through which two officers were now being led by one of the deputy directors. The enormity of the situation suddenly hit and sent him reeling. At once he had what seemed like a thousand questions to ask. His reservations about her had not quite extended this far and yet now his concerns were turning out to be well-founded. The fall-out from this would go on for months and it seemed certain that he would be dragged into it.

He watched as the police officers passed him and made their way to the office the three of them had shared. He watched as Claire stood. She looked petrified and for almost the first time he felt some sort of emotion, some warmth that had been missing before. He continued to watch as they cautioned her and then led her from the office.

There were no handcuffs and they took her away with minimum fuss, retracing their steps. Claire looked at the ground and didn't speak as she passed. Tom looked at Andy who was ashen-faced, deeply shocked and almost unable to think or speak.

'Christ', he said. Andy nodded.

'You must have questions but I don't have any answers', said Andy.

Chapter Sixteen

The truck was decked out in the blue and grey of Veolia, the company with the contract to deal with waste for the City of Westminster which made up most of central London. They closed the double doors behind them. From the metal ribs which supported the roof hung a series of strip lights, two of which did not work, one which flickered and three which bathed the scene in a sick, jaundiced glow. A puddle had formed at the door and they stood with its shallow waters leaching into their shoe leather. Khan tried to look impressed but his thoughts had become stuck at the point where he was considering murder. He couldn't quite get past a mental picture of himself choking the life out of the man before him.

'Where will you be?', he asked and it was apparent that the question caught The Tiger off guard for he blinked in surprise at his man's temerity. It wasn't for him to ask questions surely... but maybe it was reasonable that he did so in this case?

'I have to think about my security', he answered, obliquely.

'Will you leave the country?', asked Khan. He felt anger but he didn't let it show. He asked his questions as though he was making polite conversation.

'It is better if you don't know too much.'

'I can't tell anyone. I will be dead', he said reasonably, although the words shook him to his core as he uttered them.

I will be dead. I will be dead. He spoke these words in relation to himself...

'Supposing you get caught?'

This was a possibility that they had never even discussed.

'I won't get caught.'

'Why the curiosity? There is no point in you knowing such a thing.'

'Maybe I want to think about how other people's lives work out after mine has ended.'

The idea seemed to appal The Tiger but he quickly thought of a response.

'You will have eternity in Paradise to contemplate such things. That is your reward, don't forget.'

The words sounded empty and he was tempted to ask if The Tiger even believed in Paradise, but he let it pass. He looked at the man suspiciously.

'When do you leave?', he asked.

'Tomorrow.' He shook his head with a show of good-humoured impatience. 'Let's run through the plan.'

Khan said nothing.

Taking his bomber by the arm The Tiger led him forwards so that neither man was standing in the puddle.

'Tomorrow you will come back here at six o'clock. The driver will be here around the same time. You will both wear overalls so that you look like genuine council workers. The eight bombs are already loaded on the back. You drive out to the centre of London and replace the normal bins with our bombs – the driver knows the route – and then he drops you off outside Walker's department store.'

'That is where we put the eighth bin?'

'Correct. The camera is already set up. It is linked to this building and will convey your message to the internet.'

'My message? What do I say?'

'You just explain why you are doing it. Don't take too long and then press the button. The bomb will blow you to pieces.'

'And the next thing I know, I will be in Paradise?'

The suggestion seemed to catch The Tiger out, like it was something that he hadn't even considered.

'Yes', he said. He somehow managed to make an affirmative sound ambiguous.

'And the driver knows the route and where each bin is?'

'Yes. There is no detail left to chance. Nothing.' The Tiger didn't mention the fact that the security services were now alerted to the plot.

'What will happen to the driver?'

The Tiger was beginning to get irritated now but he smiled with exaggerated patience.

'Does it matter?'

'I am curious.'

'He drives off into the sunset, fades away, however you want to phrase it.'

'The plans have been made for him?'

'Naturally.'

Another hero who didn't have to die... Paradise was going to fill quickly at this rate.

***

When Tom returned to his flat that evening his mind was in turmoil. Shock had given way to dismay and confusion and he felt an overpowering need for someone to sit him down and explain exactly what was going on. Even when he tried to factor in his own vestigial suspicions, none of it made much sense to him. At worst Claire was a bit spiteful – was that even the right word? – but she wasn't whatever she was accused of. She couldn't be.

He had never known such a thing happen and by the looks on the faces of those assembled in the COBR, nor had any of them. COBR was just about the most secret place in Britain, how could someone who somehow warranted arrest ever be allowed inside?

He slumped on the sofa and put the TV on to watch the news – it was as good a source of int as any so long as you filtered out the supposition and conjecture. Tom let out a sigh, a valve to release the day's tension and shock. There had been a time when a few drinks, usually spirits, had helped him with the pain of his amputation, blurring the memory of that terrible event in his life, but these days he rarely drank. Long before he had eased off on his consumption it had been obvious that drinking was not the answer to anything and that the phrase was more than just a glib saying on the lips of reformed drinkers everywhere.

The relief alcohol had offered was of short duration, the problems it brought worse in some cases than those it helped to solve.

At one time, he had seriously thought he was turning into an alcoholic, and had stopped drinking suddenly and without any difficulty for about three months before easing himself back onto the booze. But the break had given him an appreciation of the delights of sleeping well and of waking up without a raging thirst, a pounding head and a fatigue that lasted for days. From then on, he drank rarely. He wasn't a convert to teetotalism by any means and when he was required to be sociable he would drink without inhibition, but drinking was no longer a chemical requirement in his life.

He thought about this fact as he lay on the sofa, waiting for the news to come on. He also thought about the fact that he had a bottle of Mount Gay Rum in a cupboard in his tiny kitchen. Tom reminded himself often that he didn't need a reason or an excuse to drink and that still stood. The news was on a break. An advertisement for a West End show played out in its excruciating, breathless, camp excitement on his TV. He wasn't really watching.

But it had been a hell of a day. What was wrong with having a drink?, he reasoned. He sighed again as the debate raged in the confines of his head. Finally, raising himself from the supportive comfort of the sofa, he hobbled to the kitchen, found a glass, a can of Diet Coke and the ice tray from his freezer compartment. The rum, a full bottle, was in his highest cupboard as if to keep it out of easy reach. Even as he artfully assembled the ingredients for his simple drink, he knew that it wouldn't be the answer to his prayers or anything remotely of that nature.

Drinking rum wouldn't turn the clock back to a time when he still had two feet, or when he still felt some enthusiasm for his job. It wouldn't even take him back to a time before Claire had monumentally fucked up and when he might have been able to prevent her from doing so. He was plagued by doubts but these came at him through a fog of incomprehension. Tom paused at the short length of worktop and, with a sigh, reached for a pen and pad that he kept for no particular reason. The drink untouched, he began to compile a list of questions but scratched through it before the first was even completed.

The questions remained even if he saw no point in writing them down. Who was The Bomber? And how had he managed to elude them for so long? If they found him, how would they actually foil the plot?

He tapped his fingers on the pad and then realised that what he actually needed was a timeline. He glanced at the rum, its presence strangely comforting.

Sighing heavily, suddenly overcome with weariness, he took his first sip and made his way back to the sofa. The next step was to remove his prosthetic foot and he did this quickly, allowing it to drop to the floor with a thud. Doing so had become part of his routine now. Moving around the flat wasn't a particular problem on one foot these days, although initially it had taken time to get used to this new way of living.

Tom closed his eyes and yawned, letting that first testing sip of rum find the spot. He loved that initial tiny, hesitant burst of euphoria and knew that every sip afterwards was just a lesser version of the same thing. He set down the glass on the cushion of his leather sofa and picked up the pad and pen. Tom tapped the pen on his pursed lips. His written timeline would start when he had first been given the task of tracing the missing ship. It seemed like months ago and yet everything had happened so quickly. He had found the flow and exchange of intelligence incredible; that, he supposed, was what happened when you had the help of foreign agencies. The Israelis had been straight in, and more surprisingly had shared their findings with them without question or without any suggestion of a pay-off. Was there anything from that time which might have made him think that Claire was anything other than a loyal, efficient employee of Britain's security apparatus? He tried to picture her then.

Was anything different? Only that she hadn't given him the time of day. Like a slap in the face it dawned on him. Claire's pseudo-affection, the attention she paid him, was purely to get closer to the investigation into the missing ship. For the first time he felt a sense of betrayal and this was tempered by feeling rather ridiculous. At the same time, he was glad that he had managed to keep his distance from her. Had he fallen for her, as was the intention, where exactly would that leave him now? At least this way he had no emotional attachment – ideal considering that she was likely to be going to prison for many years – and a starting point for making sense of the other events which had gone unexplained.

This was why she had made herself available to assist with the investigation. Had she used her 'feminine charms' to convince Andy that she was required? Tom took another sip of his drink and shook his head, feeling like a fool. He smiled wanly, rolled his eyes. If nothing else he could make sense of things now.

He put his concerns to one side and changed channels on the TV. The news was the usual assortment of things that had happened, things that were happening, things that were going to happen, things that were never going to happen and things that hadn't happened, although someone claimed that they had. He watched rain-soaked reporters talking about monsoons and blustery sports reporters talking about terrible football managers and their impending sacking. There was no good news, but there was no news about bombs in London either. A fire had burned down a warehouse in Leicester and extra crews had been drafted in from neighbouring counties. A man from Birmingham had been jailed for firearms offences after a long and complex trial. A politician in Northern Ireland was berating the government in London for its failure to deal with Republican terrorists.

But no one had bombed London.

By the time the news was tailing off into the lightweight end of the day's events, he had drained his glass. It was time for bed, but instead of retiring for the night whilst he was relatively fresh and knowing that drink was never the answer to anything, he limped over to the kitchen and replenished his glass, trying to replicate that first wave of euphoria, even though an inner voice told him that he could not do so.

The sofa seemed to envelop him and for a few moments he had the sensation of being adrift on a raft, surrounded by enemies if not sharks. The carpet was the sea, host to unseen dangers, and the walls were the horizon, banks of endless nothingness. He might have pulled a blanket over his body for extra protection had there been one within reach. None of it seemed too fanciful as perhaps it should have and no one would ever know that his fears had crowded around in the privacy and security of his home. An image of his mum, dead for three years now, came unbidden, and he mourned her passing anew, remembering that no one else had ever cared for him as she had done. She'd been proud of him as a soldier and probably exaggerated his importance in the army and she had worried about him when he'd done his time in Afghanistan and Iraq, despite his protestations that he was perfectly safe. Ironically, she had been right to worry.

He rubbed at the stump and looked at the ugly circle of scar tissue that led to nowhere. It had taken years to get the hang of having just one foot but although it was a great icebreaker at parties, he had never bemoaned its loss or sought to capitalise upon the sympathy factor. In part this was because he went to so few parties. He grinned at the peculiar hand life had dealt him.

The news was just background noise as he added details to his notes. He had taken over the investigation into the missing ship and then had his phone calls from Herv in Israel – it felt like he was finally hitting the big time – and then there was the stuff that had come through from Perth. Then working with Claire, the American int, the murders… he noted it down in chronological order leading to the point where Claire had been taken into custody. And yet somehow it still didn't quite make sense to him. It was all bound up to the missing computer records, which he had originally thought was the work of Wendy. But who had put that idea in his head? Claire, of course.

The news was followed by a documentary about American prisons. He watched with no interest at all and at the beginning of the second commercial break he'd had enough and finally retired to bed. His tolerance for alcohol was low these days, and his head span as he lay back on the pillow. There was something else that he had meant to add to his timeline, and he searched his memory for it as if he was searching for a path through a twisted jungle. It was there but he couldn't get to it or see it… He closed his eyes hoping for a gateway to lucidity but found nothing. He opened his eyes again and stared at the ceiling.

There was something else. Something he had missed.

A minute later he was asleep.

**

The Bomber lay on his bed and tried to avoid sleep so that he might make sense of his last night on earth but he needn't have worried because sleep didn't come at all. He had thought he might be suffused with calm, deep in some spiritual moment where he gladly handed himself over to fate, or rather over to Allah. After all he was on the cusp of something great – he would make the entire planet sit up and take note, they would talk about him for generations – and when that was done, he would be in Paradise. Khan told himself that the pain, if indeed he felt any, would be over in a split second and that his transition to something far better would be equally speedy.

He tried to think about Paradise and about what sort of reception he could expect there, for he knew that not every Muslim saw the killing of the infidel as a fast track to the afterlife. Many Muslims – most, if he was being honest – would disapprove of what he was doing. He had accepted this simply because it was foolish to think that everyone could have a clear view of the need for war. The role he had taken on was that of martyr and you had to have martyrs to make people see the truth about their situation.

And yet supposing they were right? These people who wanted nothing to do with Jihad and who preached tolerance, supposing they were right and he was wrong? He might arrive at Paradise and be turned away. And supposing they were all wrong? Supposing that Paradise was a bit of wishful thinking, designed to make the prospect of death a less bitter pill to swallow. He knew that the world's great religions were haemorrhaging followers simply because so many people thought that way. Who was to say that they were wrong and that everyone else was right?

But he still had options even if they were narrowing with each passing moment. He still wanted to kill the infidel. He found that fact reassuring. but he didn't want to die himself and saw no real need for that to happen. It all boiled down to one thing and that was the fact that those who had pushed him into this course of action would live, and it was they who would reap the glory. It was maddening.

He turned on his side and hugged the pillow protectively to his face. His last night on earth and he spent it here...

He heard The Tiger pacing about next door – prowling would have been a better word, after all he was a Tiger, was he not? Khan wondered why he didn't just go to bed. He lay still and listened. The pacing, slow and deliberate, took his mind off the events of the following day and he found that he was able to transfer his anger, frustration and irritation from his impending but unnecessary death to the noises made by this stupid man. There were other noises too, now that he was listening more intently. He heard a wardrobe door creak, and the sound of springs being compressed on an old mattress. He heard another squeak – he was back at the wardrobe – and then the sounds of coat hangers being shifted, re-arranged. He pictured clothes being taken down, folded, put in a bag and the hanger being replaced. The Tiger was packing...

He had tensed and was sitting half-upright, but allowed himself to relax and to flop down again. *Why shouldn't he pack?* He'd already said he wasn't hanging about. It made sense to pack the night before.

And yet it felt like abandonment. The Tiger had plans, whereas he had none and no need for any. Despair washed over him in a chill wave that left him almost mourning for his own forfeit life. People with planned deaths usually wanted to die, but he didn't. It wasn't a lack of religious fervour; he'd happily kill for the Jihad. He had reasoned it all through so many times.

The next sound made him jump. He was instantly tense, alert. The Tiger had unlocked his door but the snib had snapped shut with the dull smack of a hammer blow. His bedroom door creaked as did his first gentle footfall. He was trying to sneak out, thinking that his bomber was asleep. The man was running away. He'd set it up but now he was prepared to drift away, back into the shadows like a skulking coward, and yet when the history of this time was written his name would feature throughout. He was the mastermind, the great thinker, the planner, the brains, but no one would say that he had also cut and run. No one would say that he had taken to his heels long before the bombs had exploded. No one would know that.

He lay in bed, quite still, seething and still listening to all the small noises that should have passed him by as he slept. No one would ever know that the great planner had run from the field of battle. Here, the general left his troops to fight on alone. What sort of battle was that? Suddenly his anger threatened to burst out like a greyhound from a trap and he stood, getting to the door in two strides. He pulled the door open and sure enough The Tiger – looking sheepish rather than tigerish – was standing, bags in hand, outside his room.

He looked silly. He looked like a school boy caught sneaking out of his dorm.

'Where are you going?', he demanded.

'There is no point in …'

'You are running off', accused Khan. He jabbed a finger at the other man's chest.

'You knew I was leaving.'

'After! I thought you were leaving after the bomb! But instead you sneak off the night before. You send me to my death but you make sure that no harm can come to you.'

'You knew it would be this way!'

'Did I?'

'Of course, you did. This isn't anything new. You are a suicide bomber, a martyr. You know how these things are done. That is what you signed up for, so why act so surprised?'

'But you live and I die', said Khan. His anger only intensified. He didn't want to listen to any more puerile justification for the man's actions when it was clear that he was nothing more than a coward.

'And when did the plan have any other course? My job is not the same as yours. You become a martyr for the Jihad and I go into hiding to plan the next operation. You have the honour of dying for Islam.'

'Ha! We could swap if you like.' His voice almost cracked and, unbidden, tears welled up in his eyes.

'That isn't going to happen. That isn't what we have planned. Besides you are trained to carry out the mission and I am not. You have had time to prepare yourself for Paradise and I have not.' He shook his head angrily but he was obviously scared lest his plot collapse around him. If he had only known that greater danger existed. 'And keep your voice down. Do you really want everyone to know what we are doing?'

'Fuck them!', shouted Khan. 'Why should I care? I am a dead man. You get to live and I get to die.'

'You get to go to Paradise you mean, and keep your voice down.'

That instruction proved too much for Khan. The two men were roughly equal in size but The Tiger was unprepared for the punch thrown by his opposite number and fell back in pain and astonishment as the younger man's fist connected with his nose. A spray of blood erupted from a split in the flesh and he toppled over his holdall, landing heavily on the carpet. Khan was on him in a second and bent over to rain blows down. His fists were sticky-slippery with blood but he kept punching, punching, punching until his victim's feeble efforts at self-defence stopped.

Finally, he straightened and looked down at his opponent. He felt nothing, no emotion, no regret, no pain, no worry, nothing. In his mind's eye he pictured Muhammad Ali in the ring peering down at the felled Sonny Liston, the animalistic boxer he should never have been able to beat. It was an iconic image and he revelled in his own particular interpretation of it. He was mildly dismayed to see that The Tiger – a tiger no longer – was still breathing, and he thought about how he could change that, opting for a short trip to the kitchen where a selection of lethal knives sat in a wooden block, the sort of thing the police constantly warned people not to have in their kitchens lest intruders decided to arm themselves when challenged. Now someone else's carelessness played into his hands.

'Don't move', he said to the broken figure at his feet. He enjoyed the joke. He felt tough and alive. He was a killer, as good with his hands as he was with a bomb. He reached down and extracted The Tiger's fat wallet from the inside of his jacket. That would keep him going for some time. The fact that he didn't have to die was like a drug in his veins. He had never known a high like this. He was going to kill someone and no one would ever discover why the man had died, or who had done it. The kitchen door swung open easily and a few swift paces took him to the knife block. Any of the available weapons would have done the job but he selected the longest one and discarded the others before retracing his steps.

He took his time, creeping back slowly to take his man by surprise but the tables had turned, and he found that The Tiger had been in better shape than he had suspected, making his escape through the door and out onto the street. The trail of blood was short – he hadn't got far – but now he was clear of the house, staggering down the short path to the iron gate which led to the pavement. He set off after him, wearing only his pyjama bottoms. His feet were bare and the loose gravel of the path stabbed at the soft flesh as he ran. He shouted, but The Tiger, stunned though he was, continued to run, lurching drunkenly from side to side. A taxi passed, seeming to slow before pulling away again. The knife blade glinted in the headlights as he lifted it above his head and brought it down in one powerful thrust. He felt it crunch through bone and gristle as it entered The Tiger's body in the gap between his clavicle and his shoulder blades.

The man screamed and fell into the low hedge of the next door garden. As The Tiger's weight shifted, his body toppled into the garden and the knife handle was pulled from Khan's grip. But his victim wasn't dead and he tried to vault the hedge to finish the job. The hedge cut at his abdomen but he felt no pain, for the urge to kill his new enemy was so strong that mere mortal pain meant nothing and was subsumed by the blood lust he felt.

The Tiger was weakened and had become easy prey. He landed heavily on the ground next to him and took hold of the knife once again, trying to pull it free. From somewhere he heard screams and shouts but he continued to pull as the other man writhed on the ground alternately whimpering and calling out like a dying beast. No matter what he did, the knife wouldn't come loose and he had to also fend off The Tiger's increasingly weakened blows. He decided on a different tack and tried to push the knife further in. The Tiger's screams were like a banshee wail now but he sensed that the man's life force, if such a thing existed, was draining away.

The distant sound of sirens brought him up short and concentrated his mind on the need for escape. He cast a quick glance down at his foe, decided that he couldn't possibly survive his wounds, and ran back into his own house to grab a few items of clothing and an Adidas shoulder bag he kept packed. From the corner of his eye he saw bystanders keeping their distance but still eager to know what was going on. These were the people who slowed down to look at motorway accidents and who lived their lives through the vicarious pain of others. None of them had the bottle to act, although some would later claim that they had tried to intervene. The lights were on, the door open and yet the house no longer felt as if he belonged there. He ran up the stairs to his room, pulled on a T-shirt, jeans and trainers. He grabbed his wallet, a jacket and then ran downstairs to retrieve the keys for The Tiger's hire car.

The sirens were closer now and he felt the first surge of panic. The keys he found on the hall dresser and he scooped them up as he charged back through the hall and into the night. The car was right there, a Nissan Qashqai, and its four way flashers blinked as he pressed the remote fob but his attention was immediately taken by the blue flashing lights at the far end of the street. He knew his escape would be on foot. He dropped the fob and ran. He had money for the train and he intended still to complete his mission but without dying in the process. And now there was no one to stop him.

***

What else had happened? They had gone chasing round Scotland to find Jack Sullivan. It had seemed ridiculous and yet they had managed to find him. Not only that but he was now in London as part of the surveillance team.

A tiny hammer beat at his temples but this was not a severe hangover by any means, although another few minutes in bed would be welcome. A shower and a coffee would see him right. Today might be the day. What would he do when the whole thing was over? They would find something else for him to do but it would be dull in comparison. But there would also be a lot of questions to answer and he wasn't looking forward to that, especially since he himself had blundered spectacularly by not logging off his computer. A bit of dullness might be a good thing – a change was as good as a rest.

He lay still and tried to assess the amount of pain he was in. It was a relief to establish that his hangover was the most minor sort, something he could easily deal with as the day unfolded. The alarm clock informed him redly of the time – 5.54 – which left him with six minutes before he had to rise, shower, get ready and leave, but he knew that he could stretch things out for another fifteen minutes and still get to work on time.

Twenty-one minutes. Enough time to doze and prepare his mind for a new day, one in which he no longer worked with Claire. It wasn't that he expected to miss her exactly but it would be odd not to have her in close proximity. Suddenly his mind snapped him awake. He had overlooked the most obvious thing of all. The record which had been deleted and which she had intimated had been removed by Wendy, actually gave details of the real terrorist. She – Claire – had taken it out and decided that a different Asian was going to become their suspect, and all along he had just accepted what she'd said. Not only that but the man they had recruited to identify him – Jack Sullivan – actually knew nothing about the real terrorist.

Now he had to get to work and warn them. He was bolt upright. He didn't want to ring in with this news. He had to see Andrew in person. Tom tried to recall the name he had found and hoped desperately that it could be restored somehow to the database. Did she know enough to erase it permanently? Surely Claire didn't have the clearance and the access to do that? He suspected now that this marked the end of his career – he had been too careless at every step – but he still stood a chance of being the man who found The Bomber before it was too late.

***

He ran until his lungs felt like they might burst, and then he stopped for a second before continuing at a brisk pace. He was headed for the town centre and the railway station where he hoped to get a train to London. The night air rang with the sound of sirens; the police were out in force to find him, but in fact that probably only equated to a few officers and a lot of noise. He was glad.

The streets were nearly empty and, apart from a few taxis and delivery lorries taking groceries to the shops, he was alone. Only three minutes or so passed before he reasoned that his journey was in vain. After all, if the cops had a description of the assailant and if that assailant was now a murderer on the run on foot, then they would eventually swamp the area and every exit point in an attempt to catch him. This was probably their best chance to do so, for once he had escaped the confines of Winchester he could theoretically finish up in any part of the country. So, for now their brief seemed straightforward – look for a young, panic stricken Pakistani, dressed in casual clothes. There were so few people around that he would stick out like… like a young Pakistani in casual clothes. He further reasoned that the trains would shortly stop running or might already have done so, in which case he would be caught on CCTV looking up at the information screens trying to figure out when he could get a train to London in the morning. His plan was unravelling.

He stood still, pulling into the shadows, thinking, knowing that there was a solution but that it might be just out of reach. He cursed The Tiger, fervently hoped he was dead, and strained to think of a way to get to London. The euphoria of having killed his oppressor was long gone but the blood remained on his hands, slowly congealing and cracking like thick make-up. A mist rolled in, seeming to barrel down the street, over the cars and through the trees which struck skywards through the crumbling pavements. He supposed it gave him extra cover but it also brought a chill and for the first time he felt as if his body temperature was coming back down to normal and that he should put his coat on. *Was the coat part of the description the police had been given or were they looking for someone in a green Superdry T-shirt?* There was no way to know and he supposed it made little difference.

He would find somewhere to sleep, and possibly have a wash in the public toilets in the morning. Having a plan, even one as vague as that, settled his nerves. Until he remembered that he had to be in London early. He cursed beneath his breath and checked in his wallet to see if he had the cash for the long taxi ride to London. *Eighty pounds and some change in his pocket, would that do it? Would the driver even agree to take him? On the positive side, the journey could be accomplished quickly at this time of night. On the negative, he looked very suspicious. Did the police tip off the taxi drivers to look out for suspicious passengers?*

But he was running out of options. He had forgotten about The Tiger's wallet and the money it must surely have contained. He stepped out of the shadows and began walking in the direction of the station and what was left of the taxi rank so late at night.

***

Chapter Seventeen

He'd shaved roughly, wanting to get to work with as much haste as was possible in London so early in the morning. He made straight for Andy's temporary office in COBR and was dismayed to find that his boss had been delayed. Tom had wanted to avoid a phone call but now he reached for his work telephone and put the call through. As it began ringing, he stepped into the office, closed the door quietly so as not to attract attention to his presence and then parked himself on the edge of the desk where, just the previous day, Claire had sat as an integral part of the team. All of a sudden it seemed like a lifetime ago.

'Andy, it's Tom. I need to speak to you', he said. His heart thumped in his chest. According to his watch it was seven thirty and time was slipping away.

'I'm in a meeting at the minute Tom. We think we might have picked up our man.'

'I doubt it Andy. That's what I need to talk to you about. When you say that you think that you have picked him up, is this on the word of Jack Sullivan?'

'Yes. He was up early and spotted someone getting off the tube and then hanging about near Hamleys. He is dressed as a cleaning contractor but he is just hanging about and…'

'Sorry, Andy. I don't mean to interrupt but I don't think that is likely to be your man. Jack Sullivan doesn't know what The Bomber looks like. He thinks he does but this was all Claire's doing…'

'What?'

'Just let me finish. I was looking up the names we had, the ones we got according to the initials we were given from the cops in Perth.'

'Okay.'

'I found a record of the person I thought it was. I went out to the deli and left my computer logged on. When I got back the record had been deleted and when I went back in, I found that it had gone from the database altogether.'

'You shouldn't have left it logged on.'

Tom crossed his eyes and shook his head in frustration. Now was not the time.

'I know that. It was careless and I should have just come clean but that isn't important right now. Claire claimed to have found the right person so we started investigating him and that is how we ended up with Jack. He had seen this fella in Afghanistan and it was just about the only record we could link to the name, but it is the wrong man. It's bloody unlikely that the person he has spotted this morning is the guy he spoke to in Afghanistan by the way, but I suppose he feels pressured into giving a positive ID.' Tom shook his head, hoping desperately that his message was getting through. 'You can sack me later Andy, whatever you have to do, but this bloke outside Hamleys? I doubt very much if he is your man.'

'Okay. You're sure?'

'I'm as sure as I can be. If Claire hadn't been arrested, then it would never have occurred to me but now it all fits. You need to get here now with our best IT bod and try to recover the name she deleted. That is our man. Christ knows how she could ever have known that. But we have our man if we can just get that record back.'

'Listen, we'll pick him up just in case. I'm on my way. Stay where you are. I have a few calls to make. I want you to tell all this to the duty officer and let him make the decision.

If you are right it might be days before the real terrorist turns up. Or for all we know he is here already and completely at large.'

***

The fare had been over one hundred pounds – he hadn't bothered to check the meter after a while because he had decided to kill the driver when he got there anyway. Having killed so many people already gave him a degree of freedom, for now; as the saying went, he might as well be hanged for a sheep as a lamb. His one regret was that his victim this time had been a fellow Muslim but he simply couldn't take the risk of telling him about his mission or of getting into an altercation over the money. The driver was collateral damage, a phrase beloved of the Yankees when they blew apart a safe house full of civilians just to get to one insurgent or fighter.

And now the man lay behind the wheel of his elderly Volkswagen Passat, looking at peace and sound asleep but actually dead. It had taken a couple of hours to get here, plenty of time to plan the murder. It had been a simple matter to wait until he'd pulled on the handbrake before reaching forward with a nylon strap he'd removed from his bag and throttling the poor man. He had fought of course and tried to pull the cord away from his throat. His feet had kicked, kicked, kicked at the dashboard, but his strength had quickly waned and when he was still Khan sat back and spent time regaining his composure. He was out of breath and coated in sweat. That he was sitting with only a corpse for company no longer seemed strange in the context of his recent life, in which killing by any means had become commonplace and routine. He could kill as often and as brutally as he wanted to now. If caught he would die in jail regardless.

He wound the window down and let some cool air pervade the old car, washing away the body heat he had generated and the smell of sweat from both men. When he had killed Ingrid back in Germany, the effort, both mental and physical, had left him drained, but now, apart from the general fatigue he felt, it left him invigorated. It was a necessary evil, part of a larger plan, and he was glad that he had done it. He was a more rounded killer now and could bring a greater range of skills to the Jihad – and to think they had wanted him to die and let it all go to waste. The idiots.

As he waited for the driver to turn up he glanced over at the car. It might be part of his escape plan. He'd already made the phone call and, although he hadn't received a reply, he felt confident that he would get away. Maybe the Channel Tunnel would be the best way; a drive down to the south of France to get a ship to North Africa. There he would disappear. He knew he could do it. He felt the bulk in his pocket - The Tiger's wallet. *Damn*. He could have paid the man and spared his life.

Oh well. The wallet was stuffed with notes – fifties and twenties – along with cards. He was probably rich, and since no one knew who the hell The Tiger was he was free to spend his money at will. Some things just worked out better than you could ever expect.

By the time the lorry driver had arrived, he'd pulled the cab driver clear of his vehicle and dumped the body behind a set of galvanised industrial wheelie bins. He adjusted the seat and parked the Volkswagen down a narrow lane next to the lock-up. He noted with satisfaction that it still had half a tank of diesel. All of these things – these details – were signs that his mission was actually in better shape than anyone had planned for. He breathed in deeply, filling his lungs with a dank air that somehow revived him.

The lorry driver turned up five minutes early, eyeing Khan with suspicion and dislike. He didn't know why and cared less. He didn't speak as he rolled the door open and climbed into the cab. He threw down a set of coveralls and ignored Khan as he hopped around, first getting one leg in and then the other. The driver – he thought he was called Saddique – started the engine and eased the truck forwards, forcing Khan to step to one side. If he was at all impressed by the part Khan was playing in this great undertaking he kept it well hidden. He was clearly not a man given to ceremony or delay, and as Khan strode around to the driver's door to get inside he gave him a curt instruction.

'Close the garage door', he said sourly. Khan felt a moment of anger but complied. The man didn't seem to quite understand who he was dealing with, but he would someday. In fact, if he didn't change his tune he might be getting to Paradise sooner than he had planned.

The door came down slowly on its electric motor, emitting a rhythmic squeak that must have woken at least some of the neighbours. That done, he re-joined the man in the cab, giving him a look which he hoped expressed dislike. The driver looked straight ahead and said nothing; his enmity was wasted.

The driver selected first gear and pulled away. The journey to the main road was short and he was a good driver, taking his time, looking for other road users and giving them both a smooth ride as though he was on test. His driving style revealed something to Khan and that realisation led to another. Firstly, the man was driving with such care because he feared that otherwise the bombs might go off. Secondly, he was not a volunteer, hence the extreme distaste with which he carried out his task.

'Why are you doing this?', asked Khan.

The driver kept his gaze fixed on the road and for a moment it seemed as if he wouldn't reply, but eventually he said, 'I will get in trouble if I don't cooperate.'

'Trouble?'

They had stopped at a junction and the driver looked both ways before pulling out behind a police car. A few drops of rain smashed themselves on the windscreen.

'My son went to Afghanistan to fight the Americans and whoever else turned up. He soon realised that he wasn't cut out for such things but when he tried to get home, they prevented him from doing so. You can probably guess the rest. If I do this, they will not only let him go but they will arrange the travel and get him back into the country with no questions asked. I don't support your cause but I want my son back.'

'You will go to Paradise', said Khan.

For the first time the driver looked over at him.

'I will go to hell with you', he corrected bitterly

They drove the slowly filling streets in silence after that. Khan already knew how ruthless the people for whom he worked could be. He felt a pang of sympathy for the driver, but it didn't last long for they both had work to do.

'Here is the first bin', said Saddique nodding down the road. 'I will pull up alongside and put my hazard flashers on. In and out, okay? Let's not drag this out.'

When they were in position, Khan jumped down and jogged round to the side of the truck, lifting down the bomb like he had never done anything else in his entire life. It was heavy but he had to make it look as if it was empty – why would they put a full bin in place? Then he trotted to the front with the bin on his back, removed the full one, replete with fast food wrappers, and slotted the bomb in place. Pieces of litter detached themselves as he made his way back to the truck with the full bin. He slipped it into the bin area, closed the gate and returned to the cab. One down, seven to go.

***

'Look, this is probably nothing but that truck is going around emptying the bins.'

The other soldier looked over.

'What's wrong with that?'

'I would have thought they did that at night. You know, after the day's litter has been collected.'

They continued to watch, following the grey and blue truck as it turned the corner and stopped at the next bin. They were assisted by a break in the two blocks which aided their view. The truck stopped and they got a quick view of the passenger descending from the cab. He was dressed in overalls.

'Not sure if that's anything suspect but we'll ring it in. Someone else can decide.'

***

'We have a link to the database and an ICT bod is on his way. Have you remembered the name?' Andrew looked dishevelled and exhausted.

'Mohammed *Ifran* Khan. I have checked the database again and his name is still not there.'

'Ifran? You're sure about this?'

'Pretty sure.'

Andrew looked at him for a long moment and then nodded slowly.

'Okay, we're going with that name. Mohammed Ifran Khan. I'll get it out there while we're waiting.'

Andrew had logged onto Claire's computer and proceeded to send an email informing all the relevant people what had happened.

'Our lords and masters will be in at nine. We are due to see them first. You should be flattered – you're the first item on the agenda.'

'The end of my career. Great.'

'We'll have to see. You made a mistake. Compared to what Claire did that is very little.'

'Do we know anything more?'

'She's with the police now. I think she is telling them everything. After things started going wrong, they began intercepting mobile phone transmissions, yours included, probably mine too. Claire was sending texts to various people connected with ISIS, giving the game away. It seems certain that the two druggies up in Scotland were bumped off because of information she gave away. That's all I know.'

'We don't know why?'

'Not yet but it'll all come out in the wash.' Andy gave a mirthless smile. 'We might emerge from this with some credit. A bit of luck is required.'

'That would make a change', muttered Tom as his boss left the room.

***

They were at the seventh bin.

'Nearly there', said Khan. The driver just grunted. The windscreen wipers slopped across the glass in one languid motion, clearing his view of the street. Kahn hadn't bothered to tell the driver that he wasn't planning on killing himself in the explosion of the eighth bin but felt reassured that this man Saddique really wouldn't care.

He was still surprised to find himself sympathetic to the man's plight. After all, none of this was his fault and who wouldn't take extreme action to save the life of one of their children? He rarely thought about his own parents, but he did so now. They must have given up on him, but did they still feel the pain of his loss? It was a sacrifice he had taken on with ease and it made him wary about ever having children of his own. If they could leave behind their family with such ease as he had done, then what was the point? But parents never gave up loving their children…

When they stopped, he hopped out of the cab and retrieved the bomb-laden bin. He felt quite light-hearted about the whole process now, although he hadn't got a reply to his text – communications in Libya were bound to be patchy so he wasn't unduly worried. The Arabs had agreed to hide him if it became necessary and he trusted them, if only because he could pay well. Maybe there was more to it, some mutual regard, but having access to plenty of cash would seal the deal. Cash was a good fall-back in any situation and, remembering the plush hotel they had stayed at the end of their desert odyssey, he knew that The Tiger had plenty of it.

The bin slotted neatly into place and he took away the full receptacle, almost with a spring in his step. The grim-faced driver pulled away at once, plainly wanting to bring this terrible episode in his life to an end. Khan was going to speak, to offer some words of encouragement, but no words came and he clamped his mouth shut. It wouldn't be long before they never had to see or speak to one another again.

The traffic was thickening now as they merged with London's rush hour. They could not have appeared any more innocuous, no one could ever have guessed at the secret they shared or at the destruction which was about to befall the city. Khan felt a resurgence of pride and of hope. This truly was his *metier*. He was made for this moment and, simply because he no longer had to die, he would have many more moments in a similar vein in years to come. They might try to track him down but they wouldn't succeed, and to know that he was The Bomber who brought London to a standstill was reward enough for him.

'What do you do when you have dropped me off?', he asked the driver.

There was the usual delay as the man, here under duress, formulated a non-incriminating answer. He would distance himself from these events in every way possible.

'I will go home and lie low.'

'You take the truck back to the lock-up?'

'Yes.'

'The police will be looking for you.'

'They will probably find me.'

'What will you do then?'

'Nothing. What can I do? I only want to save my son's life. They will put me in jail and everyone will despise me, but my son will be freed. That is all I care about. He made a mistake – lots of young people do – but he deserves a second chance. I can't deny him that chance.'

They were approaching the eighth and last bin. Two cars were illegally parked next to it, a red Saab and an old model Porsche 911.

'Will you take me back to the garage with you?', asked Khan. He was already thinking of his own escape in the cab he had liberated from its owner the previous night.

'But you have to stay here and explode the bombs…'

'I can explode the bombs anywhere. I can do it as we drive away.'

'But aren't you supposed to blow yourself up?', said Saddique, confused. He felt a momentary panic at the thought of this attack not going ahead and of him never seeing his son again.

'Look, it doesn't matter. The bombs will still go off. I just need to get away. I don't plan to die.'

'But my son…'

'They will still let him go. They just want this attack to happen and they will be satisfied.' Saddique looked doubtful but he pulled up to the last bin, blocking the traffic as Khan jumped down from the cab and did his usual gentle trot round to the back of the truck. An angry commuter sounded the horn of his Lexus but Khan ignored him which he thought was the appropriate response for a bin man. He collected the bin with a feeling of satisfaction. He was almost light-headed with relief and excitement and already making his plans for watching the resulting devastation on the TV. That he had no TV to watch hadn't yet occurred to him.

***

'Hold on. Look at this.' Staff-sergeant Owen Lucas was a veteran of Afghanistan, Iraq and various other lesser conflicts. He knew, just knew, that something was going on. But he wanted confirmation.

'That fucking bin lorry – look. Those bins are usually emptied at night.'

His oppo, Corporal Charles, crawled over and looked directly over the parapet.

The street, ten storeys below, was packed with traffic now, a motor-driven morass congregating around an epicentre of one Veolia bin lorry. From both directions and three side streets, a variety of cars and vans had become stuck.

Charles drew a deep breath.

'Get someone in?'

'Get 'em in and quick.'

The pressel switch clicked as he sent a message to the nearest team, giving the location of the bin lorry and a brief reason for their concern. He reckoned that within thirty seconds the truck would be surrounded by armed troops.

He was wrong.

They were there in fifteen.

***

'Thunderbolt.'

'Roger.'

The four man team had been waiting for that single codeword, and upon receiving it they immediately emerged from the Mondeo with purpose. Each was armed with the ubiquitous Heckler and Koch SMG which fired a 9mm bullet with the right mix of accuracy and kinetic energy to kill a terrorist but not a bystander. That was the theory, and it generally worked out that way in the hands of specialists.

They rounded the corner, sprinting past a police control centre mounted on the back of a truck, past an optician and a pharmacy, and round another corner before fanning out, four muzzles pointed at the refuse wagon sitting to their front, maybe fifty yards away. Alert for any movement, they paused and took rough aim, the Veolia truck large in their sights, two occupants in the cab. Distant sirens rent the air.

'There they are boys', said their commander. His voice was neutral but his heart beat faster in preparation for action. He had the utmost confidence in his men as they closed in on the target.

***

Andy stood in the briefing room with the PM, Home Secretary, the Deputy Chief Constable of the Met, Maurice Gilmore and Raymond Garvin, minister without portfolio. Next to him Tom might have felt important if it had not been for the immense blunder to which he had contributed.

'Bring us up to date if you will', said the PM. She looked tired, but as ever she was immaculately dressed and totally on top of the situation.

'We have the identity of The Bomber – or we think we do – Mohammed Ifran Khan. His file has been deleted from our database but we are in the process of getting it restored, and if there is a photo of him we will get it circulated. Armed troops have surrounded a refuse wagon on Bond Street. There are two Asian men inside. No further details on that. We have established that our mole was Claire West. She is in police custody and telling them everything she has done. It seems her fiancée is being held in Afghanistan. He is a lieutenant in the army. If she fed his captors information, he would be returned unharmed. That was the deal.'

'Christ', muttered Garvin. He wasn't a totally committed fan of the security services and at times had been a thorn in their side.

'The time to pass judgement on that young lady will come', said the PM gently. 'Who knows how any of us would behave in the same circumstances?' Her reprimand, so softly delivered, had the effect of silencing Garvin. He smiled. 'What next?', she asked, directing her question at Andy.

'We await the outcome of the situation with the Veolia truck. Perhaps we have got our man.'

The PM nodded. 'Good plan. Now, any questions?'

***

Khan and Saddique sat completely still in the cab. The former had counted four automatic weapons pointed in his direction although he had no doubt that there were more. Khan thought that he could still escape, although it was not going to be easy to do so. No longer was he the invisible man. Now he had an identity, a face and a body that could be perforated in seconds by thirty or more bullets.

Khan knew that he had to communicate. They needed to know that he could blow central London sky high and they had to provide him with a means of escape. There was a deal to be made, but he had not planned for this at all and didn't know how to begin. Nor was he sure how much they understood about the potency of the weapon in his control. *Did they know anything?* How he and Saddique had come to their attention was obvious; they had created a massive traffic jam. *Why had they been looking for a bin lorry?* That was the bit he didn't understand. But it hardly mattered now.

He pressed a button in the arm rest to lower the window. They wouldn't shoot. For all they knew he might be an innocent man.

The armed men remained in place as a police officer approached on foot, armed only with a megaphone. Now came the tricky bit, he supposed. It would be easy for them to communicate with him, but in his current state he couldn't say the same for himself. He physically didn't have the voice to tell them about his situation and what he was capable of doing. He felt that if he tried to speak he would merely croak. A stab of panic punched his solar plexus. He looked over at Saddique and saw that his driver was paralysed with fear. But to have saved himself from death only to have that new hope taken away again was more than he could bear. It would have been better to have remained a suicide bomber, but that option was long gone. He was a survivor, or that was his definite intention if he could manage it.

Choked with emotion, mainly fear, he shouted out of the window, 'I have a bomb.' He wasn't sure if his words reached the ears of the armed men to his front. The street was noisy with sirens, shouts and the cop with the megaphone giving instructions that he didn't understand. The megaphone distorted his words. *What was he asking him to do?*

He felt a surge of panic as if his plan was unravelling like the rope he was using to scale a cliff. His mind was crowded with thoughts of the bombs he had planted and the devastation they would bring about.

The cop shouted through the megaphone again. The words and his meaning were lost, utterly wasted. *What is he saying? Why can't he understand me?!*

Khan recalled the Antwerp bomb and how he had watched the aftermath on TV with a mixture of detachment and satisfaction, something like ecstasy really. That had been a leap forward for the Jihad, but nothing compared to this attack. He was on the cusp of making history. Pride filled his chest but he wished that the noise would stop, for it clouded his thoughts, filled his brain when he needed to find a solution.

The pressure of the situation gave him a clarity of thought he didn't imagine possible. He needed to extricate himself from the crime he was about to commit. He needed time to think, to once again put the security services on the back foot and give him that precious opportunity.

He cut out the electronic rambling of the megaphone and focussed his gaze on the armed men who had him in their sights. It was they who needed to understand the situation. It was they who stood between him and victory. But they looked resolute, unwavering. He hoped that he looked the same to them.

'I've got a bomb', he shouted again. Even to his own ears his voice sounded weak. He thought he sounded pitiable rather than defiant...

The cop stopped talking into the megaphone for a second. One of the armed men shouted at him and he slowly moved to one side, almost apologetically.

'I've got a b...'

***

Trooper Mullan had been born in Larne in County Antrim twenty-six years previously. He had joined the Irish Guards at the age of sixteen as a means of escaping a town which he felt had no hold over him. He had done the usual tours of Iraq and Afghanistan, being mentioned in dispatches for rescuing an injured comrade during a firefight, before volunteering for 22 SAS with whom he had served for three years. It was he who heard the words shouted by the Asian man from the cab of the truck and it was he who pulled the trigger, firing two shots – a double tap.

'You didn't shout a warning', said his corporal moments later. The air was alive with sirens.

'Army, stop or I fire', said Mullan quietly and without conviction.

'*Before* you shoot 'em.'

'Fuckit.'

The time for explanations would come later.

**

A single bullet hit him in the chest, missing his heart and lungs. The second missed altogether and terrified Saddique who sat statue-still in the driver's seat and prayed for the ordeal to end. He watched in abject horror and from the corner of his eye, lest he be shot for moving too suddenly, seeing for the first time that the man he had ferried around from bin to bin held a small device in his right hand. It looked like a television remote control, of all things.

For the time being, there were no more shots, which was a relief, but of all the protagonists in this little drama, only he realised that The Bomber wasn't actually dead. Certainly, life flowed from his chest wound in a sticky waterfall, his store of energy ebbed.

But not quickly enough.

Khan was slumped but still breathing and muttering something incomprehensible. He fervently wished that the man would simply die but instead he was playing about with the remote control as if he was unfamiliar with it or couldn't quite find the right button to press.

Saddique dared not move but looked on in horror as Khan finally pushed a tiny orange key with befuddled, near-geriatric deliberation. As if matching the force of Khan's movements, a small 'crump' and a puff of black smoke wafting from the bin indicated he had managed to detonate his bomb.

But that was all. Nothing more. They were not lifted into the sky, engulfed in a fireball, torn asunder...

Something had gone wrong, and although they – the terrified driver, the bystanders and the armed men – were still alive and unhurt, a new sense of panic had taken over. The street was suddenly alive with activity but Saddique could only look on through cataracts of tears.

Saddique wanted to shout a warning. In his death throes, Khan was pressing the same little key over and over again but nothing else happened. He was like a blind man now. A second bullet, belatedly fired, caught The Bomber on the top of his head as he glared at the detonator in his lap. Saddique jumped at the impact but then fought to remain perfectly still.

More police officers had moved in and were beginning to shepherd people away from the scene of the misfiring bomb blast. In three other locations in the centre of London, similar small blasts were witnessed, but in another four locations nothing at all happened, despite the presence of recently planted dirty bombs.

The attack had been a failure. With a gun still trained on him, Saddique lowered himself from the cab to the ground where he was ordered to disrobe to prove that he was not carrying any form of suicide bomb vest. Visibly shaking, his brown skin stark against his white underwear, he complied with every instruction he was given and then the police closed in and made an arrest.

Khan's body was left in the cab until a bomb team had checked out the truck for further devices. It took until midnight, during which time the whole area was cordoned off. Much later the duty physician, Dr Pulheems, certified the terrorist dead.

***

'Can we do a deal?'

'A deal? What sort of deal?', asked the detective. He knew exactly what Saddique was angling for, just as he knew there was no deal to be made.

'I show you where the bombs are and I don't go to jail.' He sounded rightly doubtful.

'I am a police officer, not a judge', he said impatiently. When Saddique's shoulders sagged, he changed tack, trying to encourage continued cooperation. 'But it would be something we would mention. Something in your favour.'

'Okay. I understand. I was trying to save my son…'

'Let's find the bombs first and then you can make your statement, okay?'

The prisoner nodded, sadly.

'And let's be quick about it. There is a car coming to take you round. You know where they are, don't you?'

Saddique nodded again and then released a shuddering sigh. He tried to picture his route in reverse, barely noticing the unmarked Subaru that pulled up alongside.

'Get in', said the detective. 'Let's find those bombs.'

***

Saddique was able to show the police where each bomb had been planted and laboriously, with every available team at work, they were dismantled and taken away for disposal. Saddique was obsequious now, the willing helper for whom nothing was too much trouble. He hoped that he had done enough to ensure his son's safety, but he had inherited another set of masters now and they too had to be satisfied with his actions. He was caught between the forces of good and evil, even if neither side would have recognised their allotted role.

The clean-up operation happened as quickly and discreetly as the deployment. The radioactive material was taken, under guard, to a nuclear reprocessing facility in Lancashire. Its origin was never discussed at the plant and its fate never disclosed to the public.

The entire area, including the Houses of Parliament and Buckingham Palace was checked for radioactive fall-out, but the all clear was given within hours. The attack had been a total failure.

***

In a desert in North Africa, the old Bedou finally found a phone signal and immediately a message came through from the young man he had befriended. He had thought long and hard about the man's plans and tacitly agreed to help, although the chances of these vicious men he worked for actually letting the young man live seemed slight.

He looked at the text but decided not to reply. There was every chance that they were onto him now. The old Arab didn't want any trouble from the Americans or the British. Besides he had a new contract to take care of. Yet another of these psychopaths was out here testing the same sort of bomb as the last lot. This one they were going to plant in a school. When the school went up, people would be scared to send their own children off to school and the parents would have to stay at home and then no one would go to work and chaos would ensue.

They loved their plan and that was why they shared it with him, which was a mistake. He asked which country they were going to attack, but they didn't know, or so they said. He didn't approve, but money was money and besides, he had the option of passing this new information on to his friends in the CIA who were also generous with their funds. A double pay day? It wouldn't be the first time...

Epilogue

The report took some time to compile and the list of recommendations in it was lengthy. Tom was interviewed at length, as was Claire, the difference being that her interviews took place in a prison cell. Tom held onto his job, but reading between the lines it was quite clear to him that he would never get promoted and that the trust between employer and employee was gone. He found himself not caring less.

Lt Col Tony Murray was the senior bomb disposal officer involved in the operation, and with his team of experienced EOD officers and warrant officers he set about examining and compiling a report on the London bombs. The information gathered would be added to the vast canon of knowledge collected over many years by men of the Royal Engineers, Royal Army Ordnance Corps and latterly by the Royal Logistics Corps. These men and their forebears had been dealing with unexploded bombs and terrorist devices for generations, but nothing was ever discarded in terms of know-how, no matter how sophisticated the game became. From the hastily trained or untrained RE volunteers of World War Two who had dealt with the Luftwaffe's unexploded bombs, basically making up new procedures as they went along, through the EOD teams who had served in Northern Ireland during *Op Banner*, the campaign in Northern Ireland, everything was recorded. There was no one better trained or equipped to deal with bombs.

The bombs were examined in detail once the radioactive material had been removed and safely treated. It was discovered that four of the bombs had been out of range of the transmitter and could never have been detonated from the location of the eighth bomb. Radio signals naturally attenuate over distance, but with tall buildings sited between the transmitters and the receivers the signal soon lost its energy. The four bombs which did explode were faulty. The detonators were of the incorrect type for the explosive, so although a small puff of smoke was emitted from each device, the explosive force required to ignite the SEMTEX was simply not there. It was like trying to set light to a log with a single match.

Murray would have the task of writing up the report but was able to deliver his own personal findings quite succinctly.

'These bombs were complete bollocks', he said scathingly.

However, when asked to provide an estimate of the casualty rate had the bombs gone off, he reckoned eight hundred to one thousand deaths, and many more injuries. This figure was later reduced by a parliamentary committee. His estimate for the area of London put out of action – he said twelve square miles – was accepted and often quoted. The figures for the duration and cost of the clean-up operation came from a hurriedly assembled combined government and council team, who reckoned upon a month for the first and three billion pounds for the second, when lost revenue and loss of confidence in the economy were factored in.

Jack Sullivan was disappointed that, in the end, his services were not required. He didn't know that he was a diversion deployed by Claire in her treacherous plot. But he had known from the start that he couldn't really identify The Bomber. The information he had been able to provide was sparse and out of date. They got very excited when it seemed as if they had found their man and for a little while he had almost believed it himself as he watched the monitor. His brief stay with the Special Reconnaissance Regiment gave him a taste for military life once again. He rejoined his old regiment and almost immediately volunteered for the SRR.

He failed their selection.

Liz and Mark both got rapid promotions, going back into uniform as sergeants but based at different stations where they tried to battle crime with steadily dwindling numbers of police officers and resources. Burglaries, untaxed cars, domestic abuse and dog shit on pavements brought with them a certain amount of routine and certainty. They had tiny numbers of police officers to cover huge areas but they continued to do their best and soaked up all the criticism about the general lack of police presence, criticism that should really have been fielded by their political masters in Edinburgh.

Saddique was put on trial for his complicity in the terror plot, and his barrister's pleas for a degree of clemency to be considered fell on deaf ears simply because of the scale of the plot in which he had been involved. He was given a life sentence. At the age of fifty-six, he doubted that he would ever be freed.

Neither Claire's fiancée not Saddique's son was ever released by their captors. The former had actually been executed long before she was approached by an ISIS operative in London. The fate of the other man was never established.

The effect upon London was stark but short-lived. The newspapers talked about a return of the Blitz spirit, whilst other commentators lambasted them for this ridiculous analogy; no bombs had actually exploded. Within weeks, the tourists and shoppers had returned and the Queen spent some time in Buckingham Palace just to show that she could and that life went on.

Although it was clear that the bombs had been of the dirty variety, a lack of understanding about their potential, combined with the fact that they hadn't actually done any damage whatsoever, stole any harmful impact they might have made. The sections of the press not claiming a resurgence in Blitz spirit tried to stoke the fires of fear that such an attack would eventually become reality. They played down the fact that the attack had been foiled and played up that an officer from the security services was currently undergoing a trial for treason. Much was made of the fact that eight bombs had been found and no one realised that a total of sixteen had been brought into the country.

But fear, like grief, has a shelf life and things returned to normal, with the security services monitoring and intervening in any number of plots. There was always the chance that someone would get through the net and when they did… well that's another story.

Oh, and Mohammed Ifran Khan did not go to Paradise.